—[CORUSCANT NIGHTS III]—

PATTERNS OF FORCE

STAR WARS

-[CORUSCANT NIGHTS III]-

PATTERNS OF FORCE

Michael Reaves

arrow books

Published in the United Kingdom by Arrow Books in 2009

1 3 5 7 9 10 8 6 4 2

First published in the United Kingdom in 2009 by Arrow

Arrow Books
The Random House Group Limited
20 Vauxhall Bridge Road, London SW1V 2SA

www.rbooks.co.uk
www.starwars.com

Addresses for companies within The Random House Group Limited can be found at:
www.randomhouse.co.uk

The Random House Group Limited Reg. No. 954009

A CIP catalogue record for this book
is available from the British Library

ISBN 9780099492139

The Random House Group Limited supports The Forest Stewardship Council (FSC),
the leading international forest certification organisation. All our titles that are printed
on Greenpeace approved FSC certified paper carry the FSC logo.
Our paper procurement policy can be found at:
www.rbooks.co.uk/environment

Mixed Sources
Product group from well-managed
forests and other controlled sources
www.fsc.org Cert no. TT-COC-2139
© 1996 Forest Stewardship Council

Printed and bound in the United Kingdom by
CPI Bookmarque, Croydon, CR0 4TD

For
Christopher Drozd

acknowledgments

Once again, thanks go first and foremost to my editors: Shelly Shapiro at Del Rey and Sue Rostoni at Lucas-Books, who invited me to walk on the wild side of Coruscant again; to Leland Chee and the other galactic wonks who never got tired of continuity questions; a big shout-out to Maya Bohnhoff; and, as always, to George Lucas for the whole shebang.

THE STAR WARS NOVELS TIMELINE

dramatis personae

Darth Vader; Sith Lord and Emperor Palpatine's enforcer

Dejah Duare; empath, ex-partner of light artist Ves Volette (Zeltron female)

Den Dhur; ex-journalist (Sullustan male)

Haninum Tyk Rhinann; ex-assistant to Darth Vader (Elomin male)

I-5YQ; sentient protocol droid

Jax Pavan; Jedi Knight (human male)

Kajin Savaros; untrained Force adept (human male)

Laranth Tarak; Gray Paladin (Twi'lek female)

Pol Haus; police prefect (Zabrak male)

Probus Tesla; Inquisitor (human male)

Thi Xon Yimmon; leader of the Whiplash (Cerean male)

Tuden Sal; Whiplash associate (Sakiyan male)

Your focus determines your reality.
—MASTER QUI-GON JINN

A long time ago in a galaxy far, far away . . .

prologue

The voices rose and fell around him, but he paid them little attention now. He had tried to be attentive initially, but hearing the word *smuggled* had spun Haninum Tyk Rhinann off into his own private mental debriefing, on a mystery he sought to unravel for reasons of his own. The case the others were discussing—the murder of an insignificant being involved in smuggling a particularly nasty variety of spice—was of importance only to the local prefect of police, Pol Haus. Which was another way of saying that, cosmically as well as locally, it was of no importance at all.

Rhinann was almost tempted to stick his fingers in his hairy ears to block out the grating sound of the prefect's voice. There had been a time, back when he'd been the personal aide-de-camp to Darth Vader himself, when even letting such a thought cross his mind, even allowing the existence of admission of such poor etiquette, would have made all four of his stomachs turn acidic. Now he honestly had to admit that he didn't care. He wished he had self-sealing earflaps like the Lesser Houdoggin of Klatooine, so that he could shut out the sound of the prefect as easily as closing his eyes allowed him to blot away the offensive sight of him.

A poorer excuse for a Zabrak he could not imagine. In his considerable experience as an Imperial functionary he had never known a member of that species who was so impossibly *slovenly*. The police prefect's hair—what there was of it—was in wild disarray, as if he had run his fingers through it repeatedly; his clothing was disheveled; his posture was relaxed to the point of slouching; his heavy-lidded eyes made him look as if he were about to fall asleep.

He recalled hearing a rumor once to the effect that the Elomin—his people—were the descendants of a group of Zabrak who had colonized the surface of Elom ages ago. Being in the prefect's presence made him want to find whatever bescumbered ninnyhammer had started that calumny and hurl him into the nearest sun.

Rhinann sat farther back in the formchair of his workstation, noting sourly that his mind, like a child lost in a carnival labyrinth, had wandered even farther from the meander it had originally taken. He suspected that he was edging ever closer to losing his sanity. Not surprising, considering the company he kept.

He eyed the other beings in the austere living area with disdain. They were a motley group, to be sure. Besides the Zabrak prefect, who stood in the center of the room, there was the human—a Jedi in hiding, no less. Seated on one end of a low couch, he occasionally turned his head to look at the being seated at the other end—a Zeltron female, the very definition of trouble looking for somewhere to roost. The "team" was completed by a Sullustan "journalist" named Den Dhur— if one could call the sort of sensationalistic, headline-grubbing poodoo he wrote *journalism;* Rhinann had read some of his pieces in various online archives, and in his opinion comparing the little alien's writing to the Huttese term for excreta was being charitable, to say the least—and, lastly, the cause of the original detour Rhinann's mind had taken: the protocol droid I-5YQ, which everyone referred to simply as I-Five.

Rhinann's eyes narrowed as he contemplated the

droid. I-Five had once belonged to Jax Pavan's father, Lorn. Or rather, according to I-Five, had been partner and friend to Lorn Pavan. The clever mech had smuggled itself, Den Dhur, and the rare biotic panacea called bota to Coruscant in search of its partner's son, Jax. The Force-sensitive boy had—depending on who was telling the story—either been surrendered to, or taken by the Jedi as a toddler. And although I-Five's memory had been almost completely wiped, it had somehow recovered and completed its mission. Of course, it had taken two decades to do it . . .

These things Rhinann knew mostly as the result of his own careful research. What he guessed—no, the very idea of guessing gave him hives; he preferred to think of it as imaginative extrapolation—was that I-Five somehow completed a circle that included Jax, his deceased father, a mysterious Sith assassin, and the new Dark Lord, Darth Vader, whom Rhinann had recently served. What he knew through simple day-to-day experience was that I-Five was somehow, impossibly, more than a machine.

Fascinating as that was, however, it still didn't address the pertinent question, which was: did the droid still have the bota, or had it already handed that over to Pavan?

The Elomin did not pretend anymore—even to himself—that his interest in the bota was commercial. He might have hidden behind that rationale if the newest member of their mismatched team—the Zeltron, Dejah Duare—hadn't brought with her a dowry of almost unlimited funds. No, his interest was purely personal, but no less intense for that.

The literature he had found on the HoloNet had told him of the near-miraculous medicinal effects bota had on the sick and injured. Though those effects varied from species to species—including less-than-salutary outcomes for some—still, according to the twenty-year-old records he'd dredged up from the mobile med units that functioned during the Clone Wars, bota was as close to a panacea as could be imagined. With few exceptions, it was all things to all species. When administered it would simply find what was wrong in a patient's body and, ninety-nine times out of a hundred, cause it to be fixed.

Alas, this wonder was now no more than a wistful historical footnote; the bota plant evolved swiftly and, as it evolved, its properties changed. What had once been a closely guarded, much-sought-after medicinal herb was now merely an inconsequential weed . . . except to a select few.

Haninum Tyk Rhinann was one of those few.

The thing that made bota of such intense interest to Rhinann had nothing to do with its healing properties. Nor had he initially learned of that aspect of it from the HoloNet. He had—and it galled him to admit it, even to himself—gained early knowledge by eavesdropping on conversations between I-Five and Jax Pavan. In such a way he had learned of something bota could provide that the HoloNet did not catalog: a transcendent connection to the Force. Provided, of course, that the test subject had a sufficient level of midi-chlorians to make him Force-sensitive. Rhinann's own midi-chlorian count was not quite enough to access the Force unaided, but it was just possible that, with the bota extract providing the requisite boost, he might.

He'd long since come to accept, with the fatalism common to his kind, that he would die in poverty and misery, but he wanted to experience the Force just once before death. Just once, he wanted to be attuned to the power and pattern of the universe and not deaf as a dianoga; just once he wanted to have the power and presence of mind and spirit to take out those responsible for his fall from grace; just once he wanted—

"I said, 'Isn't that pretty much what you discovered, Rhinann?' "

The Elomin blinked and turned to look at Jax Pavan, who, he realized, must have repeated himself several times to have raised his voice to that level. The young Jedi was usually soft-spoken and soft-edged—a manner calculated to make him seem unthreatening. Even now there was no anger in his voice, just bemusement.

Jedi did not get angry—or so they liked to tell everyone. It was Rhinann's secret opinion that they got just as angry as the next being and simply hid it better. How could Pavan not be angry when the Dark Lord, allegedly responsible for his father's death, kept sending assassins after him? How did one possibly not rage against the universe when—

"Rhinann?" Jax repeated, his dark gaze seeking the Elomin's. His voice now held a touch of asperity.

"Pardon, I was contemplating a . . . an abstruse angle of another case."

"If you could be bothered to contemplate the rather more immediate angles of this one," said Pol Haus, "I'm sure we would all appreciate it."

Rhinann blinked again, slowly and for effect, and let out a long, patient breath. "If you could repeat the question?"

Jax did. "I was telling Pol Haus that the data you uncovered indicated that the conduit through which Bal Rado was receiving spice had dried up just prior to his murder."

"Ah. Yes. Precisely. We reasoned," said Rhinann, bringing his mind efficiently back to the matter at hand, "that his reluctance to inform his buyer—"

"A Hutt named Sol Proofrock, if you can believe it,"

interjected Den Dhur from his seat in a window embrasure.

"As I was saying," continued Rhinann tightly, "he was reluctant to inform his buyer—a Hutt with a variety of aliases—of this situation. Which caused him to try to cover it up while he sought a new source of spice—"

"Which, unfortunately for him, failed to materialize," added the Sullustan.

Rhinann favored the short, stocky humanoid with his most disdainful glare. "Well of course it didn't. Otherwise the pathetic fellow would likely still be alive. What *my* research indicates," Rhinann told the prefect, wanting it to be perfectly clear that Den had had nothing to do with the solving of the case, "is that one of the smugglers Rado contacted about his little problem—one Droo Wabbin, a fellow Toydarian, as it happens—revealed his situation to the buyer."

"That's speculation, though," Den interrupted. "Because you were unable to recover the contents of the message, all we know for certain is that Wabbin was in contact with good old Sol."

I-Five, standing just behind the low couch Jax and Dejah were seated on, made a raspy mechanical chirp that was the protocol droid's version of clearing its throat.

Rhinann ignored the subtle warning. "I suppose you think it's pure coincidence that Rado ended up dead within a day of that message having been sent *and* coincidence as well that his loyal smuggler friend received a significant sum of credits to his private account in that same time frame?"

"I didn't say that," Den objected. "I merely noted that we don't have titanium-clad proof that Wabbin's windfall had anything to do with Rado's demise. Though it does seem, you know, too much of a coincidence to be coincidental."

"Too much of a coincidence to be coincidental?" repeated Rhinann disparagingly. He snapped his long fingers several times by way of applause. "Brilliant assessment." He turned to address the prefect. "The fact is—"

"The fact is," growled Pol Haus, straightening to his full height, "that I didn't come here to listen to internecine squabbling over who knew what how. I came here to find out what you knew about the flow of spice in my jurisdiction. You *said* you had pertinent information."

"We do," said Jax Pavan quickly, including both squabblers in a quelling look.

"That's good," said Haus, "because what *I* have is a dead Toydarian 'businessman'—and I use the term loosely—and a sudden glut of pure spice in the Zi-Kree Sector. A sector *my* research indicates is controlled by our multi-aliased buddy the Hutt. If you can't provide me with good intel . . ."

Rhinann opened his mouth to reply and was incensed to see that Dhur's pendulous lips were also opening. Then I-Five made that grating sound again, which was really just too much—to be censured by a *droid* . . .

"We have provided you with only the most worthwhile intelligence, Prefect, I assure you," insisted Rhinann, far more forcefully than he meant to.

"You've also provided me with a surfeit of complaints from local merchants about harassment, more 'unknowns' than should exist in any citizen's files, and a trail of dead bodies. Perhaps I should be investigating *you*, not Sol Proofrock—or whatever our Hutt spice trader is calling himself these days."

Before any of the open mouths in the room could utter a sound, Dejah Duare rose from the couch and raised a graceful, placating hand.

All eyes turned to her, all ears tingled in anticipation of her voice, all senses stretched toward her, involuntarily desiring to lap up every effusion of her softly gleaming carmine skin—with the exception of Rhinann and Dhur, whose physiologies, though humanoid, were too alien to respond to Duare's endocrine advantage. A good thing, too, judging by the besotted looks that came over Pavan and Haus. Rhinann even imagined for a moment that the droid's photoreceptors brightened a bit, though he knew that was nonsense.

Like all Zeltrons, Dejah Duare exuded a rich potion of pheromones that she could guide willfully to affect the mood of her target audience. Right now she had brought all her resources to bear on Pol Haus.

"Prefect," she said in a voice like sun-washed synthsilk, "surely *my* citizen file is an open book. Can you imagine that I'd associate myself with beings whose scruples I distrusted in the least?"

If Rhinann didn't know better, he'd swear the Zabrak was blushing to the roots of his unkempt, thinning fringe of hair.

"With all due respect," the prefect said, "this lot did ingratiate themselves with you during the investigation of your partner's death."

Dejah uttered a cascade of warm sultry laughter that, if visible, would have been the same dark crimson as her hair. "Ingratiated themselves! Now, Prefect, isn't that understating the case? Jax and his team," she added, turning a smiling gaze to the Jedi, "solved Ves Volette's murder. And that is why I've chosen to ally myself with them. Each one of them is highly skilled at what he does. If Haninum Tyk Rhinann provides you with information, you can be certain it is both accurate and worthwhile."

The prefect looked bemused and not a little befuddled. "Well, I suppose . . . that is, of course the information is worthwhile. I've never doubted it. And I honestly don't care about the holes in your personal files as long as you continue to provide that information." This last was directed at Jax, who nodded his assurance.

"We're happy to provide it, Prefect. In this case I think the intel points to Rado's Hutt friend. I suspect what happened was that Wabbin had his own spice source and simply cut Rado out, making a separate deal with his buyer."

As Jax continued, wrapping up the package neatly, Rhinann returned to his speculations about I-Five. Droids, he knew, were not supposed to have such capacities and capabilities as this one exemplified. Nor was it simply a matter of disabling a few limitations or reprogramming the synaptic grid processor with clever learning algorithms. Ves Volette, as it happened, had been slain by a "modified" 3PO unit that had retaliated against the Caamasi sculptor for causing distress to the Vindalian mistress he had served for decades. Plainly put, with some sophisticated modifications to its protective programming, the 3PO unit had developed an attachment to its owner.

I-Five had developed far more than that. And he—*it,* Rhinann reminded himself with irritation—had somehow developed it in the hands of a man who made his living as a black-market dealer in rare commodities. From everything Rhinann knew, the droid's erstwhile "partner," Lorn Pavan, had been many things, but a sophisticated programmer was not one of them.

Which begged the question: how had the protocol droid known as I-5YQ transcended its programming?

And why?

Haninum Tyk Rhinann, much as he hated to admit it, agreed with Den Dhur about one thing: some events were too much a coincidence to be coincidental, and just about every event to which he could now connect I-Five seemed to fall into that category.

The droid would bear watching. Very close watching.

—[PART I]—

SINS OF THE FATHER

one

The library was his favorite place in the entirety of the immense Jedi Temple complex. He went there to absorb data as much through the pores of his skin as through any study of the copious amount of information stored there. He frequently went there to think—but just as often he went there to *not* think.

He was there now—not thinking—and almost as soon as he recognized the place, Jax Pavan also realized that this was a dream. The Temple, he knew, was no more than a chaotic pile of rubble, charred stone, and ashy dust. Order 66 had mandated it, and the horrifying bloodbath that the few remaining Jedi referred to as Flame Night had ensured it.

Yet here he was in one of the many reading rooms within the vast library wing, just as it had been the last time he had seen it—the softly lit shelves that contained books, scrolls, data cubes, and other vessels of knowledge from a thousand worlds; the tables—each in its own pool of illumination—at which Jedi and Padawans studied in silence; the tall, narrow windows that looked out into the central courtyard; the vaulted ceiling that seemed to fly away into eternity. Even as his dreaming gaze took in these things, he felt the pain of their loss . . . and something else—puzzlement.

This was clearly a Force dream. It had that lucent, almost shimmering quality to it, the utter clarity of presence and sense, the equally clear knowledge that it was a dream. But it was about the past, not the future, for Jax Pavan knew he would never savor the atmosphere of the Jedi library again. His Force dreams had, without exception, been visions of future events . . . and they had never been this lucid.

He was sitting at one of the tables with a book and a data cube before him. The book was a compilation of philosophical essays by Masters of the Tython Jedi who had first proposed that the Force had a dual nature: Ashla, the creative element, and Bogan, the destructive— light and dark aspects of the same Essence. The data cube contained a treatise of Master Asli Krimsan on the Potentium Perspective, a "heresy" propagated by Jedi Leor Hal that contended—as many had before and since—that there was no dark side to the Force, that the darkness existed within the individual.

Yes, he had studied these two volumes—among others. He supposed that all Padawans studied them at some point in their training, because all entertained questions about the nature of the Force and desired to understand it. Some, he knew, hoped to understand it completely and ultimately; to settle once and for all the millennia-long debate over whether it had one face or two and where the potential for darkness lay—in the Force itself or in the wielder of the Force.

When had he studied these last? What moment had he been returned to in his dream?

Even as he wondered these things, a shadow fell across the objects on the table before him. Someone had come to stand beside him, blocking the light from the windows.

He glanced up.

It was his fellow Padawan and friend Anakin Sky-walker. At least he had called Anakin "friend" readily enough, but the truth was that Anakin held himself

aloof from the other Padawans. Even in moments of ca-
maraderie he seemed a man apart, as if he had a Force
shield around him. Brooding. Jax had called him that
once to his face and had drawn laughter that he, through
his connection to the Force, had known to be false.

Now Anakin stood above him, his back to the windows, his face in shadow.

"Hey, you're blocking my light." The words popped
out of Jax's mouth without his having intended to say
them. But he *had* said them that day, and he knew what
was coming next.

Anakin didn't answer. He simply held out his hand as
if to drop something to the tabletop. Jax put out his own
hand palm-up to receive it.

"It" was a pyronium nugget the size of the first joint
of his thumb. Even in the half-light it pulsed with an
opalescence that seemed to arise from deep within, cy-
cling from white through the entire visible spectrum to
black, then back again. Somewhere—Jax just couldn't
remember where—he had heard that pyronium was a
source of immense power, of almost unlimited power.
He had thought that apocryphal and absurd. *Power* was
a vague word and meant many things to many people.

"What's this for?" he asked now as he had then, looking up into his friend's face.

"For safekeeping while I'm on Tatooine," Anakin
said. His mouth curved wryly. "Or maybe it's a gift."

"Well, which is it?" Jax asked.

The answer *then* had been a shrug. Now it was a cryp-
tic phrase uttered in a deep, rumbling voice not at all
like the Padawan's own: "With this, journey beyond the
Force."

Jax laughed. "The Force is the beginning, middle, and
end of all things. How does one go beyond the infinite?"

Instead of replying, the Anakin of his dream began to
laugh. To Jax's horror, Anakin's flesh *blackened*, crisp-

ing and shriveling as if from intense heat; peeling away from the muscle and bone beneath. His grin twisted horribly, becoming a skull's rictus. Worst of all, laughter still tumbled from the seared lips.

Jax woke suddenly and completely, bathed in cold sweat.

With this, journey beyond the Force?

That was impossible. It made no sense—and what was with the burning? He shivered, his skin creeping beneath its clammy film of sweat as he recalled one of the rumors of where and how Anakin was supposed to have died on Mustafar—thrown into the magma stream by . . . no one knew who.

"Is something wrong, Jax?"

Jax glanced over from his sweat-soaked bed mat to where I-Five stood sentry, his photoreceptors gleaming with muted light.

Jax hesitated for only a moment. It might seem a futile monologue to discuss a dream with a droid, but I-5YQ was no ordinary droid, and even if he were, there was value to talking out the puzzling dream even with a supposedly nonsentient being. If nothing else, Jax reasoned that sorting through the images, actions, and words aloud would help him understand them.

He sat up, leaning against the wall of his small room in the Poloda Place conapt he shared with the rest of his motley team. "I dreamed."

"I've read that all living things do," I-Five observed blandly.

Jax was seized with sudden curiosity: Did I-Five dream? Was that even possible? He wanted to ask but quelled the urge, instead launching into a detailed retelling of his own nighttime visitation.

When Jax at last exhausted the account, I-Five was silent for a moment, his photoreceptors flickering slightly in a way that suggested the blinking of human eyes. Finally he said, "May I point out that this would seem to contradict the knowledge you received through the Force some months ago that Skywalker was still alive?"

"Well, yeah." Jax ran fingers through his sweat-damp hair. "Although he might have been injured on Mūstafar, I suppose."

"Possibly, although other possibilities abound. It might have a more metaphysical meaning, for example. Or it might be an expression of your own inner fears."

"That's not usually how Force dreams work, but I suppose it's possible. I've never had one like this before," Jax admitted. "I mean, a dream of the past, rather than the future, for one thing. And an edited past at that. Anakin didn't say anything about the Force when he gave me the pyronium, he just asked me to keep it for him while he went to Tatooine. And I think I'd have noticed if he burst into flames," he added wryly.

I-Five's "eyes" flickered again, seeming to convey amusement.

The door chime sounded; Jax checked his chrono, but I-Five was ahead of him.

"It's oh seven hundred hours."

It wasn't a terribly early hour this deep in downlevel Coruscant where few acknowledged either day or night, but most sentients seemed to agree that some hours were impolite for calling on one's neighbor.

Jax rose and padded out of his room into the larger main living area, noticing that the rest of his companions were either asleep or out. I-Five followed him.

As he moved to the front door of the conapt, Jax sent out questing tendrils of the Force to the being on the opposite side of the barrier. In his mind's eye he saw the energy there, but he perceived no telltale threads of the Force emanating from or connecting to them.

Every Jedi experienced and perceived the Force in intensely personal ways. Jax's particular sensibilities caused him to perceive it as threads of light or darkness that enrobed or enwrapped an individual and connected him or her to the Force itself and to other beings and things. In this case there seemed to be no threads . . . though there was a hint of a, well, a *smudge*—that was the only word Jax could think of that even vaguely fit.

Curious for the second time that morning, he opened the door, smiling a little as I-Five stepped to one side to take up a defensive position where he would not immediately be seen by whoever was outside.

In the narrow, starkly lit corridor stood a short, stocky male Sakiyan whom Jax guessed to be in his sixties, dressed in clean but threadbare clothing. He blinked at Jax's appearance—he was wearing a loose pair of sleep pants and hadn't bothered to put on a tunic.

"I—I apologize for the hour," the Sakiyan stammered, blinking round eyes that seemed extraordinarily pale in his bronze face, "but the matter is urgent. I need to speak to Jax Pavan."

Jax scrutinized the Sakiyan again, more thoroughly and with every sense he possessed. Sensing no ill intent, he introduced himself. "I'm Jax Pavan."

The visitor's face brightened and he heaved a huge sigh of relief. "By any chance, do you happen to own a protocol droid of the Eye-Fivewhycue line?"

"I don't 'own' him," Jax replied cautiously. "But yes, he's here. What do you want with him, er . . . ?"

The Sakiyan executed a slight bow. "I apologize for my extreme lack of manners. My name is—"

"Tuden Sal," I-Five said, stepping out of the shadows beside the door. The droid pointed an index finger at the Sakiyan. A red light gleamed at the tip—the muzzle of one of the twin lasers incorporated into his hands. His photoreceptors gleamed brightly. "I've been waiting a long time for this . . ."

two

Kajin Savaros stood in the narrow cleft beneath a support pier somewhere in the lower levels of a cloud-scraper on the long axis of Ploughtekal Market and peered out at the rabble in the bazaar below. He wasn't sure what level he was on, truth be told. He only knew it was dark, noisome, and anonymous.

This last quality—if Ploughtekal could be said to possess "qualities"—was what had made Kaj seek it out. That, and the ease with which he could sustain himself here. Or at least it had been easy until his narrow escape from an Inquisitor the day before.

He shivered at the memory of that as he weighed the gnawing of his empty belly against the risk that somewhere in this crowd of unknowns might very well be someone watchful, someone suspicious, someone who might know what he looked like and be steeped enough in the Force to sense his presence. He had been hungry—just like now—and cadging food several levels up in the sprawling, many-layered marketplace. The Inquisitor had seen him coax a street vendor into giving him a skewer full of lovely smoked fleek belly strips, and had cornered him before he could even half devour it.

Even in his fear, the thought of the meat made him salivate. He needed to eat, but . . .

Kaj glanced up and down the overrun bazaar. Shadow and light danced in an ever-changing roil of smoke from cookpots and braziers; multicolored lights strung along kiosks twinkled and winked to tempt the eye and draw in the potential customers who thronged the thoroughfare. There was no sign of the Inquisitor or another like him—they made a point of remaining incognito.

It would seem that the sheer staggering amount of sentients, human and otherwise, that populated the city-planet would afford more than enough protection for the individual who sought a lifetime of anonymity. Coruscant—Kaj shook his head in annoyance, reminding himself again to refer to the newly renamed ecu-menopolis as *Imperial Center* in both thought and speech—Imperial Center was home to literally trillions of beings from across the length and breadth of the galaxy, and finding a single one among them all was more difficult by far than finding a single grain of sand on Tatooine, Bakkah, and all the other desert worlds combined. Hidden in the teeming multitude, he was safe—as long as he didn't use the Force.

Which was no more difficult than, say, swallowing white-hot lava.

When he went for some time without actively using the Force, but instead simply kept it pent up within, it *burned*. It was like having a big chunk of fire lodged behind his sternum. He found it hard to breathe, harder to sit still. It quite literally raised his internal temperature; after a few days Kaj found himself sweating and running a low-grade fever. If he kept it bottled down much longer than that—say, another week or so . . . well, he'd only done that once. When he'd woken up in the middle of the night, he'd felt at first blessed relief—followed by heart-stopping fear.

The bed of the cheap resiblock he'd rented for the night had been soaked with sweat, and in the far wall a circle a meter wide had been charred into the paint.

After that, Kaj tried to "bleed off" whenever he felt

the Force building up out of control. He concentrated on small telekinetics, levitating pieces of food or other objects, as those seemed to provide the most relief for the amount of effort expended. So far, it had worked— but he still quaked with the fear of being sensed by one of the malevolent Inquisitors every time he had to do it.

Kaj's gaze wandered back to a kiosk some twenty meters distant, at which several shoppers were haggling with the vendor over the assortment of produce—most of it illegal. The kiosk had food bins on three sides and was open at the back. That was unfortunate, but the booth next door had a tatty fabric awning, one corner of which was tied down not far from the back of the produce vendor's kiosk.

With his usual front-door methods rendered too risky, Kaj decided on a less direct approach. He pulled the cowl of his cloak up around his face and eased into the crowd. The stew of energies, aromas, and stenches flowed around him; the heat of someone's regard when he accidentally bumped into her caused him to cower. He tamped down the anger that seemed to crawl to the surface of his mind when he was confronted by large crowds of people intent on their own business. He supposed he was no different in that from any of the beings here.

But he was different in other ways.

He drew level with the awning and ducked sideways out of the flow of traffic, making his way around to the back of the booth. It was even darker back here than in the shadowed arcade, and he took advantage of that to slip into the deeper blackness of the narrow passage that ran the width of the booth between its fabric back wall and the ferrocrete surface of a cloudscraper's dingy exterior.

When he emerged from the narrow slit on the other side of the booth—which, from the wild dance of aromas, he realized was an herbalist's shop—he found himself less than three paces from a row of fruit bins containing little that was familiar and much that was not. Not wanting to risk discovery for something that might not even be edible to a human, he scanned the bins for something familiar. Finally he saw what he was looking for: a basket of daro root.

Mouth watering, he edged beneath the tightly pulled corner of the awning and crouched, his eyes on the treasure. Daro root grew on several worlds that humans had colonized. His had been one of them. As a child he had developed a taste for the sweet, creamy golden flesh of the root and now, as hungry as he was, he was sure it would provide the most delicious meal in recent memory.

A gaggle of shoppers was passing the kiosk, occasionally obscuring the daro from sight. He willed them to find the produce here uninspiring and to go elsewhere.

They did.

Kaj leaned forward and raised a hand toward the prize. Sweat trickled into his eyes, startling him and disrupting his concentration. He swore, swiped the salty rivulet away, and reached out again. His hand was shaking, he realized, and not with hunger. His encounter with the Inquisitor yesterday had been much more than merely disturbing. He was scared, plain and simple—scared of doing anything to call attention to himself. *Their* attention, anyway. He flattered himself that he was well capable of handling the unwelcome attention of ordinary people. But Inquisitors were not ordinary people. They were the Emperor's watchdogs, and they had powers he could only guess at.

He steeled himself. Two seconds. It would take only two seconds to procure a couple of pieces of the alluring food. He would open the way to the Force and then close it, quickly. Simple. It would be simple.

Resolved, he wiped the sweat from his palm, stretched out his hand, and *called*. A daro atop the pile wiggled, then rolled down the mound of produce to drop to the ground unnoticed. He called again, and it flew unerringly to his hand.

His heart, which had been beating out a wild tattoo in his chest, calmed. Not bad. And not an Inquisitor in sight . . . or sense. Encouraged, he decided to get more. He tucked the fat, golden root into an inner pocket of his voluminous cloak, raised his hand, and—

He felt it then, a sick trickle of dread coursing down his spine: the sudden eddy in the Force as someone nearby groped for the one who had just used it.

Kaj sensed purposeful movement in the crowded avenue before the produce vendor's stall, saw people moving swiftly out of the way of something or someone who was in a great deal of haste. He bit back his fear and threw a desperate, sharp salvo of thought at the bin of daro root. Amplified by a charge of adrenaline, the blast hit the bin like a burst from a repulsor field. Daro roots exploded into the air and cascaded to the ground, rolling every which way. Patrons milling about the booth reacted haphazardly, sidestepping, ducking, bobbing, and weaving to get out of the way, slipping on splattered fruit and stumbling out into the overcrowded avenue.

Kaj used the distraction to scoop up two more of the precious gourd-shaped roots before he hurriedly withdrew, scurrying rodent-like along behind three or four stalls in the row before finally emerging at the corner into a cross-alley. He'd secreted the daro roots on his person by that time and glided into the flow of foot traffic, straightening his cloak.

He smiled grimly, a strange mixture of relief and exhilaration flooding him with warmth. Once again he had barely avoided detection; once again he had eluded the Emperor's minions. He had a swift vision of himself as a much-sought-after prize. A shadowy rogue Force-sensitive dancing on the fringes of society, always one

step ahead of the Inquisitorius and its frustrated operatives. He could almost see himself leaping between the
sky-raking buildings, flitting along ledges—an elusive
silhouette. A powerful possessor of the Force.

A Jedi.

A sudden, almost overwhelming surge of anger arose
in Kaj's breast to swamp his relief and drown his self-
congratulatory daydreams. Once, in a more enlightened
age, he would have become a Jedi and been instructed in
the ways of the Force, honing his relatively newborn
skills—skills that had fully awakened only this past year.
But the Jedi Temple lay in ruins, and the Order had been
scattered all across the galaxy—if there were any left
alive. He alternately hoped for and despaired of that . . .
and raged at the universe and the Force itself.

He gritted his teeth, trying to suppress the seething
anger that burned through his veins.

No. *There are no Jedi left,* he told himself. *I'm alone.
Alone.*

Alone with this power that grew inside him, demand-
ing to be used. He both gloried in it and was terrified of
it. Especially in moments like these, when resentful rage
burned in him. A rage that had no target at which to
vent itself—except, perhaps, the Inquisitors. He hated
and feared those shadowy beings, but it was not safe to
attract them—not safe to target them with his anger. So
Kaj's rage remained directionless, aimed at no one—and
everyone. He held it tightly to him, because to give in to
it, to allow it to escape his careful control, would be as
good as sending up a giant flare that said to the Inquisitors, *Come get me!*

Kaj stepped out of the street as a hover-lorry approached, sucking himself tightly up against a stained
and pitted support girder that had been erected to shore
up the ruined façade of what had once been a gaming
parlor.

A tug of awareness made itself felt through the coils of control he struggled to maintain. He tilted his head up and glanced across the way. A man—a human—was staring at him from the dark, crooked doorway of the building opposite.

Before he could think better of it, Kaj erased the man's memory of him, using the Force to slide into the other's mind and rearrange his thoughts. He'd never attempted such a thing before, but it was easier by far than he'd expected it to be.

He scooted sideways and insinuated himself into a mixed group of aliens as the hover-lorry blocked his view of the staring man. With just a little more effort, he knew he could have made the other step out in front of the vehicle. It would have been easy.

Too easy.

He shuddered, put his head down, and immersed himself in the crowd.

Den Dhur stumbled sleepily into the central room of the conapt, rubbing sleep out of his eyes. When his vision cleared, the sight that met him stopped him dead in his tracks. In frozen tableau he saw Jax, I-Five, and a strange Sakiyan standing just inside the open front doorway. I-Five was pointing at the Sakiyan as if delivering a lecture . . . which was what one might think if one didn't know about the specialized lasers built into each of the droid's forefingers.

Den knew about them, however.

He shook himself more thoroughly awake, resisting the temptation to rub his eyes a second time. Had I-Five fried a circuit? And what the frip was Jax thinking? This guy could be a potential customer—this was no way to treat a potential customer.

"Uh," Den said. "Guys? Who's our new friend?"

The droid's photoreceptors blinked in a gesture so

alive that Den batted his own eyes before he could resist the urge.

Jax cleared his throat. "I-Five?"

The droid made a sound like a human sigh and lowered his arm. "I've obviously been around organics too long—I've picked up some bad habits. Such as holding grudges."

"Okay . . ." Jax said. "May I ask *why* you're holding a grudge against our guest?"

"Yeah," Den agreed, bustling farther into the room. "In fact, why don't we invite our *guest* to come in and sit down, get him a drink, and ask him to explain what he might need from us?"

"What I need, first and foremost," said the Sakiyan as he moved to sit uneasily on the utilitarian couch that graced one gray wall, "is to apologize to I-Five."

Den stared at Tuden Sal. "You what?"

"Apparently," Jax said, "Tuden Sal and I-Five have some kind of history."

The Jedi had perched on the arm of the couch, from which vantage point he could watch both the Sakiyan and I-Five. *Wise of him,* Den thought. He crossed the room to hand their guest the glass of water he'd just drawn from the tap. The Sakiyan stared at the glass as if he'd never seen anything like it before, and Den had a momentary panic attack, trying to remember if Sakiyans had some allergy to or other problem with water.

But then Tuden Sal accepted the glass, issuing a wheezy laugh as he did so. "History indeed—or the lack of it, in I-Five's case. It seems rather odd to me, too, I must admit. I'm still not quite used to the idea that I-Five, is—for want of a better term—self-aware."

"*Self-aware,*" said I-Five drily, "is a perfectly good term, thank you."

Tuden Sal nodded. "Yes. I'd forgotten how perfectly good." He looked directly at the droid, who stood facing him—probably, Den thought, about two subroutines away from firing up his lasers again.

The Sakiyan lowered his eyes and took a moment to straighten the folds of the calf-length coat he wore over his once elegant tunic. Then he looked up at I-Five again. "I'm sorry, I-Five, for what I did to you. I was . . . shortsighted and selfish."

"You can add to that disloyal, disreputable, unscrupulous, and cruel," I-Five told him. "You were, in a word, *wrong*. You can have no idea what your action ultimately cost the Jedi and the Republic."

The Sakiyan closed his deep-set eyes momentarily, veiling his thoughts. "No. I don't believe I can."

Den pulled himself up into the window embrasure adjacent to the couch. He favored this spot because it gave him the advantage of height—a rare perspective for a native of Sullust—and allowed him to study other people's faces from a proper angle. "This is all very cozy," he said, letting his short legs dangle over the windowsill, "but would one of you mind clarifying why this apology is necessary?"

I-Five canted his head pointedly at Tuden Sal, who cleared his throat and rearranged his coat yet again. "Some years ago," he said, "a . . . a friend asked me to make sure I-Five and some data he was carrying got to the Jedi Temple here on Coruscant."

Den didn't need the Force to see the effect of those words on Jax. The young Jedi stiffened.

"My father. My father, Lorn Pavan, asked you to get I-Five to the Jedi."

Tuden Sal nodded. "Yes. I didn't realize at the time that he . . . that it was something in the nature of a dying wish. Since then, I've come to appreciate that Lorn trusted me with the task because he expected not to live much longer. Unfortunately, he was correct in that expectation."

"Why didn't you carry out that wish?" Jax asked, his voice hushed.

Den glanced at I-Five. Though he gave no outward indication of tension or increased interest, his friend knew that the droid had been waiting for a resolution to this mystery for over two decades.

The Sakiyan spread his hands in the universal sign of bewilderment. "Quite simply, I saw a profit to be made from the droid, and with the hubris that often comes with success, I figured I could kill two mynocks with one blast. I had intended to deliver the holocron I-Five was carrying to the Jedi as Lorn had asked, but I first planned on having the droid mindwiped and reprogrammed as a bodyguard for use during my dealings with Black Sun. He had certain . . . modifications I had never seen in any protocol droid—not in any droid, come to it. Modifications I hadn't even realized were possible."

"Yet you failed to note the most significant of them," said I-Five.

"I did," Sal admitted. "Frankly, I couldn't believe what Lorn told me about you. I wish now that I had not been so . . . shortsighted."

"Traitorous," I-Five said simultaneously.

Den had to admit that I-Five's characterization was closer to what he'd been thinking. How could someone behave that treacherously toward a supposed friend? Den hoped he'd never become so mercenary or so jaded that he failed to put the welfare of his friends or his world before his own short-term benefits.

Tuden Sal sighed. "I can't deny it. But I did plan on getting the holocron to the Temple. I did."

"The best of intentions, I've found," said the droid, "are by themselves seldom enough to topple tyrants."

There came a silence, which was verging on uncomfortable when Jax asked, "Then what happened?"

"I had my fingers in several pies at the time—not all

of them legal. I sent I-Five to be reprogrammed, then returned to my business offices and discovered that a competitor had instigated a hostile takeover of my companies—every last one of them. I went from riches to rags virtually overnight. Quite simply, I didn't get the holocron to the Jedi Council because I no longer had the means to do so. I was under siege. I had to go into hiding and liquidate most of my remaining holdings and property—including I-Five, whom I traded to a spice smuggler with his memories wiped."

He paused to regard the droid with obvious respect. "Or so I had thought. I had spared no expense, ordered the most thorough quantum cleansing available. Apparently I-Five possesses subroutines and resources that are proof even to that."

"It took me a *very long time,*" the droid said with harsh emphasis on the last three words, "but I was at last able to recover my full memory."

The Sakiyan shook his head. "That should not have been possible. And yet, here you are. And here am I. Unlike you, I have never managed to claw my way back. Eventually, I gave up trying. Especially once I discovered that the takeover of my businesses was not, shall we say, an idea original to my competitor. I confronted him, some years down the line, and learned that he had been bankrolled by then-Senator Palpatine himself. My 'friend' was essentially acting as a proxy, though I daresay he was allowed to keep a good deal of what he took."

"Why?" Jax asked. "What did you have that the Emperor wanted?"

"I suspect I was simply an easy target," Sal said, bitterness dripping from each word. "My financial circumstances made me vulnerable, and Palpatine, while by no means in desperate straits, like all politicians preferred to use someone else's money to finance his governmental takeover." He smiled a hard, painful smile. "You know what they say: 'It's not personal—' "

" '—it's just business,' " Den finished. Yes, they'd all heard those words before.

"And I have, I must admit, used, if not those very words, certainly the spirit behind them, more than once. But I was never stupid enough to cross the government." He shrugged. "Perhaps it was that very hesitancy on my part that made me seem easy prey. Whatever the reason, the new regime ruined me. Worse than that, they black-listed me and made it impossible for me to recover. Even Black Sun wouldn't do business with me, which has implications I'm reluctant to think about." He hesitated, then added, "It wasn't just the businesses, though the gods of misfortune know how devastating that was. No, I also lost my family—my mate, my children."

"Ah," said I-Five. "Ironic, isn't it, how fickle people can be. Even those you expect to be loyal."

"It wasn't fickleness," Tuden Sal said with some asperity. "It was fear. I didn't just lose my visibility, I lost the ability to *dare* visibility. There is still a bounty on my head, I'm sure of it, though I've never been able to confirm it. When someone attempted to kidnap my youngest child, I sent my family offworld. I had no choice."

"And you've been living down here, lying low?" Jax shook his head. "I hope you weren't hoping to hide out with us. I've got a price on my head, too. And like you, I don't know why."

"I'm through lying low," announced the Sakiyan. "I'm fighting back. I've joined the Whiplash, which is how I came to find you." He nodded at Jax.

"You joined the Whiplash?" Jax repeated. "For the purpose of finding I-Five?"

Den well understood the skepticism in Jax's voice. The Whiplash—the underground organization of which Den and his companions were a part—was dedicated to undermining the Empire's doings and rescuing its victims. It was an organization that thrived on secrecy to the extent that its operatives often didn't communicate openly for long periods of time, were informed of missions on a need-to-know basis, and did not admit new "members" without having first subjected them to stiff scrutiny.

"No," the Sakiyan answered. "For the purpose of fighting the Empire. Finding you and I-Five was serendipitous. I had given up on finding you. In fact, I was convinced you were dead and the droid had been broken up for parts by some yokel who had no idea what he was holding. I would never have found you if my first assignment with the Whiplash hadn't introduced me to Laranth Tarak."

Jax reacted visibly to the mention of the Twi'lek's name, but before he could do much more than gape like a Sullustan Fluke fish, I-Five interjected: "Which begs the question—*why* have you found us?"

The Sakiyan was suddenly quivering with unwholesome excitement. Or at least the glint in his pale eyes made it seem unwholesome to Den.

"I have a mission for I-Five. One for which his special modifications—specifically his concealed weaponry and his lack of certain . . . standard inhibitions—would suit him ideally."

"And that would be?" asked I-Five.

"You, my old friend," said the Sakiyan, smiling for the first time, "would make the ideal assassin."

"You want I-Five to *assassinate* somebody?" Jax shook his head. "That's not the sort of mission the Whiplash usually involves itself in. We protect people, extricate them from unhealthy situations, find them safe passage offworld. We don't indulge people's vendettas."

"This could be seen as something in the nature of a personal mission," Sal admitted. "Though I assure you it will serve all lovers of freedom, including the Jedi, in ways you can't imagine. With I-Five's modifications and the anonymity that comes with being a droid . . . well, there couldn't be a more perfect liquidator."

"Now, just a moment here." Den raised his hands and slid down from the window embrasure, noting as he did that the wan light falling through it from outside—a weak trickle of half-dead sunlight from above and artificial illumination from below—made his shadow on the ferrocrete floor loom many times his real height. He was glad of that, because he needed to feel bigger just now. Tuden Sal's last words had turned his insides to quivering gel. "I-Five, an assassin? What kind of sick nonsense is that? He may be just an anonymous automaton to you, but to me he's . . . he's . . ."

Den hesitated, realizing that he had never articulated what I-Five was to him. He also realized that the droid's ocular units were trained right on him. "He's my *friend*, okay? And Jax's friend. And we don't want to see him put in harm's way with the callous disregard you'd show a—a . . ."

"A machine?" finished I-Five with a tone of voice that in an organic would have been accompanied by a raised eyebrow.

"Yeah. He admitted it himself not a minute ago, Five. You're not a programmable toy. We can't just pump you full of code and send you into a dangerous situation as if you were some expendable piece of equipment. You have volition. You're a *person*."

Den felt those words in that moment as perhaps he never had before, knowing to the soles of his boots that he would not—*could* not—send I-Five into a potentially no-win situation alone. A swift chill cascaded down from the crown of his head. And just what did that imply? That he would volunteer to go along?

I-Five's gleaming metal face was, as always, expressionless. "Yes," the droid said, "as you point out, I have volition. Which means that I have both the capacity and the right to determine, in consultation with the team, of course"—he tilted his head toward Jax—"what missions I will or will not undertake. But . . ." He hesitated; something he rarely, if ever, did. "Your concern is noted, Den, and the sentiment behind it mutual."

I-Five then shifted his attention to Tuden Sal so suddenly that Den felt as if a physical support had been knocked from under him.

"Obviously before we can entertain the idea of such a mission," I-Five told the Sakiyan, "we need to understand it more fully and weigh its potential for good or ill. Who, precisely, do you want me to assassinate?"

Tuden Sal smiled, and there was an almost mischievous glint in his eye now. "Allow me to test your knowledge of arcane historical esoterica. Have you ever heard of the Monarchomechs?"

I-Five did not hesitate. "Yes. An obscure sect of fanatics out in the Eastern Expansion around four hundred standard years ago. They opposed the absolute monarchy of their system of worlds, and promulgated tyrannicide. Like the B'omarr monks of Tatooine, they were not droids but cyborgs—essentially encapsulated organic brains in robotic bodies. The name, in Middle Yutanese, is a play on the portmanteau, meaning 'killers of monarchs.' " I-Five's voice was somewhat more subdued, almost speculative, as he continued, "You want me to terminate Emperor Palpatine."

three

"I beseech your courtesy," said Haninum Tyk Rhinann as he seated himself in a formchair adjacent to the couch on which the Sakiyan sat. "I cannot possibly have heard you right. You want I-Five to *assassinate* Emperor Palpatine?"

"Yes. That is essentially correct."

Rhinann turned his head slightly to look at Jax, who stood behind the couch, his face devoid of expression. Lacking the Force, the Elomin had no way of knowing what the Jedi thought of this mad idea—though the very fact of his having allowed the Sakiyan to present it proved that he did not utterly reject it . . . as he should have, in the Elomin's opinion, had he even a milliliter of common sense.

"You realize, of course, that assassinating the Emperor is not exactly a new idea," Rhinann went on.

The Sakiyan nodded. "Yes."

"And that it has been tried—with disastrous results, I might add—by people with far greater resources than we have."

Tuden Sal raised a stubby digit. "I beg to differ. None of the Emperor's would-be assassins had any of the resources we possess. True, they had material means—perhaps even more than what you command." He nodded at Dejah Duare, who had seated herself at the far end of the couch, a frown wrinkling her crimson

brow. "But they did not have a Jedi Knight in their number, or the intelligence resources of the Whiplash, or the
invaluable services of someone so recently close to Lord
Vader as yourself. And they most certainly did not possess a droid with I-Five's special talents."

Rhinann blinked at the Sakiyan. All that he had said
was true—which made it no less insane an idea. Certainly, with Rhinann's knowledge of the internal work-
ings of the Imperial Security Bureau they might get close
to the Emperor's foremost champion, and thence to the
Emperor himself. And conceivably, with I-Five's unique
qualities they might be able to make it all the way to the
core of Imperial operations . . . but no, it was still insane, there was no other term for it. If the droid were to
be captured, his memory banks could and would be
scoured for information that would bring down the
nascent resistance in its entirety.

And as for what would happen to Rhinann himself—
he trembled at the thought. The most meticulous and
thorough of the Emperor's truth-scan agents would hap-
pily don metaphoric duralumin-toed shock boots and
kick their way through the gardens of his mind and
memories, merrily trampling all the delicate neuronal
sprouts and branchings underfoot until naught but a
bloody marsh remained. Rhinann closed his eyes, wish-
ing he weren't cursed with such a vivid imagination.

He sighed gustily through his nose, rattling his tusks.
"No," he said. "This is *not* to be contemplated. It's nerf-
brained, preposterous, absurd. The risks are simply
unacceptable."

"And once again, to the astonishment of all, I find myself agreeing with the tall, scraggly critter in the weskit."
This came from the Sullustan journalist, perched back
up in his usual spot in the window embrasure. "I've
thought about this sixty different ways and every one of

them looks too risky by half. If anything happened to I-Five—"

"I-Five?" Rhinann repeated in disbelief. "All you're worried about is the droid? Have you no conception of what it would mean to the Whiplash were I-Five to fall into enemy hands?"

"Or to the remaining Jedi," said Jax quietly.

"If there are any," added Rhinann.

"The *droid*," said I-Five with subtle emphasis, "would destroy his memory core if he felt his position was compromised. I'm more concerned that failure on my part would bring severe consequences for Jax or anyone else who might be caught facilitating my mission. For that reason, *if* I do this, I wish to do it alone. *Completely* alone."

"Five!" Den objected. "That's ridiculous. You can't go it alone on a mission like this. You'll need intel, backup, an escape corridor—"

"I can provide my own intel by slicing into the HoloNet within the Imperial complex, thank you very much. I can provide my own backup as well—after all, who expects a protocol droid to be outfitted with hidden laser pistols and other defensive systems? I can also, I trust, create my own escape corridor." The droid turned to Jax. "I would argue that one of the chief reasons for the failure of other assassination attempts was that there were too many people and too many resources committed to the effort. The more individuals there are engaged on the ground in such an undertaking, the more points of discovery there are."

Tuden Sal's gaze was riveted on the droid's gleaming metal face. "What do you propose?"

"Between myself and Rhinann," said I-Five, "I expect we can gain sufficient knowledge of Palpatine's itinerary that we can safely gauge his private locations based on his more public appearances. Once I know where he's going to be, it should be a simple matter of disguising my virtual identity such that when I access Imperial nodes on the HoloNet, I do so with an alias."

"A virtual disguise," Jax murmured.

"Precisely."

"Which is fine, except that you're a discontinued model," argued Den. "You may be able to fool the 'Net, but you're still a Five series droid. I'd bet good credits there aren't too many of those near the Emperor. No doubt he's got the newest, shiniest protocol droids Imperial creds can buy. Am I right, Rhinann?"

The Elomin nodded. "Exactly right. No offense, I-Five, but you *are* a bit of an antique."

The droid actually managed to look offended. "That's as it may be, but it's not an insurmountable obstacle. The model created to replace the I-Fivewhycue series differs only in a few minor external details. For example, the ocular units are smaller and use a halogen light emission system with a characteristically blue-white radiance; the chest plate has been modified to include a repulsor unit. And lastly, the external bus couplings have been streamlined. These are things it should be fairly easy to cosmetically adapt in my own appearance. And of course, I'll need a good polish."

"All easily arranged," said Tuden Sal. "Even the polish."

"In that case, throw in an oil bath and a circuit board tune-up."

"Done."

"While you're at it, you might consider picking up the tab for our memorial services," Dejah Duare said, speaking for the first time since their impromptu meeting began.

"You sound as if you're planning a costume for a masquerade," Dejah continued. "Whether I-Five goes in alone or not, potentially he could focus Imperial attention on us and on the Whiplash."

"I tend to agree with Dejah," Jax said.

"*There's* a big surprise," muttered Den under his breath.

Jax ignored the Sullustan's grousing. "This is something we need to think through very carefully."

"I don't think so," Dejah continued, focusing her entire attention on the Jedi. "I don't think so at all. It doesn't deserve to be thought through." She had clasped her hands over her breasts in what seemed almost a gesture of supplication. "Please, Jax. Don't let your personal feelings cloud your judgment. Let this go. Tell this man no."

Tuden Sal turned to look up at the Jedi. "What does she mean—your personal feelings?"

Jax opened his mouth to answer, but I-Five beat him to the draw. "There is every chance that Emperor Palpatine— though only a Senator at the time—ordered his father's death. I should think you'd know that better than anyone here," he added wryly. "After all, you were the last person to see him alive. He must have told you what he was planning to do after he turned me off."

The Sakiyan's bronze skin darkened further—a dusky flush rising from his neck to his cheeks. "He was going after the Zabrak. I figured then—"

"That he was as good as dead?" asked I-Five.

"I don't excuse my behavior," Sal returned with some asperity. "What I did then was stupid, shortsighted, and, yes, a betrayal of a good friend. What I do now is in aid of making up for it."

"My father is dead—" Jax began.

"Which nothing I did or did not do could have changed. Regardless of my actions, Lorn Pavan would have gone after the Sith and died. Even had he not, Palpatine or his acolyte would have eventually learned he was still alive, and killed him. Believe me—that's the way these people are. If I've learned nothing else, I've

learned that." Sal shook his head. "My people's ances-
tors were warriors, but they can't match—no one in the
galaxy can match—humans for sheer bloodthirstiness.
"That said . . ." Tuden Sal hesitated, seeming to age by
a decade in the measure of breaths he took. "If I had
taken I-Five to the Jedi as promised, it is possible . . ."
His voice faltered to a stop.

"That the Jedi might not have been destroyed," Jax finished for him. "That all of galactic history might have
been changed for the better by one small action of yours."

"Yes." Sal's voice was very soft.

There was a moment of silence in which Dejah Duare
looked from the Sakiyan to Jax to I-Five with an expression of incredulity on her pretty face. When she spoke,
her words seemed to be for Jax alone. "Well, there it is.
Yet another good reason *not* to involve yourself in this
absurd, hopeless plot. For all you know you could be
the last Jedi on the planet."

Jax shook his head. "I'm not."

"The last *real* Jedi, then. Yes, I know you think the
world of the Twi'lek, but she's not Temple-trained."

"That doesn't make her less a Jedi."

Dejah blinked at him, obviously taken aback. "That's
irrelevant. You're missing my point—or dodging it intentionally. If this plot were to be discovered and I-Five
captured, it would lead straight back to you. It might en-
able the Emperor to snuff out the light of the Jedi entirely."

"The light of the Jedi?" Jax repeated. "Is that what
I'm supposed to be? Well then, should I hide out, doing
nothing, until I die at a ripe old age . . . having done
nothing?"

"New Force-sensitives will be born," said I-Five
philosophically. "Someone has to train them if they are
not to fall to the dark side."

Jax looked up, startled.

By the nine gods of fury, Rhinann thought, *has he really never contemplated that before? Or did it just stun him coming from a soulless hunk of metal?*

"Which," I-Five continued, "is all the more reason that, if I were to undertake this . ... mission, you should be as far away from me as possible."

Rhinann blinked at the tone of the droid's voice. Was that really wistfulness? The shadow of impending loss? He shook himself. "I think it's all the more reason," he said to I-Five, "for you to forgo this 'mission' and do what you're best at: watching his back." He tilted his horned head toward Jax.

Tuden Sal cleared his throat. "As I-Five so aptly pointed out, he is an independent being."

"With an OFF switch," muttered the Elomin.

"An independent being," repeated Sal, "with the capacity to make his own decisions."

I-Five turned to Jax. "I do have that capacity, but in this case I'd like to hear the opinions of all concerned parties. Especially yours, Jax. In making this decision, I'll give your vote the most weight."

"Vote?" Dejah let out a peal of false laughter. "If we're to vote, I vote *no!*"

"As do I," said Rhinann.

"Ditto," said Den.

All eyes turned to Jax.

He met each gaze in turn—last of all, the droid's—then shook his head. "I don't know," he said quietly. "I just don't know." He glanced down at the Zeltron. "I think I need to go someplace where I can think this through."

And I, thought Rhinann, *need to go someplace where I'm not so likely to be killed.*

Probus Tesla knew the peace of the Force.

He had surrendered himself fully to its dark currents and, in moments such as this, he felt the power of those currents moving about him and within him, buoying him up, tugging at him, washing through him.

Cleansing him.

The Force was contentment. It was purpose. It was all. To be an instrument of justice, to believe absolutely in the righteousness of that justice, conferred great power . . . and without the concomitant responsibility. He was a young man, barely into his twenties; young enough that power without accountability was a heady combination. Young enough that the speed of his rise through the Inquisitorius filled him with fierce, hot pride. To be picked out of a literal army of applicants and made the personal factotum of the Dark Lord himself—it was a dream come true. To hone his power under the tutelage of Darth Vader was to drink from water very pure, very close to the Source, indeed.

Now he stood in Vader's presence and felt that purity of power flowing over him in thrilling waves. It was all he could do not to grin drunkenly with pleasure, but he kept his face composed and his spirit calm as he received his orders from his master.

In fact, he noted with bemusement, his mentor seemed less serene than he was. The Dark Lord had been pacing when Tesla had entered the room, and had not ceased doing so in the time the young Inquisitor had stood silently, awaiting his lord's pleasure.

At last Vader spoke, his voice washing over his acolyte like a deep, cooling tide. "I have sought Jax Pavan for some time now. I have, indeed, made it a priority, for reasons I have not shared with you. I commend you on your sense of duty, Inquisitor. Ever since I brought you in on this, you have not questioned my orders, though I sense you are curious about them.

"Now I have a new quest for you."

Tesla blinked. A new quest? He had yet to complete the old one. "My lord, I am close to finding Jax Pavan," he said in cool, even tones. "I am sure of it. I've been working one sector at a time, and—" A horrific thought occurred to him. "Do you believe me incapable?"

Vader paused in his pacing and raised a gloved hand. "Nonsense. I believe you quite capable. It is because of that that I am giving you this new mandate. When you find Pavan, you are neither to challenge him nor to harm him. Your mission will not be complete until you have found the protocol droid that has been his sometime companion—the I-Fivewhycue unit that reportedly was the property of Pavan's father. Pavan is a means to an end: find Pavan and let him lead you to the droid. Of course, if you should be able to locate the droid in some other way, Pavan can wait."

Had he heard right? Tesla shook himself mentally. It took every bit of discipline he possessed to remain stone-faced. He was somewhat taken aback when Vader sensed his dismay.

"Is there a problem, Inquisitor?"

"No, my lord." No, no problem, save that he had just been assigned to the scut work of locating a droid.

A *droid*.

You sent a stormtrooper on a fetch-and-carry mission like that. A lackey, someone with no special skills. Droids had no affinity with the Force, so sending a Force-sensitive on an errand like this was . . . well, at best, it was a waste of resources. At worst, it was a slap in the face.

"I am aware," Lord Vader said, the insectoid lenses of his mask trained on the Inquisitor, "that this presents more of a challenge. A droid is not Force-sensitive and thus will not reveal itself in that way to someone who is. But I have had it suggested to me that this is no ordinary droid."

As if that made it any less an insult. More of a challenge, indeed. Did Vader imagine he was speaking to a drooling Padawan?

But Probus Tesla was a professional. Despite his young age, he was a veteran of many such missions. He would perform whatever duty his lord deemed necessary, no matter how demeaning it was.

He raised his head to watch Darth Vader stride to the well-camouflaged window of his sanctum, where he looked out at the cityscape below and beyond. There was no reading the face hidden forever behind the obsidian mask, no body language to observe beneath the folds of the soot-dark robes. Nothing but that earlier pacing, which indicated a certain disquietude.

It occurred to Tesla that this was a test, not of his Force abilities, perhaps, but of his loyalty and his perseverance. He squared his shoulders and aligned his spine. One thing he was sure of—something about this particular quest agitated the Dark Lord. Perhaps if Tesla completed his mission, he would find out what it was.

With that in mind he bowed deeply from the waist, knowing that his lord could see his reflection in the window. "Regardless of what kind of droid it is, my lord, I will find it for you. And when I find it?"

"Bring it to me," his master said shortly. "In one piece and operative. And if possible, bring Pavan as well—in the same condition."

"As you wish, my lord," Tesla said and bowed yet again. He did not let his emotions show—not his disappointment, not his curiosity, not his hope that this was merely a gateway to greater things.

The Force would be with him, as it always was. Perhaps it would help him find this droid, somehow. And just maybe, he'd get lucky and catch a Jedi as well.

four

Probus Tesla.

There it was again—that name. That face.

Haninum Tyk Rhinann increased the magnification of his holodisplay and peered at the freeze-frame image of the Inquisitor he'd heard other members of the Whiplash refer to as "the Bloodfiend."

This was a human designation, originally a variant breed of terentatek used for tracking down sentients with an affinity for the Force—in particular, humans. The idea that humans hunted their own kind did not surprise Rhinann overly much, but knowing the provenance of the sobriquet in relation to Probus Tesla chilled him to the bone. Tesla was called the Bloodfiend because of his ability to "sniff out" his prey—Force-sensitive humans. He was steeped in the dark side, and it was said his sense of the Force was so delicately and exquisitively balanced that he could pinpoint its usage by a single being in a crowd of a million.

Rhinann didn't believe it, of course, but he was self-aware enough to know that this was largely envy on his part. He was certain that, were he human, he could stand right in front of the Inquisitor and raise not so much as a ripple in the Force—no more, say, than a droid or a doorpost. The knowledge galled him.

He reapplied himself to his surveillance. Here was Probus Tesla entering the Imperial Security Bureau yet

again. According to the scanner records Rhinann had
accessed, each time Tesla passed through the various
checkpoints in this hive of Imperial activity, he visited
not the offices of the Inquisitorius, nor the administra-
tive centers of the Emperor's functionaries, but rather
the palace quarters belonging to Darth Vader.

This was interesting to Rhinann because he had also
recently discovered, via a combination of HoloNet research and scuttlebutt from the streets, that Tesla had
been asking questions about one Jax Pavan, not to mention a droid who might be keeping company with him,
as well as an erstwhile Sullustan journalist . . . and, last
but unfortunately not least, an Elomin who might or
might not be seen with one or more of these individuals.

Interesting was not the operative term, of course. The
information he was uncovering was, in a word, terrifying, because it indicated that Vader knew more about
the company Pavan kept than was healthy for any of
that company—most of all Rhinann. Not to mention in-
dicating that Vader had narrowed his search for the Jedi
to this very sector of Imperial City.

Rhinann made a minute gesture that flipped the display to a frame in which he had been compiling a map.
This was a set of locations at which Tesla had been seen
or had asked a series of seemingly random questions
about a group of miscreants whom one would hardly
expect to find in close proximity. The bright dots on the
map formed a nearly circular pattern around the very
neighborhood in which Rhinann sat at his HoloNet
console.

No doubt about it—since Vader had brought in the
Inquisitorius, the net was tightening. He wondered why
the Dark Lord had waited this long to introduce the
heavy guns in his search for Pavan, and shrugged. Who
alive could fathom the mental machinations of Palpatine's second in command? No doubt Vader had his rea-

sons for prolonging the search this long. Perhaps he had been waiting for other arrangements and affairs to be concluded, or perhaps he merely enjoyed the whisperkit-and-mouse aspects of the hunt. It didn't matter; what did matter was that his former employer was obviously tired of fencing and was going in for the kill. Through Tesla, Vader had learned the names and occupations of all of Pavan's team of misfits, save one: as far as Rhinann had been able to ascertain, the only one whose name had not figured in Tesla's careful questioning was Dejah Duare. Which was a good thing, because if she was linked to the Jedi in some way by the Inquisitorius, her seemingly bottomless well of funds might be unexpectedly siphoned dry.

The Elomin's pulse quickened and a choking tightness seized his throat, uncomfortably close in sensation to one time when he had felt Vader's phantom grip close suggestively there. The connection between Dejah and the rest of them, he realized, could be made at any moment. If he was going to get out of this situation, he should act now, while the Zeltron's wealth was still available to him.

Quaking, he selected one of his newer aliases randomly from a cache of carefully compiled profiles of deceased and nonexistent persons, then accessed a travel broker's HoloNet node and prepared to buy himself a ticket offworld. Just shy of completing the transaction, however, he hesitated. If he left now, he might save his sorry hide, but he would forever forgo his chance of experiencing the Force . . . unless he found the bota and took it with him.

Rhinann sat back in his chair and stared, unseeing, through the travel brokerage's colorful HoloNet "storefront" to the dingy gray wall of the conapt and contemplated the full implications of that.

He had no moral problem with lifting the substance

and fleeing with it. His only problem was that he wasn't certain who had it. He suspected I-Five still carried it, but he couldn't be certain that the droid hadn't already revealed its existence to Jax Pavan.

Even if he had, Rhinann realized, I-Five might still be the safest entity to guard it. There was no way that even a dark-side-sensitive such as Probus Tesla could disinter stray thoughts to any meaningful degree from a droid brain.

The simplest thing to do, then, would be to kidnap I-Five.

He gave a half laugh, half snort that rattled his nose tusks. When kidnapping a freakishly sentient machine became the easiest of your options, you were in more trouble than you knew. Especially when the droid in question was contemplating regicide. Still, I-5YQ was, when all was said and done, a mechanical device, and like most mechanical devices he had an OFF switch. That switch was hardwired to the droid's consciousness template and couldn't be removed without irreparable damage—in other words, killing him. Therefore, for all of Lorn Pavan's clever manipulation of the droid's programming and firmware, that master switch must have remained untouched. If Rhinann could contrive to get the droid alone long enough to somehow deactivate him, he could go through his pockets—so to speak—thoroughly and without fear of reprisal.

That, of course, was the trick: I-Five's reflexes were preternaturally quick compared with even the dazzling reaction time of an Aleena. Next to Rhinann, who was a diplomat, not a warrior, he was bottled lightning. And unlike the average droid, he wasn't programmed against shooting first and interrogating the result at his leisure.

Rhinann backed out of the travel node and returned to his map. He considered the proximity of the Tesla hit closest to their bolt-hole. How long? he wondered. How long did he have before he completely ran out of time?

There was no way to know. He considered the sequence of his informants' reports about the Inquisitor and the amount of time that had passed between each of them. Based on this, he gave himself twenty-four standard hours to come up with a plan—or to have circumstances present him with an opportunity to isolate, deactivate, and rob I-Five. If he hadn't gotten the bota within the next day, he would simply leave. He was, after all, a practical being.

He returned to the travel node and purchased a one-way ticket for the next outbound freighter on the Perlemian Trade Route to Lianna, which was the closest planet to the Outer Rim in the sector nearest Elom. This time tomorrow, Rhinann promised himself as he transferred funds from the account Dejah had set up for them, he would be on that freighter, with or without the bota.

Jax made his way along the narrow, serpentine length of Snowblind Mews. It was a running joke among the members of the team that the namers of the narrow passage couldn't have had even the vaguest idea of what the appellation meant; no one on Coruscant had seen snow for uncounted centuries. It was Den's opinion that the name shining from street signs at the occasional corner was actually a ribald phrase in Shistavanen or some other planetary dialect that just sounded like *Snowblind Mews,* and that whenever Basic speakers uttered the phrase in the hearing of the aliens, they would howl with laughter.

Jax walked slowly, tentacles of Force-sense curling outward toward the walls of the densely packed resi-blocks that rose to dizzying heights on either side. It was not the worst neighborhood in which to live. In fact, the

ornate stacks of conapts that lined the mews and looked
out on the cul-de-sac plaza known as Poloda Place still
wore a shadow of their original elegance. Their once
gleaming walls were age-dulled and grimed, but there
was a certain shabby respectability about the place that
Jax felt was to their advantage. Most people who hid
out from the Imperial eye went to the lowest levels of the
city and dived into its deepest, darkest haunts. So when
Imperial forces went shopping for criminals, that was
the first place they looked. They did not often think of
poking their noses into the more affluent areas around
Poloda Place—usually a haven for artists and other creative types.

Until now, Jax reminded himself. Rhinann had told
him of the shadowy personage who had been nosing
about recently only one or two levels below. A human
named Tesla. A man well versed in the Force.

An Inquisitor.

Jax felt himself tighten up reflexively at the thought,
and wondered at the vagaries of fate. If Tuden Sal had
fulfilled his promise to Jax's father, he and Tesla might
have been peers, possibly even friends. Now he was set
at odds with a man he didn't even know.

He reached the street and began to walk aimlessly,
trying to process Sal's proposal and the reactions to it of
his teammates. Den, Rhinann, and Dejah were obviously dead set against the idea. That was understandable. They were afraid. It was just as understandable
that I-Five, who felt no fear, was willing to entertain the
idea.

Dejah's alarm, however, had been palpable. He could
still feel it tugging at him, imploring him. He wondered
if it stemmed from the fact that the Zeltron's late partner, the light sculptor Ves Volette, had been killed by a
domestic droid. The droid, which belonged to the house-
hold of one of Volette's most loyal patrons, had some-

how come to reason that it must use deadly force to protect the interests of its mistress.

It made emotional sense in the abstract that Dejah should have a fear of droids, but somehow the theory felt wrong under her particular circumstances. The crimson-skinned Zeltrons were a markedly hedonistic species of humanoid, whose unique combination of exceptional beauty, empathic ability, and pheromone production made them often seem shallow. Dejah was not shallow. She had grieved the loss of her partner, and had stayed on Coruscant out of loyalty to the man who had solved his murder. It was surely that same loyalty, Jax reasoned, that caused her to argue so vehemently against Sal's plan, and not an irrational fear of putting a droid in a position where it could kill. In the brief time she had been living with Jax's team in their roomy conapt she had shown no uneasiness around I-Five.

He was flattered, Jax realized. Flattered that Dejah had become so attached to him that she had not returned to her homeworld as she had planned. He chided himself for the emotion. He'd gotten past the need to draw on the Force to counteract Dejah's heady combination of pheromones and telempathic subtlety, but occasionally he caught himself having silly, almost adolescent thoughts about her. The fact that she had begged him not to leave the conapt just now, expressing fear for his life with the Inquisitors at large, had likely contributed to those thoughts.

He replayed their recent parting at the door of their apartment: her gazing up at him, worry on her lovely face, her deep red lips parted, her eyes glittering with fear, her hands fluttering between them like startled birds. He had felt her willing him to embrace her and had deflected the impulse, though perhaps not as successfully as he'd thought. It would have been the most natural thing in the world to lean his head down and kiss her. It was a moment out of a romantic holovid.

He chuckled and shook his head. *Gotta watch that.*

He knew his Jedi discipline and the detached state it supported frustrated the empathic Zeltron, and he suspected she'd be pleased to know how attractive he found her. He was not numb to her pull—he felt it as a tingle on the skin, a flutter of his heart, a quickening of his pulse—but he was a Jedi, after all, and it took just a touch of the Force to deflect her attempts to influence him.

He looked up to find himself at a crossroads: left, right, up, down. Which way to go? He struck out at random, stepping into the down tube. As he slowly descended he found himself thinking, unaccountably, of Laranth Tarak.

The Twi'lek Jedi had been absent from his team for several months now, and while this wasn't the first time he'd thought of her, it was the first time she'd come to his thoughts with such strength. He hadn't seen her since the day she'd quit the team to work full-time with the Whiplash and its leader, Thi Xon Yimmon, a charismatic Cerean who—to hear his associates tell it—possessed the fighting prowess of a trained soldier and the wisdom of a Jedi Master.

Strange, Jax thought. It hadn't occurred to him before to wonder why Laranth had abandoned their group. He recalled she'd been impatient with him about something— he'd never discovered what, exactly—and there had been a moment when he'd visited her in the medcenter after her encounter with the bounty hunter Aurra Sing, when he'd wondered if their relationship was sliding toward . . .

He drew himself up short, recalling the day: Laranth lying on the medcouch, patched and tubed and pale, and him at her bedside, a roil of emotions turning him inside out.

Had there been a moment when she had read him and feared he had grown too attached to her? Or had she already felt the pull of Yimmon's personality? Or both? Or neither?

He looked around and realized that his steps had taken him down into Whiplash territory. In fact, he was only a block or so from the charity in whose headquarters the group occasionally held clandestine meetings. It was one place of contact between the insurgent organization and those who needed its help.

It struck him, in that moment, that what he wanted most right now was Laranth's take on this whole business . . . and her opinion of the trustworthiness of Tuden Sal himself. After all, they had only Sal's word that he was really a new Whiplash member and that Laranth had sent him to their door. And even if she *had* sent him, that was no guarantee that his plan was sound.

Jax directed his steps toward the community kitchen that served as one of the Whiplash's windows on the world. He was about three long strides from the door of the charity when an unseen compulsion abruptly settled violently about him like a bola, all but spinning him about. For several seconds he felt like a feather buffeted in a strong wind. He put a hand out and steadied himself against the façade of the nearest building, reaching out with his senses to locate the source of the disturbance.

Down. Down and to the west. That was *where* it was.

What it was, was easy.

It was the Force.

five

Probus Tesla returned to Ploughtekal Market despite the fact that his target had been changed. After all, he reasoned, the droid and the Jedi he sought surely were in close proximity to each other. The droid belonged to Pavan, or so reports suggested.

Which led the young Inquisitor to wonder why his lord had changed the target in the first place. Find one, logic suggested, and you would eventually find the other. The Force had been telling him for weeks that a powerful sensitive was present in the environs of the marketplace. The chances of that being anything other than a Temple-trained Jedi were vanishingly slim. Tesla's own Force sensitivity was the surest means of finding Jax Pavan, so why would Darth Vader set him on this detour instead? Was it a test, or was his lord simply guiding him to use his sense of the Force in a different way than he was inclined to do?

The idea set him back on his heels, mentally speaking. Perhaps it was not his ability that Darth Vader doubted, but his loyalty. Perhaps what was being tested was not his skill but his obedience.

The thought raised a tendril of shame. He had doubted Vader's wisdom, if only for the briefest moment, and even as he went about seeking the protocol droid—asking questions of his contacts and sifting through the answers—

he was hoping to encounter the presence he'd come so close to touching mere days before.

He stood now in the shadow of a support pier listening to the marketplace chatter, sniffing its panoply of scents—greed, acquisitiveness, anger, satisfaction—tasting the subtleties of those emotions, hoping to encounter the vibrancy of the Force.

He experienced the Force that way—as scent, sight, sound, and savor. Every nuance of it thrilled his senses, playing darkly in his head, exploding on his tongue, dazzling his eyes with color and light. Because of the sheer power of those things, he'd had to learn at an early age to filter and control the impulses the Force evoked in him. It had been a lifelong struggle to work through the potency of those impulses, and he often wondered if all Force-sensitives experienced it in this way.

It was not the sort of question one was encouraged to ask other aspirants during Inquisitorial training. He had spoken of it to his master, of course, for he had to learn the discipline of his gift.

Master Kuthara had not commented on whether his particular experience of the Force was unusual or common. He had only said, "The Force flows through you, around you. You must learn to sail its currents and harness its winds without letting them swamp you or blow you off-course. Your discipline is a vessel, and you are the being whose hand is on the tiller."

He had been about fourteen when that conversation had taken place and had suspected that his master experienced the Force in just such a way—as a current to be ridden. He had been naïve enough at the time to ask, "But wind and wave have no motive, do they, Master? We speak of an ill wind, but isn't that just a pretty conceit? The wind and waves are random."

"Your point?" his Falleen master had asked, oddly puzzled.

Tesla had grown used to Master Kuthara answering his questions before he could even frame them; the uncertainty thus expressed had been a bit unnerving.

"Can the Force be said to have dark and light sides? Winds are neither dark nor light; currents are neither dark nor light, they simply *are*."

There had been a moment of suspended time in which he waited for his master to applaud his intuition, punish his audacity, or simply astound him with an answer of the utmost simplicity and profundity. He had more than half expected the latter. So the answer he got had stunned him.

"You disappoint me, Probus," his master had said. "It is the most elemental of understandings that the Force is a duality. You have mouthed that duality yourself, apparently without understanding it. Light and darkness simply are. It is that elementary."

Impulsively Tesla had blurted, "But isn't darkness merely the *absence* of light? Light is made up of photonic particles. Darkness isn't made up of anti-photons, is it?"

For that question he had been instructed to take his lightsaber and spend six hours practicing Shii-Cho—the most basic of combat forms.

Later, when he had lain on his bed aching with fatigue and numb with boredom, his master had come to him in an odd frame of mind—if not apologetic, at least conciliatory.

"You will understand in time, Probus," he'd said, "that the Force is neither as simple nor as complicated as we want to make it. It falls into the realm of neither science nor mysticism. Its use is at once an art and a discipline."

"Like sailing," Tesla had suggested.

His master had nodded, a wry smile curving his thin

lips. "Like sailing. Or like learning to sort through and comprehend the world of the senses."

Tesla sorted through his senses now: peering, scenting, tasting, listening, and still hoping that he would catch—

He raised his head and turned to look out over the marketplace, eyes narrowed. Through a veil of multicolored light he saw a flash of blue-white radiance moving away rapidly. The scent came next, pale and sweet and tangy at once. A sound that was almost musical danced and shimmered at the fringes of his hearing.

He smiled in anticipation and dived after the sensory ghost. The crowd of shoppers parted before him as people recognized the uniform of the Inquisitor—cloak and cowl of an indescribable hue that seemed to shimmer with phantom color, the Imperial crest upon one shoulder.

Across the width of the teeming square he trailed the bright target, determined not to lose it as it dimmed. He suspected the Jedi must have used the Force for something to have sent up such a vivid little flare just now. That puzzled him. It had puzzled him since the first time he'd picked up the telltale signature of a Force-user. A trained Jedi would surely know better than to give in to displays of power in so public a place, and it was hard to believe he would have need to.

This gave Tesla some pause; it was just possible, if not likely, that Jax Pavan was intentionally luring him somewhere.

He bit back a chuckle of dark mirth. That would be futile. Probus Tesla knew without ego—or nearly so—that his abilities were exceptional. He had been trained by one of the greatest masters in the College of the Inquisition, and he had earned his place in the Inquisitorius by utterly defeating that master.

Regrettable, that, and it had drawn from Tesla the

pledge that one day he would take Master Kuthara's place in the college himself, training aspiring Inquistors. He would never, he promised himself, give any of them any knowledge of himself that could be used for his undoing. Oh yes, he'd come to understand well why it was best not to speak to others about one's own relationship with the Force. To understand others' sense of the Force was to understand how they could be defeated.

He was dismayed to realize that the sensory target was dimming still further—its scent was all but gone, its taste turned to dust, its music muted. Only the light of it pulsed at the fringes of his awareness from white to blue, paling against the mundane palette of the market.

He hastened his pace, zigging and zagging through the crowd until he reached a long, dark alleyway with a dim rectangle of light at its nether end. Gouged into the ferrocrete walls of the surrounding buildings, the alley seemed to lead nowhere. And yet this was where his quarry had gone.

He pushed into the tunnel, senses groping before him as he moved. Once again, he suspected a trap, and once again he discarded the idea. He was, after all, effectively shielded from detection by his taozin-scale necklace.

The taozin were huge, segmented creatures that inhabited deep underground caverns beneath the planet-city and whose scales rendered their life force transparent to a Force-sensitive. Tesla's synthsilk necklace didn't possess enough of the rare and dangerously gotten substance to block him entirely from another Force-sensitive, but it was enough to scramble whatever emanations of the Force he leaked and render them almost unreadable. Jax Pavan—or any other trained Jedi—would have to work awfully hard even to get a fix on him.

He fingered the strand of synthsilk as he dived farther into the darkness of the passage, hastening toward its end. The rectangle of dim light grew ever larger. It was hypnotic, so much so that when he reached the aperture, Tesla very nearly stepped across the threshold to his death. The floor beneath his feet ended abruptly, and he had a momentry impression of a gaping chasm hemmed by unending walls and a drop into sheer nothingness.

His reflexes were such that he was able to catch himself, but it was the wind that saved him, not the Force. A veritable maelstrom spiraled up from the abyss, ripping his cowl from his head and lifting him bodily, tossing him backward into the tunnel like a piece of chaff.

He lay against the wall of the tunnel for a moment, heart hammering, breath coming in short, staccato bursts that echoed harshly against the stone of the walls. Then he picked himself up and approached the end of the tunnel with care. He poked his head through the door to nowhere and looked out.

Above was a pale blur of eternal twilight. Below, he could see the vertical flank of the cloudcutter through which the tunnel bore disappear into darkness. Hundreds of yards away across the chasm stood another cloudcutter, its broad flanks sweating dank grime.

There was no one in sight and no place anyone could have gone. Anyone except a Jedi.

He looked up, reaching out with his Force sense. He stretched across to the far building. He angled a look down.

And there it was, far below and to his right: that tiny point of light, the barest whiff of the perfume of power, the merest tinkle of sound. Hair rose up on his half-shaven head and down the backs of his arms. He smiled. *Good try, Jedi,* he thought, and stepped from the aperture into thin air.

The Force lowered him like an invisible turbolift. The violent updrafts of the abyss buffeted him occasionally, tearing at his robes, but still he rode silently, swiftly, his senses on that spot where one building ended and another began. The target had paused there below but suddenly began to move again, away from the chasm.

At the crumbling intersection of the two buildings—at a point where their buttresses seemed almost to intertwine—there was a gap. Just enough of a gap for a humanoid of Tesla's size to pass through. Tesla jackknifed and threw himself through the air toward the gap, unclipping his lightsaber as he flew but not igniting it just yet. He erupted through the needle's eye and into a cavern filled with rubble. His target had moved on ahead. He took only a moment to orient himself. The sheathing of the wall of the mammoth building on his right—the one from which he had dropped like a stooping raptor—had come away from the substrate and fallen in huge stone and duracrete panels against its nearest neighbor. What had once been a maintenance alley between the two had been transformed into a cavernous tunnel. But where the previous route had been narrow and human-sized with regular surfaces, this was a cave built by decay. Immense and asymmetrical, its ceiling ending in darkness far above his head, its uneven walls canted and uncertain, its floor littered with random chunks of rock and twists of durasteel eroded and fallen from the buttresses.

The wind sobbed inconsolably here, and the buildings seemed to groan and tremble at its passing. Above this there was another sound—no, not a sound exactly; more of a sensation, almost a *tingling* in the air.

Tesla hovered, perfectly still, listening, sensing, *feeling*. It was not the Force he felt, but some type of kinetic energy. He could feel it dancing across his cheeks and the backs of his hands, raising the narrow strip of red hair that ran from the crown of his head to the nape of his neck. A force field of some sort?

He moved slowly downward, senses probing the way before him, eyes watchful. His boots touched down lightly on the rubble-strewn floor, and he strode forward. The cleft was about twenty meters long and ended in a dim wash of light that seemed to flicker and weave like the shadow of a fire. At random points along its length, dark apertures suggested other means of egress and regress. He eyed them suspiciously, but none of them held anything of note. Armored rats. Hawk-bats, perhaps. Nothing sentient.

The only sentient target he sensed was ahead somewhere in or beyond that wash of inconstant light. Tesla activated his lightsaber. The blade hummed to life, the color of a sunset he had once seen on his homeworld of Corellia. It was also the color of the lava flows on Mustafar. He moved forward with cautious anticipation.

The target had stopped.

The threads Jax followed were slender and impossibly bright, but they seemed to flicker and pulse as he trailed them down into the depths of Ploughtekal Market. When he reached the lowest levels of the structure that housed the rambling bazaar, they were little more than the ghosts of threads—like an afterimage burned into the retina.

They were on the point of vanishing completely by the time he dived into the warren of crevices in the towering resiblocks that roughly defined Ploughtekal's borders. As he stood at the gaping mouth of one such crevice, several levels below where the marketplace petered out, he saw the threads break altogether.

He stood for a moment, trying to decide what to do next, then froze at the sudden sense of *presence* behind him. He swept his lightsaber into his hand, activated it, and spun 180 degrees in one smooth movement.

"I see I'm not the only one who's had her aura tweaked today." Laranth Tarak faced him from an alcove in the dirty wall of the junction in which he stood. She had a blaster in each hand and holstered one of them as she stepped out of the alcove.

Over her shoulder Jax could see a set of steel rungs embedded in the alcove wall. Okay, not an alcove, then—a chimney or access tube. He used the trivial observation to hide his reaction to seeing Laranth so suddenly and under such circumstances, and couldn't decide if he was excited or dismayed.

"You felt something, too?" he asked stupidly.

"I think I just mentioned that." The green-skinned Twi'lek's truncated left lekku shifted slightly on her shoulder and Jax had the irrational feeling that she was laughing at him, despite the fact that her mouth formed a familiar grim line . . . as it ever did. Also irrationally, he was finding it difficult to look away from her face.

He did so with a will, clipping his lightsaber back on his belt and nodding toward the crevice he'd been about to explore. "I lost it right here. What do you think it is?"

She shook her head, moving to peer into the darkness. "No idea."

"Inquisitor?"

"I suspect most of them carry taozin wards these days," she said.

"They what?" There he went, sounding stupid again.

She turned and looked at him, her eyes—which were the same rich shade of green as her skin—showing no amusement. "I noticed it about three days ago. I saw one of them plain as day about three levels up, snooping around in the bazaar. Saw him, but couldn't *sense* him."

Jax nodded.

"So, how . . . how have you been?"

She tilted her head to one side, right lekku curling slightly at the end, whatever that meant. He wished he knew how to read the sophisticated subtext that Twi'lek head-tails were said to convey.

"You can't tell?" she asked.

"No, I . . ."

"I can tell how you've been," she said cryptically, then jerked her head at the crevice. "You want to check this out or what?"

He nodded and let her precede him into the dark gap.

They'd gone maybe ten meters along its stygian length when Jax remembered that he'd thought of looking for her earlier. "Laranth," he said quietly, "about Tuden Sal . . ."

"What about him?"

"You know him."

"He came to us about three weeks ago. Got in touch with us through our contact at Sil's Place."

"Sil's Place," repeated Jax.

"A dive near the Westport. The Amani pubtender is an operative."

"And you trust him?"

"I wouldn't have helped him find you if I didn't."

He let that settle for a couple of beats. "Did he tell you *why* he wanted to find me?"

"He didn't want to find *you*, exactly. He wanted to find I-Five. To repay an old debt, he said. He told me what he'd done . . . or rather what he failed to do." Her voice was grim, cold. It took Jax back to the night he and the Gray Paladin had met in the ruins of the Jedi Temple complex amid the death and smoke and flame. She knew as well as he did that what Tuden Sal had failed to do may have been responsible, among many other things, for what they referred to as Flame Night. Responsible for the deaths of all those innocent Jedi and Padawans.

"Did he tell you how he plans to repay that debt?"

She shot a glance back over her shoulder. "I figured that was between him and I-Five."

"No. Not really. It's a lot more complicated."

He was about to explain just how complicated when the Force nearly yanked him off his feet for the second time that day. This time there was no question what direction the pull was coming from—the tether stretched away into the darkness of the crevice.

He didn't have to ask if Laranth had felt it, too; the Twi'lek Paladin was already in motion. Jax unclipped his lightsaber and hurried to keep up.

Tesla stepped from the shadows of the fallen buttressing into light that was brilliant only in comparison with the midnight gloom he'd just traversed. The sight that met his eyes was confusing at first. Stretching away from him for perhaps a hundred meters was a debris field roughly twenty or thirty meters wide, formed by the gap between two massive resiblocks. It made what he'd just passed through look like a well-tended garden path; twisted lengths of duralumin and gigantic shards of transparisteel, some thicker than his body, lay like strange, misshapen skeletons over and around chunks of masonry and plasticrete. The two resiblocks on either side were apparently in an advanced state of decay, and this bizarre landscape was the result.

But there was more to it than that, Tesla sensed as he drew closer. The air here was charged with electrostatic energy that made every hair on his body stand on end and created strange creeping halos around the pieces of debris. As he continued to move, he found it more difficult, as if the very molecules of the air conspired to push him back. He realized that this was a repulsor field, subtly tugging and twisting due to an everlasting state of flux, which had, over the centuries, warped the huge pieces of various metals into the agonized postures that lay all about him.

Peering down the length of the cluttered swath, Tesla saw the source of the weird auroras. At the far end of the wreckage a repulsor field generator thrummed, the subtle, light-bending contours of the region pressing against the canted walls of the buildings and coating them with shimmering iridescence. A faulty field generator would explain the state of flux that caused the visible effects. Under normal circumstances the field would be invisible.

He smiled. If his quarry had come in here thinking to escape him, he had erred grievously. That repulsor field would thrust back whatever approached too closely. The Jedi had come to a dead end, and the slice of darkness that marked an exit, which Tesla could just make out through the writhing veil of the energy barrier, might as well be on another world—he would never be able to enter it.

Tesla started forward again, his lightsaber at the ready. He was halfway across the open expanse when he saw a figure emerge from the crumble of rock and steel, to clamber up and stand atop a huge chunk of ferrocrete. Two things struck him simultaneously: One was that the figure thrown in relief against a rippling curtain of light was not Jax Pavan, but a teenage human boy with a wild mane of pale hair. The other was that there were two field generators—one on each side of the canyon formed by the two resiblocks. At a point just beyond where his unknown target stood the two fields overlapped, creating a sort of hole through which the boy doubtless intended to flee . . . unless Tesla did something to stop him.

That he *should* stop him was obvious. No, this was not Jax Pavan, but it was a Force-user of such power that he had drawn Tesla to him as a lodestone draws iron.

In the moment of decision, Tesla flung himself into the air in a graceful Force leap calculated to carry him within striking distance of his quarry. But instead of landing at the foot of the ferrocrete block, he was met in midleap by a resilient energy barrier that slapped him to the ground. Hard.

He fell between a gleaming shard of transparisteel and a twisted spur of durasteel buttress, only his finely honed reflexes and a sweep of his lightsaber saving him from serious injury. He thought for an instant that he must have connected with the repulsor field, but realized the impossibility of that as quickly as the thought occurred to him. His quarry had been standing at the edge of the field—the barrier he'd struck had met him several meters from that verge. He hadn't collided with the repulsor field; he had been struck down by the Force, wielded by someone who had remarkable strength in it.

Someone he could not afford to let get away.

He gathered himself and leapt again, up into the charged air of the ersatz canyon. He lit upon the block of ferrocrete as lightly as a bird, ready to fire a bolt of Force-lightning at his opponent.

His target was gone.

Tesla reached out with his senses toward the interstices of the two repulsor fields. He found his prey with eyes and the Force simultaneously. Two strides took him over the edge of the block of debris and down onto the ground behind it. Above him the energy fields pulsed and flickered, making him feel as if fire gnats crawled over his body. But directly before him was a warped corridor of safety—a buffer zone in which the opposing fields canceled each other out.

It writhed and shifted as if alive—a twisted gullet that bent light and refracted color. It conjured the image of two deep pools of troubled water kept back from each other by an invisible and uncertain barrier. How in the name of the Force was the boy able to navigate it?

It hardly mattered. Tesla reached out with the Force and grasped the fleeing figure, yanking it to him. The boy fell backward, his tattered cloak fluttering about him. Tesla could feel the presence in his hand almost as an actual, tactile sensation. He tightened his Force grip and dragged the boy toward him.

One pale hand reached out of the tattered cloak as if to try to arrest his headlong slide. Tesla smiled grimly and squeezed—then cried out in surprise and consternation as his feet were wrenched out from under him. He landed hard on his back, air driven from his lungs, and dropped his lightsaber.

He took only a second to recover, by which time his quarry was gone again. The boy might be young, but he was obviously no novice; Tesla would not allow himself to be lulled into stupid complacency again.

He picked up his lightsaber and hooked it to his belt, then went after the boy with both hands. This time he would not be deflected or caught off-guard. He would capture this prize for his master. Failure was not an option.

At the mouth of the energy corridor, he reached out anew with the Force, using one hand to restrict his target's limbs and the other to haul him in. Concentrating his full attention on his task, he almost failed to catch the sudden movement of a five-meter-long section of fallen buttressing that swung suddenly toward his head.

Tesla whirled, using both hands to deflect the deadly length of metal. In his frustration and anger he did more than deflect it—he sent it flying. It hit the edge of one of the repulsor fields and exploded skyward. By the time it fell, hitting the ground with a shriek of metal on stone, Tesla was in motion, pursuing his elusive quarry into the wriggling corridor of energy.

It was an unnerving place—an ever-changing passage of creeping light and shadow through which the external world could be seen as if through a thick wall of gel. Now the walls were rippling toward him; now they flew away like a sac swollen by a breath of ionized air. Far above—forty stories, perhaps—he could see a thin sliver of twilight sky. Then that was wiped from view in the rippling distortions of the walls.

The sounds, too, were distracting; deafening screeches and roars, like metal sheets being ripped asunder, and his nostrils were constantly assaulted by the stench of ozone. He ran, using the Force to speed him along and deflect the billowing walls of the passageway. He tried nothing else until the boy was perhaps three meters ahead of him; then he reached out and tripped him. Or tried to . . . It was as if the boy could read his intentions and knew just when to defend himself; this time he simply lifted his feet from the ground and somersaulted up the passage several meters before turning, touching down, and doing something that changed Tesla's mind utterly about the nature of their contest.

The boy *reached into* the transparent energy fabric of the repulsor field—something that should have been impossible—and literally wrenched out a blazing ball of energy, molding the mass of writhing static between his hands as if it were made of modeling gel instead of highly charged energy particles. Then he flung the blindingly bright ball at Tesla.

The Inquisitor whipped into a defensive position, erecting a barrier against the salvo. It seemed to matter little; it still took him by storm, knocking him backward almost to the entrance of the corridor. Only his own well-honed control of the Force kept him from tumbling out of control. He jackknifed in the air and came at the boy again, this time with his lightsaber lit.

He saw the boy's face clearly as he charged. The cowl of his cloak lay back on his narrow shoulders, his hair floated wildly about his head, and his eyes were huge with fear and fury.

Feeling the youth's anger, Tesla was exultant. He had a fleeting thought of what a prize this child would make for his lord, but the proud thought was swamped by survival instinct—and by his own wrath. He would not be bested by a mere boy! He roared aloud, using the Force to amplify the sound, and saw the teenager's eyes widen farther.

Tesla was ready when the second ball of repulsor energy came flying at him. He raised his lightsaber to parry it—and was blown upward into the heights of the field tunnel in a flash of searing crimson light. At a height of seven or eight meters, he collided with a ripple in the energy barrier that deflected him downward again with just as much force. He came down on the gritty duracrete surface face-first, only just gathering the presence of mind to wrap the Force around him like a cocoon. It was all that kept him from breaking bones.

He levitated back to his feet, enraged, and threw back his own cowl. "Fool!" he roared at the retreating form. "I offer you freedom and you choose to hide with the vermin!"

The youth hesitated and turned. "You're an Inquisitor." His voice came to Tesla's ears warped and tortured by the skittering, moaning sounds of the warring repulsor fields.

"So could you be, with your power."

The boy's unspoken scorn was immediate and powerful, as if it, like his unlikely ability, was fed by the Force. He started to turn away.

"Return with me or die!"

The boy turned back, his gaze meeting Tesla's so strongly that the Inquisitor heard it as a rending sound in his head and felt it as a searing pain behind his eyes. His heart pounded, his breath was suddenly constricted—

he felt like a lidded vessel filling with some white-hot substance until it must surely burst. The fire gnats were crawling over him again, inflaming every nerve in his body.

"Leave me alone," the boy said quietly, and the words sounded in Tesla's head, each one like an icy dagger in his paralyzed brain. "Just *leave me alone*."

Then suddenly he was free. He stumbled to his knees, fury and humiliation sweeping through him in waves. Tesla lifted both hands and fired a bolt of Force-lightning at the corridor just above the boy's head, uncaring of the result. If the wretch would rather die than be taken by an Inquisitor, then so be it.

The lightning struck the rippling surface and bifurcated, each sizzling lash recoiling to strike again centimeters apart. They twinned again, then quadrupled.

Tesla cut off the flow of Force-lightning from his body, but it had little, if any, effect. Suddenly the corridor was filled with a dozen random lightning strikes, then twice that many. They were advancing on him in a trenchant storm, eating up the passageway before him. He couldn't see what had happened to the boy; his figure was lost in the erratic pulses of light. Tesla threw up a defensive barrier and backed swiftly away from the advancing lightning. Surely, with its motive energy cut off, it would soon fade.

He kept moving, staying just ahead of the searing, draining discharges until he was certain the exit must be directly behind him. He glanced over his shoulder. It was not. In fact, only a meter or two farther along the passage, what had been an open passageway seemed to end in a pocket of charged and warped air.

He hesitated, heart thudding. How was this possible? The interstice in which he stood was formed by a cancellation effect. The two fields' overlap was unstable, but the instability was linear. There was no way the two opposing fields could meet and meld in that way, no power that could—

He peered beyond the barrier, through the fluctuations in the cul-de-sac. Beyond them, out in the open debris field, he saw a lone figure standing atop a slab of ferrocrete. A figure with a bright mane of pale hair, rippling and warping as if viewed beneath the surface of a storm-tossed sea.

The dance of energy on the left side of his face alerted Tesla to the fact that he had hesitated too long. He had barely enough time to stiffen his Force shield against the lightning before it struck, exploding the tiny pocket of relative calm in which he stood—

When Jax first emerged from the cut into what passed for daylight at this level of the city, he wasn't sure what he was seeing. At the far end of the plaza, between the walls of two massive buildings, a pair of indistinct figures struggled within what looked like a writhing bowl of transparent, gelatinous light. It looked like the interstice between two force fields, but Jax had never encountered such a thing except in theory.

He glanced at Laranth, who gave the Twi'lek equivalent of a shrug, both lekku lifting slightly before settling again, the shorter one just brushing her shoulders.

That both combatants possessed the Force in abundance was obvious. They knocked each other off their respective feet several times before one hurled a ball of such brightness at the other that it was painful for Jax to look at it, even from meters away.

Laranth stopped in midstride, peering at the unstable slot between the fields. "What was that? It didn't look like Force-lightning."

A second charged ball erupted toward the figure nearest the entrance to the flux. This time the would-be victim met it with his lightsaber—his bright *crimson* lightsaber.

"Sith," hissed Jax under his breath as the repulsor fields lit up like a festival barge. "Or an Inquisitor."

"Then who's the other guy?"

"I'd love to know." Jax activated his lightsaber and moved cautiously toward the fray, keeping low and moving from cover to cover, Laranth at his back.

They had reached a particularly large block of ferrocrete when the fault between the two fields erupted in a fitful blaze of blue-white light that seemed to grow exponentially.

"Now that *is* Force-lightning," Jax murmured.

"From the Sith?"

"Must be. The other one just disappeared."

The other one reappeared suddenly, shooting out through the narrow interstice at a height of at least two stories. Clear of the repulsor fields, he executed a perfect somersault in midair and landed on the slab of ferrocrete beside which Jax and Laranth sheltered. With a motion that suggested the closing of a curtain, the youth—for he couldn't have been more than about fifteen or sixteen—closed the lips of the flux zone, sealing the Sith within. A heartbeat or two later, the fields blazed brighter than the noonday sun on Coruscant's uppermost levels and gave a sound that made Jax think the sky was splitting. The concussion hurt his ears and buffeted him even in the lee of the ferrocrete block, and it knocked the boy from his high perch to the ground.

He wasn't unconscious when Jax and Laranth got to him, but he was stunned. Aware of the other's obvious power, Jax projected feelings of calm as he knelt beside him.

"That was a pretty neat trick you did with that field back there," Jax said mildly. "Is that dead end going to last much longer?"

The boy blinked and shook his head.

"Then we'd better get you out of here. That Inquisitor's going to be pretty mad when he comes to."

"If he's still alive," Laranth murmured.

"Who are you?" the boy asked, confusion and fear intertwining in his voice and invading his gray eyes.

Jax held his lightsaber up between them, then deactivated it. "I'm a Jedi Knight," he said. "My name is Jax."

six

Jax and Laranth stopped to reconnoiter in the confluence of corridors where they'd met on their way to the Force eruption. The boy, who'd mumbled that his name was Kaj, seemed less dazed now. His eyes kept going to Jax's lightsaber.

"Which way from here?" Laranth asked, jerking her head toward the alcove terminus of the shaft she'd descended earlier. "That comes out in Ploughtekal. Near the heart of it, in fact. If the Inquisitors are looking for our friend, the market might offer us the best cover. How did you come down?"

Jax grimaced. "I barely remember. Kaj here sort of swept me off my feet."

"If you're a Jedi, where's your lightsaber?"

Laranth and Jax turned in unison to look at the boy. He actually blushed.

"Strictly speaking," Laranth told him, "I'm a Gray Paladin. We have a somewhat different approach to a few things, lightsabers being one of them. A Gray Paladin isn't married to a particular weapon. We simply use the Force through whatever tool we prefer. I like blasters." She patted the pair holstered at her thighs. "Though I've been known to use a vibroblade from time to time."

The boy turned his eyes to Jax. "Your lightsaber is red. *His* was red." He flicked his gaze back the way they'd come. "How do I know you're really Jedi—either of you? How do I know you're not Inquisitors?"

Jax could feel the uncertainty and fear building up behind the pale eyes. Building toward panic. He'd already seen what this Force prodigy could do when panicked.

"I'm not," he said. "Touch me. Use the Force to reach out and read me. I won't stop you." He saw Laranth's eyes widen just before he closed his own and opened himself to this strange boy. He felt her trepidation as a cascade of cold lines down his back, felt the boy's tentative touch as a cool tendril of uncertainty.

Blue. The Force manifested in Kaj as amorphous blobs, blue tending toward violet. Jax saw them in his mind's eye reaching out for him, encircling him, probing.

After a moment the touch was withdrawn and he opened his eyes to see the boy looking at him, perplexed.

"What did you sense?"

"There's no anger in you. No rage. I have so much and I have to fight it so hard sometimes. And he . . ." Again, the flicker of attention back toward the debris field with its possibly dead Inquisitor. ". . . he was like a *furnace*. He burned with it. Why are you so different?"

"Because I'm a Jedi," Jax answered him. "Our Inquisitor friend is—something else."

"A Sith?"

Jax glanced at Laranth. "What do you know about the Sith?" he asked Kaj.

The boy shrugged. "Legends. Myths."

"Well, there are all kinds of Sith. As far as I know, an Inquisitor isn't actually a Sith. But they do use red light-sabers. It's a function of the crystal that's used. Different crystals produce different colors."

"So . . . it's a choice you make."

Jax and Laranth traded glances. "Yes," Jax said. "Usually. Only I didn't choose this lightsaber. The one I had, the one I built and trained with, was destroyed. This one"—he patted the hilt—"was given to me by . . . someone who knew I needed one."

Laranth moved restively. "I hate to break this up, but we have a logistical problem—how to get Kaj onto friendly turf."

"Yes, but which friendly turf?" Jax met her eyes, which made his stomach feel strange. "I can take him back with me, or you can smuggle him to Thi Xon Yimmon."

"Yimmon has a lot on his plate," the Twi'lek said. "I can't conscionably give him yet another consideration without asking."

Kaj, who'd been sitting against a pile of rubble, scrambled to his feet. "I'm not a consideration. I'm a Jedi. At least, I *want* to be a Jedi," he amended when the weight of dual gazes fell on him. "I want to be trained. I want to—to learn to use the Force. To control it instead of having it . . . burn through me like it does. It—it scares me sometimes. The way I feel. The way *it* feels."

He ran down, his hands tugging at his cloak, his eyes pleading. He looked and sounded so very young and fragile . . . which made what he'd done to the Inquisitor back there all the more astonishing.

I-Five's words came back to Jax at that moment— what the droid had said about Jax being needed to train the next generation of Jedi. Perhaps that need was already presenting itself.

"We'll take him to the conapt," he told Laranth. "But be sure to give Yimmon a full report. Maybe it's best for him to train with you, learn the ways of the Paladins."

"Maybe it's best he gets the high points of both philosophies," said Laranth. "Circumstances being what they are, mutual exclusivity is a luxury the Jedi can't afford."

She was right, of course. They were stronger together

than apart. Which brought Jax's mind forcibly around to the fact of her leaving their team. He opened his mouth to say something about it, to suggest that she come back, but she was already moving into the alcove, craning her long, graceful neck to scan the vertical shaft with its inset hand- and footholds.

She flicked her green gaze back to Kaj. "Can you do a controlled leap when you're *not* under attack?" she asked, and Jax thought that her lips curled slightly at the corners.

The boy moved to peer up the ferrocrete tube. He nodded. "I think so. At least I've leapt as high as that cross-shaft." He pointed straight up.

Jax joined them in the small access, following the boy's gesture to a point roughly ten meters up, where a durasteel catwalk skirted the shaft, halving its diameter.

"Good," Laranth said. She drew one of her blasters. "I'll go first. Follow me up."

She leapt, reaching the metal platform easily and lighting on it with a soft tap of her booted feet. Kaj glanced at Jax, who nodded encouragingly, then followed, overshooting the catwalk by almost a meter. Laranth snagged his cloak and reeled him in before leaping away to a higher perch.

Jax took that as his cue to move, and joined Kaj on the catwalk. The boy peered at him in the twilight gloom, his eyes betraying fear.

"Won't they feel us? The Inquisitors, I mean. Won't they feel us using the Force?"

"Probably. But they certainly felt that big explosion you set off back there, and hopefully that's where they'll concentrate. It'll take only a few seconds to reach the bazaar, and once we're there, we can blend in. Now go on up. Laranth is waiting for you."

They got him back to Poloda Place without incident. The market was, in fact, curiously empty of Imperial presence, and Jax, despite stretching to the limit of his Force senses, detected not even an Inquisitor—or, rather, the "hole" in the Force that would suggest the use of a taozin cloak such as some of the Inquisitors used to hide their presence from other Force-sensitives.

Jax was surprised when Laranth accompanied them all the way to the conapt. Rhinann and I-Five were both connected to the HoloNet when they entered the living area. Rhinann glanced up with obvious surprise, whether at seeing Laranth or their guest or both, Jax couldn't say. I-Five's photoreceptors blinked once, then settled on Kaj.

"Are Dejah and Den around?" Jax asked.

"Dejah Duare is out," said I-Five in his obedient-protocol-droid voice. "Den Dhur is in his room composing a correspondence."

Jax smiled at how jarring it was to have this particular protocol droid behaving in ways that were normal for a protocol droid. "It's all right, I-Five. Kaj is . . . Kaj is a friend. And he's a Force-sensitive. He just took down an Inquisitor single-handedly and unarmed."

"He did what?" Den Dhur stood in the doorway to his quarters, his already large eyes looking huge in the wash of full-spectrum light from the room's cleverly concealed indirect illumination.

"Kaj, this is Den Dhur. A member of our team."

The short, stocky Sullustan came farther into the room, his eyes on the newcomer. "Oh, great. Sure. Let's make polite introductions while every Imperial stormtrooper on Coruscant is out looking for him."

Jax shook his head. "Den, didn't you hear what I said?"

"Yeah, I heard what you—"

"Kaj is a potential Jedi," said Jax patiently. "The Inquisitor was after him. He didn't get him. That's *good* news."

"Good news? He's a potential time bomb, Jax. Can't you—" He cut off as I-Five's metal hand came down on his shoulder.

"Den, it's rude to talk over someone as if they weren't there. I know—people do it to me all the time. What Jax is telling us is that the Emperor failed to get yet another valuable prize. For all his trying, he has failed to capture Jax, and now he's failed to capture our new friend—" The droid tilted his head toward the boy, who blinked.

"Uh," Kaj said. "Kajin. Kajin Savaros."

Jax steered Kaj around the Ves Volette light sculpture that Dejah had installed in their living space and into the seating area. He sat him down in a formchair, then moved to sit on one corner of the couch, facing him. "Are you hungry, Kaj? Thirsty? It can't be easy living out there on the street like that."

"I'm starved actually. I'd stolen some stuff from the market, but the Inquisitor smoked me out before I could eat much of it."

Jax started to rise, but I-Five waved him down. "Allow me. Laranth, would you also like some refreshment?"

The Twi'lek opened her mouth, glanced at the droid, then simply nodded and followed him over to the beverage dispenser.

"The Inquisitors are after you, too?" Kaj asked Jax, pulling his eyes from the light sculpture's kinetic, ever-changing display. "Because you're a Jedi?"

"That's the official reason, I guess. It's really a lot more complicated than that. What about you? How long have you been dodging Inquisitors?"

"Since I turned fifteen six weeks ago. That was when the Force really woke up in me. Before that, I was just another street kid who occasionally made strange things happen."

"But you haven't always lived on Coruscant."

Kaj shook his head, his eyes lighting up at the sight of the plate of ghibli fruit and a tall glass of some sort of red tea that I-Five carried toward him on a tray. One of I-Five's soothing concoctions, Jax figured. The boy accepted the food and took a healthy bite before answering Jax's implied question.

"I got here about . . . oh, seven months ago, I guess. From M'haeli." The expression on his face froze, and Jax could feel the cold, swift stab of grief that lay behind it. "My parents' farm was destroyed by Imperial troops. My father was a local elder. They wanted to make an example of him—show that they were the leaders now. So they sacked the farm and drove us off it. Mother and Father put me on a transport to Coruscant, hoping . . ." He shrugged, swallowing a mouthful of fruit. "I'm not sure what they were hoping. My parents knew I was different. Since I was a baby I'd occasionally, like I said, make strange things happen—you know, levitate something to make it come to me, that sort of thing." He drank most of the tea in a single gulp. "They knew the Jedi Temple was gone, but I think my mother was hoping I might find someone . . ." His eyes sought Jax's, then moved to Laranth, who had come back into the room behind I-Five.

"Someone who would train you," Jax finished.

"Train who to do what?" Dejah Duare swept into the room, unwinding a long, pale scarf of translucent golden synthsilk from her deep crimson hair, which blazed when the light hit it.

Jax felt his throat constrict and used a tendril of the Force to fend off the effects of Dejah's sensual aura. At first he thought she must have caught something of the tenor of their discussion and that concern had caused an unconscious spike in her pheromones. Then he realized that her gaze was not on Kaj, but on Laranth.

The Twi'lek didn't so much as twitch a muscle, but

she disappeared from Jax's sense of the Force almost as effectively as if she'd put on taozin-scale armor.

"I need to report to Yimmon," she said. "Let me know what you decide, Jax. Good-bye, Kaj. May the Force be with you. You've found a good teacher."

She glided past Dejah without so much as a glance. Jax opened his mouth to call after her, but couldn't think of anything to say. He shrugged mentally; that was just Laranth's way. He should be used to it by now.

"Report what to Yimmon?" Dejah asked coming farther into the room, settling the scarf about her shoulders. "Decide what? What's she talking about?"

Den, who'd been hovering between anteroom and living area, scuttled quickly out of her way and took a seat next to Jax on the couch.

Only when she'd rounded the chair Kaj was sitting in did her eyes fall on him. She smiled, radiantly, her smile like a benediction.

Kaj's eyes widened, then flicked toward Jax as if seeking instructions. "You're a Zeltron," he said with something like awe in his voice.

"Oh boy," Den muttered.

Jax elbowed him. "Dejah, this is Kajin Savaros from M'haeli. He just had a narrow escape from an Inquisitor. Laranth and I were lucky enough to have witnessed Kaj's powerful use of the Force in defeating that Inquisitor. Alone. Unarmed."

Dejah drew in a deep breath and exhaled, her eyes meeting Kaj's. "Remarkable. Then . . . are you a Jedi?"

"I *want* to be. I'm hoping Jax will teach me."

Dejah's regard swung to Jax. "That's what you meant, then. Teach him to become a Jedi. You want to take him on as a Padawan. There, you see, it's just like I-Five said: if the Jedi Order is to be rebuilt, you'll have to have a hand in it. Surely you can see that now."

"I wasn't blind to it before," said Jax gently. "I was just aware that there are other priorities."

"What could be more important than that?" Dejah demanded. "What could be a more valuable thing for you to do than to train this young man?"

She was trying to make points with him by flattery, of course, Jax realized. Trying to convince him to stay out of Tuden Sal's plottings. He smiled, warmed by the fact that she cared so much for him.

Den growled. "What a bunch of bilterscoot."

I-Five stirred and made his throat-clearing sound. His sudden reappearance in the conversation startled Kaj. Jax saw the boy's reaction as a sudden appearance of a multitude of Force spikes that darted out and receded as soon as he registered the source of the sound and movement.

Jax frowned. That had been an involuntary reflex; Kajin Savaros was wearing the Force awfully close to the surface. If it was that easy for Jax to sense him, how much easier would it be for an Inquisitor?

"While I agree with Dejah Duare in principle," I-Five said, "it does seem to me that in light of the way Kaj came to be among us, we should be prepared to move him—and ourselves as well—if it becomes necessary."

"Why would it become necessary?" asked Dejah, looking from Jax to the droid to Kaj.

"Maybe you didn't hear Jax clearly, Dejah," said Den acerbically. "Kajin, here, defeated an Inquisitor. Which probably means that the entire College of Sith flunkies is about to come down on our heads."

Dejah swung around to look at Kaj. "But you killed him, surely?"

"I—I don't know," Kaj stammered, then looked to Jax. "Is there a way we can tell?"

Jax shook his head. "All I can tell you is that he wasn't

conscious when we left the area. I didn't detect any Force threads from him at any rate."

"Force threads?" repeated Kaj.

"Metaphorically speaking."

"What difference does it make if he's dead?" Den asked sharply. "The Inquisitors aren't loners. They stay connected to their boss. If you killed him, then he just became a big, fat blank spot on Vader's sensors, and if he's still alive, he'll go scurrying back to his lord and master to make a full report."

"He's already a big, fat blank spot, Den," Jax explained. "Laranth told me that the Inquisitors have started using some sort of taozin by-product to block detection."

"How much danger do you think we're in?" Dejah asked.

"No more than we were before. But I do need to start Kajin's training."

"Good," said I-Five. "That should give you incentive to complete the lightsaber you've been working on. And, if we can find another crystal, you might even be able to retrofit the lightsaber you're carrying now to emit a less sanguinary hue."

Dejah laughed, the sound trilling and warm. "I resent that remark," she said without rancor. "I find crimson a most appealing color . . . don't you, Kajin?" She cocked her head pertly to one side, sending a thick lock of burgundy-colored hair over one eye.

The boy nodded mutely.

"Oh please . . ." Den slid off the couch and disappeared into his room. After a moment, I-Five followed him.

Jax looked at Kaj. The boy's eyes were still on Dejah, but they seemed unfocused, vague. "You up for starting your career as a Padawan?" Jax asked.

The boy shook himself visibly. "I'm pretty tired. Is there someplace I could sleep for a while?"

Jax took Kaj to the sleep alcove in his own quarters and bedded him down, hoping he wouldn't have any Force dreams. With power like Kajin Savaros had shown, a Force dream could wreak havoc on their homestead.

He'd soft-pedaled that just now, he realized, and he said nothing of his concern to Dejah when he returned to the living room to find her sitting in the chair Kaj had lately occupied.

"This is a good thing, isn't it, Jax—this boy?" Her eyes were eloquent with the need to be reassured.

"It's a very good thing. Once he learns to use his ability—well, I can only imagine the sort of things he'll be able to do. You should have seen him, Dejah. He was nothing short of astounding. I've never seen anyone do what he did—just by instinct, I think. He handled repulsor energy as if it were malleable—clay in a sculptor's hands."

"Or light?" She smiled up at him, obviously thinking of her late partner, whose light sculptures had been the pride of Coruscant's elite collectors, and to whom she'd been completely devoted.

That devotion was an unusual trait in a Zeltron. As a species they were naturally inclined to swift, passionate relationships, torrid love affairs, brief obsessions. Dejah was different, and Jax suspected at times that she had not completely transferred her devotion from Ves Volette to him—that beneath her air of sultry flirtation lurked a deeper current of mourning.

He shook the thought away. He was a Jedi. He didn't want her to transfer her devotion to him. It was dangerous—to both of them. But he answered dutifully and with a smile, despite the chilling thought: "Like light. In fact, it looked as if he were molding light in his hands. Then he hurled it like a weapon. He manipulated

the repulsor fields as if they were curtains made of this."
He moved closer to her chair to lift a corner of the
synthsilk scarf that lay in soft folds over her shoulder.

She gazed up at him raptly, eyes bright, lips parted. A
frisson of something indescribable tickled the back of
Jax's neck. He dropped the scarf. "And he's only just
turned fifteen," he said quickly, stepping back from the
chair and the female in it. "He has no training, no for-
mal practice in how to control the Force. Only his instinct, and his instinct is apparently very good."

"He must be very powerful," Dejah murmured,
lowering her eyes. "Yes. Yes, I can see. That much raw
power would have to be trained, controlled, channeled." She smiled again and shook her head, sending
the light dancing through her hair. "You certainly have
your work cut out for you, young Jedi Master."

Jax flushed. "I'm not a Jedi Master. Barely a Jedi
Knight. But you're right—I do have my work cut out for
me. I'm going to have to train Kajin Savaros to be a Jedi,
whether I'm up to it or not."

"What's the matter with you?"

At the sound of the mechanical voice, Den turned to
find that I-Five had entered his room on silent droid feet.

"What's the matter with *me*? I was gonna ask what
you thought was the matter with everybody *else* around
here. Well, not everybody. Just Jax and—well—*you*, not
to put too fine a point on it."

"Ah. Of course there's never anything wrong with
you, is there? You're Den Dhur, the journalist. You
observe all and are touched by nothing."

Well, that took the scathing prize. "Look, you mean-
spirited bucket of bolts, I've never claimed to be untouched or completely objective or any of that nonsense.
Any journalist who claims he's impartial or uncaring or
uninvolved has got hash for brains, is lying to himself and

the Universal Mind, *and* is betraying the very purpose for which he became a journalist in the first place. A jaded journalist is a journalist who should frippin' retire." He paused to take a breath. "*I* should frippin' retire."

I-Five managed to make his stationary metal eyebrow ridges look as if they had arched in feigned surprise. "Really? I should say you're too far from jaded for that. Something has obviously set you in a high dudgeon."

Den stared at the droid, wondering if this was a golden opportunity to spill his guts and receive reassurance, or just a solid-brass opportunity to look like a complete idiot.

"It's that Duare woman. She's—she's . . ."

"Yes, yes, I caught the childish mutterings. That's nothing new. This is."

Den crossed to his bed and threw himself onto it, folding his hands behind his head and staring up at the duracrete ceiling. It had, at some point in its existence, been painted a soothing shade of gray-green that reminded him of the color of the cavern ceilings back home on Sullust. He could be there, he realized for the thousandth time, reclining on a formcouch in his own cave, having a peaceful conversation with Eyar and not in enemy territory, hiding out in a dive, staring with nostalgia at a ceiling, and having a frustrating dialogue with a protocol droid.

What had he been thinking when he decided to stay here on Coruscant? Oh well, he knew what he'd been thinking—that I-Five would never leave Jax and that he would never leave I-Five. Jax was Five's—what, adopted nephew? Adopted *son*? How twisted was that?

No more twisted, he supposed, than that his best friend in the whole universe was made of metal and had a synaptic grid network instead of a cerebral cortex.

"Well?" said his best friend in the whole universe, looking and sounding arch.

Den sat up. "In case you hadn't noticed, our young Jedi has brought home a stray human. A potentially dangerous stray human. I don't know if you caught the subtext of what Jax was saying—or, rather, trying *not* to say—but I did."

"The boy is being sought by the Inquis—"

"Not that. *We're* being sought by the Inquisitors. The boy is freakishly powerful and untrained."

I-Five cocked his head to one side. "He's a raw talent, yes."

Den sighed. "Are you being intentionally obtuse, Five, or have you fried some capacitors? Jax and Laranth are very careful about when and how they use the Force—around our neighborhood, especially. Our houseguest apparently drew the Inquisitor to him through an injudicious use of the Force. Who's to say he won't suffer a similar breach of protocol here?"

"Jax."

Den opened his mouth to protest that Jax was not omniscient, but I-Five raised a hand.

"Trust, Den. This whole team that Jax has gathered around him is based on trust. If Jax thinks he can train this boy, then I have to trust that he can."

Den snorted. "Trust? You think you can trust Rhinann or Dejah or Tuden Sal?"

"No. Not even as far as I could throw them—which would be a considerable distance, actually. But every one of us knows that we can trust Jax. He's the core. The heart. All our threads connect to him. Of course, you also know that you can trust me; and I know that I can trust you. But in the final analysis, it's our trust in Jax that holds us together."

Den swung his legs off the bed and leaned closer to

the droid, his mind reaching for something he'd been trying to articulate for some time.

"But *can* we trust him, Five? Can we trust him when *she's* working on him? Reading his emotions, playing to them, maybe manipulating him?"

"By *she* you mean Dejah Duare, of course."

"Who else? She's a *Zeltron,* Five. I'm not saying she's got ulterior motives when it comes to our Jedi. Her motives are perfectly clear. She wants him. I just think she's a distraction. And under the circumstances, Jax can't afford a distraction like that. *We* can't afford a distraction like that."

I-Five's metal face was as unreadable as it was supposed to be. "Jax has noted, as have I, that Dejah does not seem to be a 'normal' Zeltron. She seems capable of a longer emotional attention span, for one thing. And in Jax's estimation, capable of a surprising amount of loyalty. Jax would remind you that she could be back on Zeltros or some other world far removed from the Empire's dark heart. She has chosen to remain here with us instead. He would also remind you that she has been very useful both in our relations with Pol Haus and with the various informants—willing or otherwise—that we have occasion to use."

"I know what Jax would remind me of, thank you. I'm just surprised that *you're* reminding me, too."

"Are you? Well, something I will assuredly remind you of is that Dejah Duare agrees with you about Tuden Sal and his plan to terminate Emperor Palpatine. I'm surprised you haven't seized on that as a means to forge an alliance with her."

On that note the droid turned on his metal heel and exited the room, leaving Den to ponder his last words: Forge an alliance with Dejah Duare?

Could be useful, he supposed. Might even occasion

him to undercut her obvious attempts to slip into a more intimate relationship with Jax.

He thought about it for a while, but contemplating a possible physical relationship between Jax Pavan and Dejah Duare only made him lonely for Eyar Marath. He got up from the bed and crossed to his workstation, more determined than ever to contact her. He had half a letter composed already and now he was certain he would send it—would find out if the beautiful Sullustan singer was still awaiting him on their homeworld.

Rhinann slouched in the formchair at his workstation, mulling over the last half hour's worth of conversations he had eavesdropped on. Oh, he'd certainly not been in hiding. With as much notice as the others paid him, he could hide in plain sight.

What was that Kubaz expression? An insect on the wall? An arthropod on the ceiling? Something like that. At any rate, something that was right in front of everyone's nose, yet went completely unnoticed.

Not that he was complaining. His social invisibility had given him an unprecedented opportunity to observe interactions that he might not have overheard if he had been a notable entity.

What had he observed? He cataloged the items carefully, ticking them off in his mind.

There was the growing antagonism between the Zeltron female and Den Dhur, of course—well, at least Den's antagonism toward her. He had the feeling that Dejah Duare found the Sullustan more amusing than annoying. No accounting for taste.

There was the obvious tension between Laranth Tarak and Dejah Duare—now, *that* was interesting.

Dejah was still angling for the Jedi—nothing new there, but now she seemed to be casting her net at the younger adept as well. Was that merely a reflex, or did she do it to a purpose?

Then there was the boy. He clearly had everyone spooked. Understandable; Rhinann was feeling far from sanguine about his sudden appearance himself. And truthfully, he was torn: instinct told him that the boy represented either a magnificent opportunity or a potential disaster—which it was largely depended on how well the youngling responded to Jax Pavan's attempts to educate him. He was certainly an intriguing variable. What might be made of a Force-sensitive of such strength that he could overcome an armed, Sith-trained Inquisitor?

Rhinann was turning these thoughts over pleasantly in his head when an idea occurred to him that was so chilling he very nearly swooned. What if it was all a setup? What if the M'haelian boy had been planted where Jax Pavan would notice him, find him, bring him home?

What if Kajin Savaros was a mole?

Breathing gustily enough to rattle his nose tusks, the Elomin turned back to his workstation and connected to the HoloNet. It would cost an extravagant amount, but he would make certain that when he reached the Westport, there would be a ship to take him away from Coruscant at a moment's notice.

He made his travel plans hurriedly, while in the back of his mind considering ways he could accelerate his search for the bota.

seven

Jax started Kaj's training the next day with a series of meditations geared toward getting the boy in touch with his own center. He recognized the great difficulty of what he'd set himself up to do. He had trained as a Jedi since the age of two; spent years in meditation and study of Jedi history, Jedi philosophy, Jedi strategy. He had spent months and months in combat training, which consisted largely of learning the defensive forms from Shii-Cho to Juyo. He had spent countless hours on mental, physical, emotional, and spiritual control.

There was obviously no way to teach Kaj all of that in the compressed amount of time they might have. And there was no way to teach it at all without using the Force.

He had to find a solution to that problem somehow, but at the moment, as he watched Kaj sit cross-legged, attempting to master his breathing and control his heart rate, he could think of none.

"The Jedi have a code that we live by," Jax said now, his voice soft, calming. He sat opposite Kaj on a woven mat in his room in a meditative posture, head up, eyes closed, hands lying open on his knees.

"There is no emotion; there is peace.

"There is no ignorance; there is knowledge.

"There is no passion; there is serenity.

"There is no death; there is the Force."

He felt the boy stir and remembered his first real meditation on the Jedi mantra. He had been about six and the words—which he had heard over and over again for four years—had suddenly struck him and resonated . . . and raised no end of questions.

"Ask," Jax said.

"There is no death?"

"What do you know of the Force?" Jax asked in return. "What have you heard or been told?"

Kaj looked uncertain. "I know only that it moves through me—sometimes like a quiet stream; sometimes like a raging river. I've heard only that its power can be channeled."

Jax listened carefully to the words the boy used to describe that which he possessed but barely understood. "The streams and rivers flow into a great ocean. That ocean is the Force. It is the end of all journeys."

There was a moment of silence in which Kaj digested what Jax had said, and in which Jax kicked himself several times for the simplistic metaphor. He'd been trying to follow Kaj's lead.

"I'm from a farming family," the boy said. "I understand what water means. How it permeates everything, how its presence gives life and its absence brings death. Is that what the Force is like?"

"You tell me," Jax said. "Is that what it's like for you?"

Again, the boy paused for thought. "Yes . . . and no. I mean, sometimes it's like that if I just sort of . . . swim in it, I guess. But when I try so hard not to let it out, then it's like water behind a dam—building up, building up, wanting to be let out. And that's when it gets away from me. Then I think it's more like fire. It burns."

Jax pondered that. He'd never experienced the Force that way himself, nor had he ever heard anyone describe experiencing the Force that way. He wondered if the dichotomous images were partly explained by the fact that Kaj had had no early training—that his talent had grown up like a wild thing, untrammeled and free; a late bloomer compared with most. The visualization exercises that every young Padawan was taught to help him or her harness the Force were new to Kajin Savaros.

Just as teaching them was new to Jax Pavan.

"Right now try to think of the Force as water," he said. "Water you can channel. You're . . . you're the high mountain lake in which the river starts. You determine how fast it flows, where it channels and erodes, whether it sings or roars. If you can learn to turn the water, you can keep it from transmuting into fire. You can control it. Now—can you see the lake?"

"Uh . . . ," Kaj said. Then suddenly as if in discovery, "Yes! Yes. I can see the lake."

"Good. Let's follow the river . . ."

They went on like that for some time—hours, in fact—during which Jax was certain Kaj would become bored or sleepy or confused and impatient. He did none of those things. He followed his river, making it go here and there, rise and fall, ripple and sing, without ever allowing it to become a white-water rapid.

After a time, Jax set a Sontaran song ball out on the floor between them and had Kaj perform the placid, soothing ritual of using the merest tendril of the Force to roll the ball back and forth between them. As they did this, they recited the Jedi Code as a call and response. The ball—which was made of a rare titanium alloy of great tensile strength—was composed of a sphere within a sphere. The two touched as the thing moved, creating a low, sonorous note that rose and fell like the breathing of an immense flute.

Jax gave the ball the barest nudge with the Force, rolling it to Kaj: "There is no emotion; there is peace."

"There is no ignorance," said Kaj, rolling it back, "there is knowledge."

"There is no passion; there is serenity."

"There is no death; there is the Force."

The boy had hesitated at first, sometimes forgetting the words, sometimes unable to push the ball in the right direction. But he had mastered it quickly, as someone with the reflexes of a youth rather than a toddler can, and now the ball sang between them in the weaving of Jax's threads and the gentle push of Kaj's currents.

It was a safe-enough exercise; even an Inquisitor standing in the street below their aerie would have trouble reading the gentle warp, woof, and tidal surge of the schoolroom practice. But what they would do when more rigorous training was called for, Jax couldn't yet imagine. Sooner or later he would have to train Kaj to control his impulses in the heat of combat, and that would take a good deal more than gentle nudging.

Still, it was, all in all, a good start. Jax was congratulating himself when Dejah tapped at the door, then entered without waiting to be admitted. Simultaneously the song ball shot past Jax, barely missing his right thigh, and hit the wall behind him with a resounding *crack* and a loud thrum of the inner resonator sphere. Dejah leapt back a step with a high-pitched squeak.

"Kaj—the river. Mind the currents," said Jax, keeping his voice pitched low, but the boy was already on his feet, his composure shattered to pieces.

"I—I'm sorry," he stammered.

"No, *I'm* sorry," Dejah said contritely. "I was just wondering if you were hungry. You've been in here for hours. I thought maybe you could use a break."

Jax glanced from her to Kaj, whose face had gone almost as red as the Zeltron's. He knew he should send Dejah away and make Kaj resume his meditations. It's what his own Master would have done. Master Piell had not been a grim authoritarian, by any means, but had known that a Padawan must learn early how to retrieve lost composure or shattered concentration.

He opened his mouth to say the words *We have more work to do,* but a look at Dejah's face stopped them in his throat. Instead, he nodded. "You're right. We've been at this a long time. I'm sure Kaj could use a break and a good meal—right, Kaj?"

The boy nodded mutely, his eyes never leaving the Zeltron.

"Well, come on then!" she said pertly and curled a finger at Kaj before disappearing through the door.

Kaj scrambled after her, giving Jax an apologetic sidewise glance. "It won't happen again," he murmured.

Not true, Jax thought. With Dejah around it most likely would. And if it did . . .

Jax crossed the room and picked up the now slightly dented song ball. The plasticrete wall, supposedly resilient up to a metric ton of pressure, had sustained equal damage. And who knew how loud the roar of that white-water surge had been? Jax had been deep in his own meditation and he had felt it. His thigh still tingled with the residual energy.

In the outer room Dejah uttered a throaty laugh that was followed by a diffident echo from Kaj. Something stirred uneasily beneath Jax's breastbone—something he couldn't quite put a name to. One of the first things he was going to have to teach Kajin Savaros, he decided, was how to block or at least filter Dejah Duare's heady "perfume."

Rhinann had no reasonable expectation that the droid would divulge any information about the bota, but on the off-chance that some vestige of his original programming had survived Lorn Pavan's tinkering, he asked anyway. Nothing ventured, nothing gained, as the humans said.

So when Rhinann and I-Five were alone in the workstation alcove, the Elomin decided there would be no better time. Everyone else seemed to be engaged in the current pursuit of smuggling a Togrutan female with nascent Force abilities offworld via the UML.

He thought of his travel arrangements, of how easy it would be to simply pack up and leave . . . were it not for the arrival of the Force prodigy and the fact that Rhinann had been less than aggressive in his search for the bota. It wouldn't do to be slavish in sticking to a timetable. That sort of tunnel vision could lead to missed opportunity—like the one he was now presented with.

Deciding that honesty—or something close to it—was the best policy, Rhinann seized the moment, sat back in his workstation formchair, and said, "I am troubled by the amount of attention that may soon be trained upon us."

After a moment of hesitation, I-Five disengaged from whatever online information he had been pursuing and responded. "Really? Why is that?"

"Why is that?" Rhinann repeated. "I should think that would be obvious, particularly to you." He ticked the reasons off on his long, spatulate fingers. "Our houseguest is a Force-sensitive—that makes him a prime target for Lord Vader's continued purges. He has been pursued by an Inquisitor—ergo, he has drawn attention to himself. Ergo, Vader cannot help but know of his existence. He has killed an Inquisitor—"

"We don't know that for a fact," I-Five said with maddening imperturbability.

"Then he's injured one, at the very least. *And* he drew Laranth and Jax into his association. How can you possibly think that we are *not* at increased risk of exposure?"

"I can, because one thing has not changed: Vader has no more information about us or our activities or location as a result of Kajin's appearance than he had previously." I-Five gestured at the HoloNet link. "I monitor several different bands that convey classified intel, and none of them has given me any reason to suspect otherwise. Trust me: so far, Vader knows nothing of this."

"He does if his Inquisitor saw Jax and Laranth come to the boy's rescue."

"A moment ago," said the droid drily, "the Inquisitor was dead. He can have hardly observed anything in that state."

Rhinann kept calm. "If he was only injured, he might have seen Jax and Laranth save the boy."

"At the time that Jax and Laranth arrived on the scene, the Inquisitor was being blown sky-high by a blast of repulsor energy. Jax was blinded standing outside looking into the blast. I can't imagine what the Inquisitor might have seen from inside the blast zone, but I doubt it was Jax and Laranth."

The stupid droid was apparently bent on being utterly uncooperative. Rhinann strove for composure. "But he sensed them, surely. He would have known other Jedi were involved."

"Perhaps he did. But he was incapacitated, or so Jax sensed."

"How do we know that wasn't the taozin effect?"

The droid had to think about that, and Rhinann felt absurdly pleased. "Jax has told me," I-Five said, "that once you know what to expect, the effect can be sensed."

"I heard him. He said it could be sensed as a complete absence or blockage of the Force—as if someone were no longer there. As if, perhaps, they had been knocked senseless?"

The metal face was completely opaque. "That is a possibility, I suppose."

Thank the gods! At last, an admission of uncertainty. Rhinann pounced on it. "Well then, perhaps you can understand my uneasiness. If the Emperor's henchmen were to locate us, it would be disastrous for more than just our company. The Whiplash would suffer as well, and a great many precious things would fall into enemy hands—Jax, that extraordinary boy . . . you. And of course, there is the Sith Holocron Jax is guarding and that bit of pyronium Anakin Skywalker gave him—and . . ." Rhinann turned to look at the droid directly. "And the bota."

The droid's only reaction was a cocking of his head and a brightening of his optics. "What do you know about the bota?"

"I know that Jedi Barriss Offee gave it to you to transport here to the Jedi Temple. I also know what properties the bota is supposed to have and their value to the Jedi . . . or to Darth Vader. I think we are both in agreement that for the Dark Lord to come into possession of such a prize would be beyond disastrous. It has the potential to render him virtually omnipotent."

The droid studied him for a moment, then said, "Rhinann, we have no idea what the bota will do to one as steeped in the Force as Vader is. None."

"Well, it can't be good."

"We agree on that, at least."

Rhinann leaned forward in his chair. "Have you given no thought to what might happen if Vader should possess not only the bota, but the pyronium and the Sith Holocron?"

"I have given it as much thought as it deserves."

Rhinann bit back his frustration. This was like talking to a cryptogram generator. "And has it not occurred to you that these items should be separated?"

"Yes. Some time ago, in fact."

Rhinann feigned relief. "Then you've distributed them to several different hiding places."

"I've done what I thought necessary."

Maddening, perverse, obstinate . . . the list of vices that no droid should *ever* possess grew exponentially in length. What in the name of creation could Lorn Pavan have been thinking?

"So you've given the bota to Jax already?"

"I have seen to its safety. That's all you should know, don't you think?"

Stung, Rhinann opened his mouth to protest, but I-Five continued, "After all, if I tell you who has the bota and you're captured by Darth Vader, then the dark side would alert him to the fact that you had information he wanted. Information he would cheerfully scour your skull to get."

Rhinann felt the blood drain from his head. "You're right, of course," he murmured, surrendering. There was no use in interrogating a thing that would not permit itself to be interrogated. "I certainly wouldn't want to be caught with any information Vader might find useful."

"No," said I-Five. "You wouldn't."

It was evening by the chrono and everyone was home from their various tasks when the door chime sounded. Jax felt a thrill of mingled dread and anticipation course through him. He'd been working with Kaj at improving the boy's ability to concentrate, and Jax wryly realized that the interruption had disturbed his meditations far more than it had the boy's. Kaj remained seated cross-legged, apparently a few centimeters or so above the mat upon which they meditated. Jax had dropped to the floor.

Silly, really: the enemy would not chime politely and

ask to be admitted, so this was not an attack. Why the reaction? He thought of Tuden Sal and Laranth in the same heartbeat—Sal might be back to press for an answer to his proposal, and Laranth . . .

He stood and found Kajin's gaze on him.

"Stay here," Jax instructed. "We don't want to advertise your presence, okay?"

The boy nodded and returned to his contemplations, bobbing slightly higher above the mat.

Jax shook his head as he went to the living room—Kaj made it look so easy. It had never been that easy for him.

Den had answered the door by the time he reached the outer room, admitting Pol Haus. The Zabrak police prefect looked positively grim. The emotion behind the expression on his face was so intense that Jax realized it was what had pulled him from his meditations. Haus was wrapped in dark Force threads that, though as insubstantial as smoke, were troublingly sinister and seemed to be in constant motion. They went nowhere; they simply wound themselves around the prefect in a visible analog for the tension that showed in his face as pale gray lines bracketing his mouth.

The prefect stepped through the conapt doorway and let the door glide shut behind him before he spoke.

"We've got a situation," he said without preamble.

Jax exchanged glances with Den. "A situation?" he prompted.

The Zabrak fixed him with a steady gaze. His eyes, usually distracted and unfocused, were as sharp as the pointy end of a vibrosword. This, Jax realized, was the real Pol Haus—the man who lived beneath the carefully cultivated air of shambling disorganization.

"One of your lot has murdered an Inquisitor."

"One of *my* lot?"

Haus tipped his horned head to one side. "C'mon,

kid. Do I have to spell it out? A Jedi—if not officially, then a pretty powerful Force-sensitive. Seems he or she fried this Inquisitor with the energy siphoned from a couple of badly aligned repulsor fields. Is that in your repertoire?"

"Oh *frip,*" muttered Den.

Jax very nearly took a step backward but, sensing no hostility from the Zabrak, stood his ground. "I don't know what you're talking about," he said. "Of course that's not in my repertoire. I'm not—"

"Save it, Pavan. I don't have time to let you blow smoke at me, and you don't want to make me mad at you. Look, I'm not going to give you up to the Inquisitorius, if that's what you're wondering, so let's just see if we can't work past this momentary awkwardness and get to the heart of the matter."

That had, in fact, been what Jax had been wondering— if he was looking a threat in the face. Now, reaching out toward Haus with tendrils of Force, he wasn't so sure.

"Jax . . ." Den shifted nervously from foot to foot, glancing up at the Jedi's face. Apparently not liking what he saw there, he swore again, this time more volubly.

"No," Jax said, in answer to Haus. "No, it's not in my repertoire. I don't have that kind of ability."

Pol Haus nodded. "That's sort of what I figured. The perp was described to me as a rogue Force-sensitive, dangerous and out of control. It was suggested to me that I do everything in my power, move every resource at my disposal, to run this rampaging adept to ground."

"Suggested by . . . ?" Den asked.

Haus kept his gaze on Jax as he answered Den's question. "Darth Vader."

Den made an incoherent sound somewhere between a groan and a growl. Jax blinked and gave Haus's mantle of Force threads a more careful look. Yes, they made more sense now. The prefect had been touched by the emissary of the dark side. The touch still stained his personal aura—and obviously disturbed him a great deal.

"So that's why I'm here," the prefect continued. "If a Jedi or some rogue Force-user offed this Inquisitor, you're the best person to help me find them before they assassinate another one."

Jax gestured at the room behind him. "Why don't you come in and have a seat and we'll discuss it?"

Out of the corner of his eye he could see the expression on the Sullustan's face. *Dumbfounded* didn't even begin to cover it. Jax nudged Den into motion as he turned to follow the prefect into the living room.

What are you doing? Den mouthed at him.

Jax waved the journalist back, mouthing in return, *Get I-Five and Dejah,* and nodding toward the workstation alcove. Den scurried away while Jax led the prefect into the living room.

Jax knew that Den had no idea what he was doing. Truth be told, Jax himself wasn't sure what he was doing, but he was painfully aware that the object of Pol Haus's search was sitting not six meters away, separated from them by a meager plasticrete wall—a wall that would prove to be no barrier at all should Kaj panic and invoke his connection to the Force.

Prefect Haus would learn then mighty fast where the rogue Force-sensitive was hiding. Assuming that he survived the discovery . . .

eight

"How did you know I was a Jedi?" Jax stood where the kinetic light from Ves Volette's sculpture played across his face, obscuring his expression from the police prefect, who paced up and down the center of the living room, his dingy topcoat swirling about his legs. "Who—or what—gave me away?"

"Do you really want to know?"

"Yes."

"No big proof. More like a body of evidence. A lot of little things. The way your companions and associates react to you. The way you carry yourself. The way you observe what's going on around you. The way you react to it. The way you seem to disappear from my radar sometimes when I know you're there. The way your hand hovers over your left hip when you sense danger. The speed of your reactions . . ." Haus shrugged. "Someone sent a bounty hunter after you—a Sith-trained bounty hunter. You came back alive; she didn't."

Jax knew Haus was talking about Aurra Sing. He had wondered if the Sith lightsaber he now carried hadn't belonged to her—the fact that he'd gotten it from an anonymous source just prior to his confrontation with Sing surely couldn't have been a coincidence. He didn't ask how Haus had known about the connection. He was the police prefect; it was his business to know that sort of thing. Jax just hadn't expected that he *would* know it. Apparently he had underestimated Pol Haus.

Haus continued, "When someone like that shows up on your turf you find out why as quickly and quietly as you can. I knew she was trailing a Jedi—a young Jedi who matched your description. I called in a few favors, got a list of Jedi who still haven't been run down. Guess whose name was on there." He looked at Jax with a cocked eyebrow. "Did you *want* to be found? 'Cause I'm thinking you sure didn't go to a whole lot of trouble to make yourself scarce."

Now that he'd laid it out, it did seem to Jax that he'd done a remarkably poor job of covering his tracks. He wondered what Haus had divined from how his companions reacted to him. He glanced from Den to Rhinann to Dejah to I-Five. He wasn't going to ask that just now.

Instead he asked, "Vader came to you directly?"

Haus snorted. "Get serious. He sent one of his goons—oh, excuse me—one of his Inquisitors to fetch me. He made sure the meeting took place on his turf and that I was suitably impressed with his security measures and clout."

Jax stiffened. "You were at Vader's headquarters?" Images flashed through his head of tracking devices and furtive tails. Judging from the expression on Rhinann's and Den's faces, their thoughts had taken the same path. Dejah, bless her, seemed not to have caught the sinister implications of the prefect's words. Her lips were parted, her eyes bright, as if he'd just told her she'd been awarded a prize.

I-Five, correctly interpreting Jax's concern, said, "He's clean. Any tracking devices would have pinged the sensor net at the entrance to the mews."

Haus, his gaze never leaving Jax's face, said, "Don't worry. I'm a professional. I went back to my own headquarters and had myself carefully and completely debugged—and yes, there were some stowaways on my person. They're gone now and, no, I don't really give an armored rat's behind what Vader thinks of me removing them. What I do care about," he added, "is that a rogue Force-user—a truly rogue Force-user—might be a little overexcited by his ability to take out Inquisitors. He might develop a taste for it. He might strike again. Which would be very bad for all of us."

Jax felt Kaj's presence on the other side of the door to his room, felt the chill spikes of his sudden fear. He split his attention, sending the youth calming thoughts.

"So," Haus continued, "I'm sure it comes as no surprise, Pavan, that I need someone of your unique ability to help me find the assassin."

Haus's words fell into the room like a gigantic boulder into a placid stream. Kaj's reaction hit Jax in a cold wave of terror. Apparently Dejah sensed it, too, for she rose from her seat, her crimson eyes wide.

"Jax . . . ," she murmured, but anything else she might have said was interrupted by a loud thud from the next room and the unmistakable sound of a Sontaran song ball being abused.

Pol Haus frowned, turning to look in the direction of the open doorway. "You have more houseguests?"

"Oh no," said Dejah looking apologetic. "It's my whisperkit droid. I've forgotten to deactivate it—again," she added with charming self-deprecation. "I do that so often, you really should remind me, Jax, not to leave it playing with its toys. I'll just go turn it off."

She swept across the room to Jax's door and disappeared inside. Her voice came back to them lightly—only Jax caught the undertone of agitation. "Oh, there you are, you poor thing. Come down from there now. Everything's just fine. Did that nasty song ball scare you?"

They heard the soft chime of the Sontaran meditation device, then Dejah said, "Good droid. Come to Dejah."

Both Den and Rhinann had turned a pale shade of blue-gray and looked about to leap out of their respective skins. I-Five was as impenetrable as a droid was supposed to be.

Jax felt laughter born of relief bubbling up from his throat. He pushed it back down. Without doubt, Dejah was the only one among them who could have walked into that room just then with the least chance of being felled by the frightened boy's power. Dejah was, at that moment, the only one Kajin trusted. Jax almost shook his head in bemusement: a Zeltron empath accomplishing what even a Jedi Knight most likely could not.

He turned back to Pol Haus. "You were saying you wanted our help finding the assassin. What do you intend to do with him if we catch him?"

It was not Jax's imagination that everyone in the room held his breath.

After a moment of close scrutiny, the prefect said slowly, deliberately, "Turning him over to Vader is out of the question. He killed an Inquisitor, so he's clearly not a Sith or a Sith sympathizer. That means his abilities could be used by the Jedi."

"Prefect," Jax said quietly, "I don't know that there are any other Jedi on Coruscant—or anywhere else for that matter."

Haus lowered his horned head and gave Jax an almost sly look out of the corners of his eyes. "I have it on good authority that there are other Jedi about. Can't tell you where or who, but I'm convinced they're there. And this powerful an adept shouldn't be lost to them, I'm thinking."

Den leaned forward in his window casement. "So you'd—what—help smuggle him offworld? Go underground? What? I mean, Vader would expect you to turn the killer in, right?"

"Yes, he would. Which is why when I tell him that the killer died while we were in pursuit of him—fell into the materials hopper of a fabber at the spaceport, say— he would most likely believe me."

Jax blinked and met the prefect's golden eyes. He swept him again with his Force sense—which he was convinced the Zabrak knew he was doing—and again saw the swirling ribbons of smoky darkness encircling him. They were dimmer now, less active, but they were still there.

Darth Vader's residual touch, or something else? Something dark that emanated from Pol Haus himself?

Jax knew the prefect was asking for trust, for cooper- ation, but he also knew the consequences if those were mistakenly given. He couldn't take that chance, even though Haus seemed to have disinterred a great deal of information about their activities—at least insofar as they concerned Aurra Sing.

Did he know these things, or was he merely guessing, hoping Jax would reveal more?

"You'll understand if I'm reluctant to jump into this," Jax said. "You're talking about a potential Jedi, and I've only your word that you mean this person no harm."

The Zabrak nodded. "Yes, though I might be able to get someone else's word. Someone you trust. And be- sides, I've shown that I mean *you* no harm, Jedi. I've sus- pected that you were more than you made yourself out to be for some time. I could have run to Vader and said, Hey, check out this bunch. They've got connections on their connections, and their leader seems to always land on his feet no matter who's trying to stomp on his toes. I haven't done that."

"Maybe because we're too valuable to you," sug- gested Den. "Up till now, anyway. Now you've got a

chance to maybe look like a big hero to His Dark Lord-
liness. And maybe if we help you find this . . . this person, you'll just hand him over to Vader, figuring there's
nothing we can do without putting our own lives in
jeopardy. And if we *don't* help you find him, maybe you
just hand over Jax instead."

That thought had also occurred to Jax and filled him
with a sinking dread. To have to leave Coruscant, to
run away from all he wanted to accomplish, away from
the chance at finding out the truth about his father's
death . . .

"Oh, I don't believe Pol Haus would do anything so
dastardly."

All eyes turned to where Dejah Duare stood in the doorway of Jax's room, gleaming like a red sunset. She crossed
back to the seating area, wafting so close to the prefect
that her translucent gowns brushed his disreputable
duster.

"As he noted himself," she continued, "he's had reason to suspect our situation here for some time and he's
done nothing. The plan he suggests might even satisfy
Darth Vader and make it even less likely that we'll be
discovered. I feel we should consider his job offer."

"Dejah Duare is absolutely right," Haus said, smiling
crookedly. "I have no reason to want to disband this
group or sever my ties with it. You get results that my
forces can't. Besides, if I were to betray the Inquisitor
killer to Darth Vader, you'd just try to rescue him. With
all due respect, you put your lives in danger every day of
the year. Your lives are in danger at this very moment.
Things move out there in the dark," he added, sweeping
a broad gesture toward the city outside Den's window
casement. "You know that as well as I do. And some of
them are looking for you."

"How kind of you to remind us," said I-Five, speak-

ing for the first time. The sound of his voice made Den
start visibly and nearly topple from his window ledge.

The Zabrak prefect laughed. "I've had opportunities
to help them find you. I haven't. I won't. Your choice on
whether you believe that or not."

Jax glanced at Dejah. She could sense the emotional
subtext of Haus's message; what did she think? She gave
the slightest nod, the merest glimmer of a smile.

"All right," Jax said. "We'll help you find your Force-
user. But if he's as powerful as Vader says he is, then he
may be impossible to find . . . unless he wants to be
found."

The unseen listener in Jax's quarters coiled and un-
coiled, still teetering on the edge of terror.

"Understood." The prefect turned on his heel and
started for the front door, the job interview apparently
at an end.

Jax moved with him, side by side, to the door and saw
him out into the hall. "Tell me, Prefect," he said, "what
about my companions' reactions hinted to you that I
was a Jedi?"

Pol Haus turned to look at him, a wry almost-smile
on his lips. "You're the youngest of them, but they all
look to you for direction. Even the Gray Paladin did
when she was here. A question is asked, they all watch
your face as if the answer is there. And though you are
also the most soft-spoken, the least verbose—" A glance
back through the door. "—you're the one who makes
and speaks the decisions. I can think of no one of your
age who would be accorded that respect if he or she
were not a Jedi."

"Oh," Jax said, showing some of the eloquence for
which he was not famed. "I see."

"So do I. But relax. Most people don't notice things
like that. Just avid students of sentient nature like me."

He gave a sloppy half salute with one hand and turned to go.

"Whose word?"

"What?" The prefect arrested his shambling gait and turned to look at Jax over his shoulder.

"Whose word would you give that we'd trust?"

"Now, that would be promising what I might not be able to deliver. Or it might be revealing an important source of information. *Or* it might be betraying a friend. Or all or none of the above. Have your droid patch into the 'Net in about an hour. I'll be sending you what I've got on the murder from the Imperial Security drones."

Jax nodded, then watched the police prefect make his way down the corridor, looking nothing like what he was. There had been a time when Jax Pavan had regarded Pol Haus as a disorganized, easily befuddled Imperial functionary. Now he wasn't sure what to make of him.

nine

"He's gone," Jax said as he reentered the living room. "It's all right, Kaj, you can come out."

A moment later the boy appeared, looking highly spooked.

Jax smiled at him reassuringly. "It looks as if we may have another ally."

"I'd withhold judgment on that," advised Rhinann. "You can never be too careful."

"Actually, you can," I-Five said. "And you can miss opportunities that way."

Still keeping tabs on Kaj through the Force, Jax turned his objective attention to the droid. "And is this an opportunity or a risk?"

"Aren't they two sides of the same coin? Opportunity rarely comes without risk."

"Oh, stop it, Five," said Den. "You sound like a carnival oracle droid. Opportunity, my aunt Freema's dewlaps. All this is, is one more person—one more person with a link to His Evilness—who knows Jax is a Jedi. I see no particular upside to that. I think we should relocate immediately."

"Ah. Somewhere not on this planet, I assume."

"I'm willing to compromise. I'll consider the same galactic sector."

"But where would *I* go?" Kajin asked. He hovered at

the very edge of the seating area, the light sculpture washing him with lambent hues.

"No one is going anywhere," said Jax.

Den stared at him. "Haus could be on his way to Vader right this minute."

"Den," said I-Five, "you're showing every sign of rampant paranoia."

"You know the difference between paranoia and realistic concern? Breathing. The way I see it," Den said, "Haus has little to lose by tipping Vader to us and much to gain in the way of prestige. I don't trust him."

Behind Jax, Kaj uttered a sick moan and, much to Jax's astonishment, disappeared entirely from Jax's Force radar. Startled, the Jedi turned just as the boy slid into a formchair, simultaneously coming back into sight, as it were.

Had Kaj just disconnected from the Force? Could he do this at will? From his attitude he seemed unaware of what had just happened. Even so, the implications were stunning. Jax opened his mouth to say something, but Dejah had launched into a disagreement with Den.

"That's because you can't sense him, Den. Not like Jax and I can. Right, Jax?"

"I . . ." Jax pulled his attention away from Kajin, who continued to brood. "What I sense from Haus is . . . anomalous. He's got some dark ribbons of Force around him, but they don't seem to be connected to Vader, or anyone else, which is unusual. There's an underlying agitation there, though. My sense of it is that he's more disturbed by Vader than he cares to admit."

"Well, *I'm* not sensing anything anomalous," Dejah said. "I don't sense any duplicitous emotions from him at all."

"You're not getting your psychic impressions of him through the Force," Rhinann pointed out.

"Which leads me to trust them all the more."

A moment of somewhat stunned silence followed this. Then Jax said, "Before, when he was playing the bungling detective, did you realize that's what he was doing? Did you sense duplicity then?"

Dejah stared at him in surprise. He felt suddenly contrite and nearly apologized aloud.

"I sensed no malice," she answered.

"But neither did you realize that he was concealing his true nature," said I-Five.

Anger flashed briefly in the Zeltron's eyes. "I sensed he was hiding no hostility," she repeated.

"Why would you assume that anyone who meant us harm must necessarily feel hostility for us?" the droid asked. "Beings often hurt each other for reasons other than emotional impulse. Some of the greatest atrocities in history have been orchestrated with complete dispassion. The Emperor's annihilation of the Caamasi homeworld, for example, or, to put it on a more personal level, Tuden Sal's betrayal of Jax's father. In the latter case, Sal certainly held no malice toward him. If you had been privy to the last meeting Lorn and I had with him, you would very likely have come to the same conclusion: we were in no danger, because Sal wasn't hostile toward us."

"What about you, I-Five?" Jax asked the droid. "You're a student of humanoid body language. Do you think Pol Haus is enough of a threat that we should leave Coruscant?"

"I think we may wish to relocate somewhere else in the city, perhaps keeping this place up as a front. But not so much because I distrust Pol Haus as because I trust Vader to be hypervigilant. I also think that if Pol Haus is our enemy, he has the potential to be a bad one, because he will most certainly have all the usual means of escape watched, if not already closed. Getting offworld cleanly is probably not a realistic option at this point."

Jax again felt Kaj's emotions spike. Then he winked out again. Jax swung around to face him.

"What are you doing?"

The boy, Force-visible once more, froze as he was rising from the chair. Liquid light from the sculpture splashed his face.

"I was just—" he started, but Jax cut him off.

"No, I mean how did you shield yourself from the Force just now?"

The boy swallowed in obvious confusion. "I . . . I didn't do anything."

"Twice in the last couple of minutes you have virtually disappeared from view through the Force. Are you sure you didn't make that happen?"

"I didn't do *anything*," Kaj repeated, a note of sullenness creeping into his voice.

"Not consciously, perhaps," said I-Five, regarding the young Force prodigy with obvious interest. "But it could have been an involuntary part of your fight-or-flight response. What were you feeling just now?"

"Afraid. I was feeling afraid. Nervous. I don't want to leave Coruscant. My parents said they'd try to come here to find me. If I leave . . ."

"Fear?" Jax looked at the droid. "You're suggesting he disappears when his fear reaches panic proportions? I've never heard of any Force-sensitive who could do that. Besides, when he was confronted with the Inquisitor he didn't just disappear. He fought. He used the Force to fight, not to hide."

I-Five turned to the boy. "You've been dodging the Inquisitors for some time now. Are you certain there isn't some trick you use—something that may even seem second nature to you—that allows you to hide yourself from them? Something that's allowed you to escape them?"

"I've escaped them by knowing where they are and

using the Force as little as possible when they're around."

Jax and I-Five exchanged glances. "You mean you've learned to read the taozin signature?" asked Jax. "The damping field? In other words, you know where they are by sensing where they're not?"

"Is that what it is?" Kaj shrugged, apparently unwinding a little bit. He cast a shy smile at Dejah, who continued to hover in the background. "It feels like ripples to me. Like weird little splashes—water flowing around a rock." He looked into the light sculpture and took a deep breath. "Y'know, looking at this thing is relaxing. Maybe I could use it for meditation."

He moved a step closer to Ves Volette's masterpiece . . . and disappeared for the third time.

"What is it?" I-Five asked, and Jax realized he was staring once again at the boy.

"He just disappeared, didn't he?" Dejah asked, her voice hushed. "You can't feel the Force from him while he's standing that close to the sculpture."

"How do you know?"

"I lost him telepathically, too. Or nearly so. He's . . . muted. Gray."

"I'm gray?" Kaj looked at his arms as if expecting to see himself in black-and-white.

Jax felt a rising tide of excitment wash through him. "Kaj, step away from the light sculpture."

"Huh?"

He waved the boy back with one hand. Kaj looked puzzled but did as asked. He reappeared in the Force as soon as he had cleared the dance of light by about half a meter.

"Dejah?" Jax murmured.

She nodded solemnly. "He's back. Vividly."

Jax motioned at Kaj. "Now walk around behind it."

Kaj obeyed, moving behind the light sculpture at a distance of about a meter. His Force threads broke like so many strands of hair-thin synthsilk. With his eyes, Jax could see him vaguely through the kinetic display, but he couldn't see him at all with the Force.

"Walk away from the sculpture," he told Kaj. "Move toward the wall."

The boy did, and remained hidden from the Force.

"Incredible," murmured Dejah. "I had no idea Ves's light sculptures possessed this property." Brow furrowed, she moved slowly around the display, stopping only when she stood next to Kaj opposite Jax. Then she peered at the Jedi through the moving pattern of lights.

"I can't sense you," she murmured, then glanced from Den to Rhinann. "Any of you." The idea seemed to disturb her. Wrapping her arms about herself, she left the room without another word.

"What was that about?" Den asked.

"Perhaps," said Rhinann, "one of us should inquire. She seemed . . . unhappy. I'll go," he added, before anyone else could respond, then moved after Dejah with an alacrity that was no less surprising than the gesture itself.

To his further amazement, Jax could swear that Den had also made a move in Dejah's direction. He didn't have time to give headspace to the Zeltron woman's peculiar reaction to their discovery, however. The overall implications of it as far as their current predicament was concerned were too important.

Jax, I-Five, and Kaj all gathered around the undulating display of colorful light. A moment later Den joined them, and they all stood looking at the thing like a flock of art gallery patrons gawking at the newest exhibit.

"Any theories, I-Five?" Jax asked the droid. "Any idea how or why the light sculptures might cause this sort of damping effect?"

"The display itself uses a combination of electro- and bioluminescence, so I suppose there is a possibility that it could somehow warp the kinetic energies of biological entities. But I think it more likely that it's the power source. The light sculpture creates a cohesion field capable of bending light to the desired shape by using a lightsaber crystal. Perhaps it bends more than light."

Jax stared at the droid. "You're saying the Force might not be blocked, but instead shunted somewhere else?"

"Possibly, but not necessarily. I would suggest, given the challenges inherent in training your Padawan, that you may wish to conduct some simple experiments. There are still at least half a dozen of these sculptures in Ves Volette's studio. It would be interesting to know if they all create the same effect, and if they damp telekinetic and other psionic forces—or, as you suspect, shunt them off somewhere else."

"What I'm wondering," said Jax, "is what would happen if a Force-user was surrounded by them. Would they make an effective wall?"

"A redistribution enclosure?" suggested I-Five. "Something like an EM cage?"

"A what?" Den wanted to know.

"An electromagnetic cage is an enclosure lined with conducting metal designed to block various frequencies of radiation," I-Five explained. "It's extremely versatile and has been used for millennia. What Jax is postulating is essentially the same concept, applied to the Force."

"Hard to believe that someone hasn't stumbled across such a basic concept already," Jax said.

"Not really. For centuries the only ones really interested in the Force were the Jedi, and their R and D was much more esoteric and theoretical than practical. Their emphasis was always on ways to augment the Force, rather than restrict it." The droid looked closely at the light structure. "We'll no doubt have to tweak the frequency for optimal results."

Jax glanced toward the closed door to Dejah's quarters. "Not without her permission. She loves those sculptures. They're all she's got left of Ves Volette."

"Naturally, we would get her permission," I-Five conceded. "But I can't imagine she would withhold it. She has, after all, been an outspoken proponent of you pursuing a serious training regimen with Kajin."

"You really think a shield of these things would work?" the boy asked, staring up into the play of light.

"There's only one way to find out," Jax said, and turned toward Dejah's quarters.

I-Five put a pewter-shaded hand on his shoulder. "I think perhaps you should wait until Rhinann has had a chance to ascertain what's bothering her."

Jax felt a twinge of remorse. He'd been so wrapped up in their discovery that he hadn't given thought to Dejah's apparent discomfort with it. He should have gone after her, he supposed, but this . . . he gave the light sculpture another appraising glance. This could be the perfect solution to his current quandary.

He wondered how the Elomin was faring in his attempt to comfort the Zeltron. He'd thought Rhinann completely immune to Dejah's gentle emotional tugging and prodding. Apparently he'd been wrong.

"Dejah, are you unwell?" Rhinann stood on the threshold of the Zeltron's room and peered in at her.

She had gone immediately to sit in a false window seat, staring at a projected image of her late lover's equally deceased homeworld, Caamas. The Empire had seen fit to all but extinguish the elegant and gentle Caamasi, Rhinann recalled. Only a handful of those living on the planet, and emigrants to other worlds, had survived the scourge.

"Hiding," she said softly. "Ves was hiding from me, Rhinann. He had surrounded himself with objects behind which he could hide from me emotionally—withhold himself from me—whenever he wished."

"Perhaps he didn't realize that," Rhinann said. He felt excruciatingly uncomfortable—the only species that found speaking about emotions more anathema than Elomin were Givin.

She shook her head. "No, he knew it. He must have known it, to have used it so carefully that I never suspected. If it were a random effect, he would have disappeared emotionally at random moments, not . . . merely when he wanted to. Not merely *how* he wanted to." She seemed to struggle for a moment with the idea, then added, "I thought I was party to his private thoughts and feelings, the direct reflection of his soul. But he was only allowing me to catch a muted echo."

"Oh, surely he wouldn't be so cruel."

"He wasn't being cruel." She looked up at him with wide, tear-filled eyes. "He was just being private, independent. It's too much to expect a non-Zeltron to be as—as public as we are. He just wanted to keep some of himself . . . for himself. And so he died, surrounded by his barrier of light. It has always bothered me that I didn't feel even a touch of fear or pain from him that day, and now I understand why. Even the day his world died . . ." She put a hand up to her mouth.

"I doubt you would have wanted to feel that, my dear," said Rhinann, trying to go for an avuncular impression. "Your kind are not known for their tolerance of negative emotions."

"No, and right now I'm feeling . . . betrayed. I know I shouldn't. I know it was just his way of retaining a sense of privacy, but . . ."

"Consider your friend's kindness in sparing you the full brunt of his grief," Rhinann suggested. "Perhaps that will assuage your feelings of betrayal."

She smiled wryly and wiped her nose on the sleeve of

her garment—a gesture that Rhinann found strangely charming, given his usual distaste for such things.

"Count my blessings, Rhinann?" she murmured. "An odd sentiment, coming from you."

Yes, it was, rather. He caught himself, realizing what was happening. In her agitated state, Dejah Duare was undoubtedly pumping more pheromones into the atmosphere than she usually did, so much so that some of them were creeping past his natural immunity. He shook himself. He must not be distracted from his goal.

"My dear," he said, retaining the endearment because he thought it useful, "can you be thinking that Jax Pavan also might use this technology to hide from you, as you put it?"

She blinked up at him, eyes sparkling with tears. "It—it . . . Now that you mention it, yes, he certainly could. He has the Force to hide behind, of course." Her mouth turned up at the corners and her eyes shed bereavement as if it were a transient film, to be flicked away with a wink. "But that's entirely different. The Force, even used to filter or block, has such interesting . . . textures. In some ways it's more satisfying to the touch than the emotions it conceals."

Rhinann was intrigued and annoyed simultaneously. This hedonistic telempath clearly had a higher midi-chlorian count than he did. If she did not possess a capacity for Force manipulation herself, she clearly could sense it.

"Textures?" he repeated. "How interesting."

"Oh, more than interesting." She drew her knees up under her chin and hugged them. The gesture was at once child-like and seductive. Or would have been, if the Elomin were capable of being seduced.

"Even when Jax pulls the Force across himself like a curtain," she continued, "it's a curtain of amazing depth and nuance. Like . . . a warm bath, like sun-heated sand beneath your feet, like morning grass at the first touch of the sun, or—" She looked up, caught the look on Rhinann's face, and laughed. "I don't do it justice and still you think me overimaginative and overemotional."

"No, my dear, of course not . . ." He did think those things, but they were potentially useful things, so he tried not to dispense with them. "I was merely wondering how you would perceive the effects of the bota extract if Jax were to use it."

"The what?"

Rhinann gazed into the Zeltron's eyes. Ploy or honest puzzlement? He couldn't tell which. "The bota. The plant extract once deemed a panacea—"

"Yes, I know what bota is—or was. It's pretty much just a weed in its current form, isn't it? It mutated or something. Years ago."

"It did. But I was speaking of its ability to enhance the use of the Force. I thought perhaps you'd know about that—being, as you are, so close to Jax."

She shook her head, her burgundy brows drawn together above her eyes. "*Enhance* the Force? What are you talking about? Jax has never mentioned anything to me about such a thing."

"Ah. That's odd. According to the droid, a Jedi named Barriss Offee serendipitously discovered that an injection of bota extract amplified or expanded a Jedi's Force perception and ability exponentially. While they were on Drongar together, she gave a vial of the extract to I-Fivewhycue to bring to the Jedi Temple. By the time he arrived, of course, Order Sixty-six had been implemented, and so—"

"So I-Five has it? And Jax knows this?"

"I assume one of them has it. Though I could be wrong. The droid might have given it to someone else, or hidden it somewhere." Rhinann shrugged as if the location of the bota were of no interest to him at all. "I've no idea."

"But why hasn't Jax used it? If it amplifies the Force as you say, mightn't that make him powerful enough—" She paused, took a deep breath, then continued with a lowered voice, "to destroy the Emperor?"

Rhinann was no thespian, but he put every gram of acting ability he had behind his next words. "Indeed it might. Perhaps the droid isn't the best candidate for an assassin, after all."

"So why hasn't Jax taken the bota?"

Gazing down into the Zeltron woman's avid face, Haninum Tyk Rhinann had an epiphany: if something was missing, the more people you had looking for it, the better.

He frowned and tapped his thin lips with one flat fingertip. "Perhaps because he doesn't know where it is. I begin to suspect that the droid has not yet given it to him. That perhaps he has hidden it instead."

"Why would he do that?"

Rhinann shrugged. "Who knows? Were he a normal droid, the answer would have to be because someone instructed him to do it. But I-Five is not a normal droid, so that opens up a score of possibilities. Perhaps he wants to be the hero, instead of Jax. Perhaps he wishes to exact vengeance on the Emperor and Darth Vader himself."

Dejah looked thoughtful. "No. That's not like him. More likely he's trying to protect Jax."

Feign innocence, Rhinann instructed himself. *Project guilelessness.* It, along with his natural immunity to the Zeltron's wiles, seemed to be working. "Protect him from what?"

"From making himself a tool of vengeance. To do that would be to give in to the dark side, wouldn't it? Or maybe he's afraid of side effects. *Are* there side effects?" She glanced up at him askance.

"I don't know," he said, irritated by the digression. "I do know—or understand from the little I've learned—that the extract would make the Jedi who takes it . . . well, very nearly god-like in power and abilities."

"But for how long?" she murmured, her eyes going to the static view of the dead world projected into the niche above her "window" seat. "And at what cost?"

"Cost?" repeated Rhinann.

She gave him a gamine look from beneath her long, blood-red lashes. "Nothing is without cost, Rhinann. Nothing." Her eyes moved back to the image of the world that no longer was. "It's all a matter of trade-offs. Of knowing what something is worth."

"Different things are of varying worth to different people," he observed neutrally.

"Yes," Dejah murmured. "They are." She reached over and tapped a small touch pad next to the image niche. The view of the once verdant surface of Caamas disappeared, to be replaced by a panorama of a junglescape in which the dominant color was red. Rhinann assumed it was an image of Dejah's homeworld, Zeltros. Sitting before the landscape, she all but disappeared into it.

She turned her gaze back to Rhinann. "Do you think I-Five is wrong to keep Jax from the bota—if that's what he's about?"

"Wrong?" Rhinann splayed a thin, spidery hand over his heart. "I can't judge the wrong or right of the situation, my dear. I only know that it exists as a possibility. And as for what the droid is about, look at the evidence: Jax wants nothing more than to destroy the Emperor and Darth Vader and to restore not only the Jedi, but the fortunes of the Republic. The bota could give him the means to do it, but he hasn't used it, or even *suggested* that he use it. The only logical reason I can think of for that is that the droid has hidden it from him. If the droid were a biological life-form, Jax could influence his thinking. But he isn't, and he follows orders poorly or not at all. Therefore, he is impervious even to Jax."

"Yet I detect no strain between Jax and I-Five," Dejah observed. "At least, Jax doesn't seem to have any negative feelings for the droid."

"Perhaps because our mechanical friend has done a good job of convincing him that withholding the bota is for the best. I-Five can be quite persuasive when the need arises. After all, he is—or was—a protocol unit."

Dejah shrugged. "Perhaps he's right. Perhaps it is for the best."

Rhinann's smile was so brittle, he feared it might crack his lips. "I'm sure of it, Dejah," he said. "After all, who knows the Jedi better than I-Five?"

Dejah Duare merely smiled.

"My, look at the time," Rhinann said, glancing at his chrono. He left quickly, on the pretext that he was expecting a data dump from one of the Imperial intel links he was monitoring, and went away unsure of what, if anything, he had accomplished. Clearly Dejah Duare had known nothing of the bota until he had mentioned it. Had that mention fueled a further sense of betrayal? Had it intrigued her? Amused her? Frightened her?

He gave up his maundering. Who knew what a creature like that was likely to do? She was, as Pavan was wont to note, an atypical Zeltron. In some ways that made her as hard to read—and as frustrating—as Pavan's metal guardian.

He exhaled gustily, then winced. His nose tusks were vibrating so much lately from sighing that the anchoring flesh was getting sore.

"The prefect removed our tracking devices within minutes of returning to his headquarters."

Darth Vader's gloved hand moved in a dismissive gesture. "That was to be expected."

"He's a traitor then. He's chosen his side."

"Has he?" The Dark Lord turned, and Probus Tesla saw his distorted reflection in the curved black surfaces of the Dark Lord's optic panels. His image was warped, but the marks of his brush with death were still clearly visible on his face, notwithstanding the hours spent in a bacta tank. No matter. The scars served their purpose: they reminded him that hubris was a failing he could not afford and that false assumptions based on hubris could be deadly. He would not forget that hard-learned lesson.

"Or," Vader continued, "is he just being a prudent and cautious officer of the prefecture? Do you imagine that those we seek would not check for tracking devices? If they found them, Pol Haus would become useless to us. They'd never trust him."

"Then we still don't know where he stands."

"No."

"How will we know?"

"If he continues to evade our attempts to track him, we'll know he's Thi Xon Yimmon's man. But if one day he is less than vigilant about such things . . ."

Tesla smiled. The gesture hurt, tugging at the new flesh on his barely healed face. The pain, like the scars, was also good. It was a reminder of his personal goal: with or without the help of Prefect Pol Haus, he would track down the Force prodigy who had done this to him—be he Jedi or not—and either bring him as a prize to his master, or destroy him utterly.

ten

"I don't get it," Den said. "Why are you asking *me* this?"

"Obviously," Rhinann replied, his face, his posture, his entire *person* saying that he thought the question idiotic, "because I thought that perhaps you knew."

Den gestured at the virtual SEND icon on the holo-display and watched his message to Eyar Marath soar away on wings of . . . well, whatever such messages soared away on. "I don't know," he said. "I suppose I assumed that Five had it or had done whatever he thought appropriate with it. Maybe he gave it to Jax."

"Doubtful."

"Why doubtful?"

Rhinann shrugged. "Jax has said nothing about it. And he obviously hasn't used it."

"Well, yeah. I kind of think we'd know if he had . . . considering what it's supposed to do. But he wouldn't just use it without warning us."

"What makes you say that?"

Den gave the Elomin a withering glance. "I know Jax Pavan." He got up from his workstation. "I just remembered it's my turn to do the shopping. Gotta run. I'll see you later."

"You must realize what could happen if that substance should fall into the wrong hands."

The words turned Den around in the doorway of the

workroom. "Yeah, Rhinann. I'm not a total milking moron. I do get it. But frankly, there's not a whole lot I can do about it . . . other than trying to talk my good friend the droid out of doing something abysmally dangerous."

"So you're not even curious?"

Den shook his head. "No. Not even."

"An odd state of mind for a *journalist*, don't you think?"

Heat flashed up the back of Den's neck and around the rims of his ears. "Now, that was just plain *low*."

"I only meant—"

"You only meant that you don't think I'm much of a journalist. Well, maybe I'm not. And maybe I don't want to be anymore." *Oh, now* that *was a mature comeback.*

Rhinann's eyes narrowed. "*You* have it, don't you?" he murmured. "You've got the bota."

"And you've got a loose sanity chip, big guy. There's no way that I-Five would trust me with that stuff."

"Nonsense. I can think of no one else he'd trust more."

Den shook his head. "Well, then you've been into the dreamspice, Rhinann. Because I don't have it, and I don't much care who does."

The Elomin didn't try to stop him again. Den managed to get out of the conapt and make his way down several levels to a little café on the fringes of the Ploughtekal that he frequented. There he ordered himself a hot caf and a steamed bun stuffed with vegetables and meat—the provenance of which it was wisest not to inquire about—and sat at a metal table under an arbor covered with plants that were no more real than the "meat" in the bun.

He had finished his meal and was working on his third cup of caf when he felt watched. He looked up nervously, his eyes drawn to a hooded figure at a booth across the way. The cowled head was turned partially away from him, and he was beset with the sudden fear that he was looking at an Inquisitor. The noise of the market seemed to suddenly grow in volume, and his face felt flushed and hot.

That's ridiculous. Why should I be afraid of the Inquisitorius? I'm not a Jedi.

Maybe not, said a snarky voice from the back of his head. *But you know where one lives.*

What should he do? Get up and leave? Order another cup of caf?

The figure turned, presenting a comely profile, and Den slumped in relief. Then again, he could just invite her to join him. I-Five had suggested he make nice with Dejah Duare. Why not start now? She turned away from the booth, and he waved.

Seeing Den sitting in front of the café, Dejah seemed to hesitate; then, at his beckoning gesture, she came to take the seat opposite him.

"Can I buy you a drink?" he suggested, feeling utterly foolish.

"All right," she said graciously. "A caf?"

He got up to place the order, returning to the table with a steaming beverage and a possible, though utterly lame, way of starting the conversation: *Hey, what do you think of our new boy wonder?* He set the cup of caf in front of Dejah, slid back onto his chair, and opened his mouth.

Dejah preempted him. "I'm worried about Jax," she said.

"Why is that?"

Dejah folded her hands around the thermo-cup, making it appear as if the steam rose from her fingertips, and looked at him earnestly. "I'm terrified that I-Five is going to convince Jax to opt into Tuden Sal's ridiculous . . .

scheme. Do you have any idea of what that could mean?"

Didn't I already have this conversation? Den asked himself. Aloud, he said, "Well, it could put both I-Five and Jax in harm's way. And us, by extension."

Dejah took a sip of her drink and glanced up at Den through her lashes, which he could swear were getting longer by the minute. "Yes, by extension. But I was thinking more of Jax himself, the thing he holds most dear." She leaned forward over the table and lowered her voice nearly to a whisper. "The continuation of his kind."

"You mean the—" Den glanced around, then made a surreptitious gesture with one hand imitating someone wielding a lightsaber.

She nodded.

"What makes you think he'll go for the scheme? I mean, there's every reason *not* to do it—don't you think?"

"Of course. Apart from the danger to himself, there's the risk to the Whiplash, the others of his kind, and the boy. The fact that failure would even more deeply enslave us all. And failure," she added, "is the most likely result."

Den blanched. "I-Five seems to think it would work."

"I-Five is thinking like a biological life-form, not a droid. It's wishful thinking. The odds against him succeeding are astronomical. If there were only some way to make certain of his success, and of Jax's survival." She shook her head.

"I'm sure Five has a plan . . . ," Den said weakly.

She frowned. "Rhinann said the same thing. He talked about something called . . . um . . . bota—is that right? Yes, bota. He said it would make Jax invincible."

Startled, Den snorkeled hot caf up his nose and went into a fit of sneezing and choking.

"Wind spirits bless you," Dejah murmured after Zel-tron custom, bowing her head almost into her cup.

"Thanks," Den said when he could talk again. He wiped his nose on his sleeve. "Rhinann said that? He told you about the bota? I wasn't sure he knew."

"Yes, poor thing. He's worried, too. He said the bota is the only real chance that Jax has to survive if I-Five and Sal go through with this ridiculous plan. If he's able to take it at the appropriate time, he'll be able to blow our enemy away."

Den tried not to look stupefied. "Really? He said that?"

She nodded again. "So I asked him if he was sure the bota was where Jax could get to it easily, and he said he didn't know. He had to trust that I-Five had done something with it to keep it safe."

Den shrugged. "Well, sure. I trust I-Five, don't you?"

She fixed him with a look that all but curled the rims of his ears.

Den exhaled explosively, feeling as if she'd gut-punched him. "Point taken. So you think I-Five's not fir-ing on all thrusters?" A delusional droid—was that even possible?

He remembered how Dejah's partner had been mur-dered, and felt more blood drain out of his head.

"I think that as much as I-Five loves Jax Pavan," she said, "he loves his father's memory more. Remember, Den—I-Fivewhycue doesn't have the same sense of time that we have. He doesn't forget anything—no matter how unpleasant the memory is or how long ago it was made. Organic sentients can count on the passage of the days, the months, and the years to create a comfort-ing buffer zone that softens the reality for us, makes it bearable. Time heals all wounds—except those of droids. Ordinarily, this wouldn't be a problem, since a droid has no emotional ties to the past. But once again,

I-Five's sentience makes him unique. Lorn Pavan's betrayal is as fresh to him today as it was twenty-odd years ago—or as fresh, anyway, as it was the moment he recovered that particular memory and realized what it meant."

There were tears sparkling in the Zeltron's eyes as she finished. Den realized his own eyes had grown moist and his breath had all but stopped in his throat. It had never occurred to him that there had to have been a singular moment in which that particular memory, as Dejah put it, had resurfaced for his friend, never to be put aside again. Nor had it occurred to him that the one way in which I-Five was all droid was in his capacity to relive his past in vivid, perfect detail. Combined with his ability to imagine and theorize like an organic, well . . .

He couldn't even begin to imagine how much pain I-Five must be in.

Den drew in a long breath. I-Five may not have seen Lorn Pavan's death in real time, but Den was willing to bet he'd imagined it time and time again. And because he was a droid he could not escape it, even in sleep, since droids didn't sleep. The only other respite was temporary deactivation, which was not a real respite at all, since no subjective time was lost.

I-Five could not forget his loss, or gain perspective on it through the balm of years. Ever.

Which left only one course of action open to him.

"You think I-Five wants to avenge Lorn Pavan."

"If someone destroyed I-Five, or killed Jax, wouldn't *you* contemplate revenge?"

Would he? He liked to think that he'd only contemplate justice, but who knew? He considered the idea now and nodded. "Yeah. Yeah, I guess I might, at that. Okay, so we may have a vengeful droid on our hands. What can we do?"

Dejah shrugged. "I don't know that we can do any-thing before the fact, though I suppose we can try."

"You bet we can." Impulsively, the Sullustan reached across the table and put his hand over the Zeltron's. "If the two of us, along with Rhinann, keep up a united front, and if we all vote down this mad idea, Jax *has* to listen, doesn't he? Especially if you—you know—help out a little with that seductive sweat of yours?"

She cocked her head to one side and smiled in be-musement. "You *want* me to influence Jax?"

"In this case, yeah. And I'm perfectly willing to admit it's a slimy, hypocritical thing to say, but I'm willing to say it: do your best. If it'll keep Jax and I-Five out of deep ronto poodoo, I'm all for it."

Dejah's eyes twinkled at him, and she laughed, the sound trilling lightly in his ears before cascading down into a sultry purr. "You're an odd one, Den Dhur," she told him. Then her tone became serious again. "I sup-pose there's a chance we could fail, even united, but . . . there's always the bota."

He nodded. Truth to tell, he didn't like even thinking about bota—the very word conjured memories of Dron-gar and his time served on that plaguey world in vivid detail. The recollections might not be as realistic as I-Five's, but they were more than enough for him.

"Rhinann thinks you have it," Dejah said bluntly.

What—was she eavesdropping on private conversa-tions now? He didn't ask her that; instead he fell back on his usual refrain. "He said that?"

She tilted her head. A nod? A semi-nod? A maybe? Den wasn't sure. The Zeltron was humanoid enough to share a great deal of body language with most hominid species, but there was always a chance of misreading something.

"Well, Rhinann is wrong," he replied. "I don't have it

and I don't know who does. For all I know Five still has it."

Dejah gave him another ear-curling look. "Our would-be assassin? That hardly seems wise."

"Look, if that bota represents what you think it represents—the survival of the—" He made the lightsaber gesture again. "—then I-Five will hide it where it will come to no harm and do the most good—if he hasn't done so already. Our job is to try to talk him out of Plan A so he doesn't need a Plan B . . . agreed?"

He put out his hand as if to seal a business deal. She regarded the hand solemnly for a moment, then placed her own in it, sealing the bargain.

"Agreed."

They parted then, Den shaking his head at the twisted situation. I-Five had been the one to suggest he forge an alliance with Dejah Duare and now they had forged one—against him.

Plenty of nuance to savor there, if you're into irony, he thought.

eleven

There was a certain amount of guilt in Jax's concern for Dejah after the discovery of the light sculpture's damping properties. He'd intended to talk to her directly after Rhinann had, but he'd been experimenting with the sculpture and hadn't noticed her leaving the conapt. It wasn't until he had satisfied himself in a small way that further experiments were warranted that he left Kaj meditating in his quarters and went looking for the Zeltron, only to learn that she had gone out.

"Did she still seem upset when she left?" he asked Rhinann.

"Upset?" The Elomin shrugged his bony shoulders. "I can't honestly say. You know how Zeltrons are—they tend to be mercurial."

"What was bothering her?" Jax felt odd discussing the issue with someone other than Dejah herself, but Rhinann *had* gone in to check on her . . .

Rhinann considered that for a moment, then said, "Well, as near as I can tell, she felt renewed bereavement because she supposed that her late partner was holding out on her—emotionally speaking, that is."

"Hiding behind his creations."

"Precisely. It made her realize, I think, that her understanding of her relationship with Ves Volette was fundamentally flawed. She felt . . . left out."

"I hate to say it, but that may make her more inclined

to let I-Five and me tinker with the mechanics of the remaining light sculptures."

"Unless she's now fearing that *you're* going to hide behind them, too."

Jax smiled wryly. "I hide behind the Force. Or at least I'm pretty sure that's the way she sees it. Well, I'm going to trust that she'll realize it's for the greater good."

Rhinann merely tilted his head and shrugged.

Jax had turned and started for his room when every hair on his body stood on end. Something was happening within the confines of his room—something so anomalous he couldn't grasp it. He had heard a blaster overload once—had heard the sound of it grow from a staticky buzz that made his teeth itch to a piercing whine that threatened to remove the top of his head. This was like that, but it was in his brain, in his bones, in his blood.

It was a buildup not of sound, but of the Force.

Jax leapt for the door to his room and flung himself inside. Kajin Savaros lay in the middle of the floor in a fetal position, hands to his head, eyes squeezed tightly shut, rocking back and forth while the Force built up within him like water behind a dam.

In all his years of training with Master Piell, in all the time he had been on his own, Jax had never encountered anything like this. He had no idea what to expect, no idea what to *do*. On the opposite side of the room the items atop his storage bench began to vibrate. Even as he watched, a hairbrush, a chrono, and a book of Caamasi poetry jigged their way to the edge and fell.

Jax was in motion again before they hit the floor, pushing the Force ahead of him as he dived for the writhing teenager. He wrapped Kaj in soft folds of the Force, projected soothing, velvet calm. Then he grasped the boy's shoulders, his grip firm but gentle. He felt a backlash almost immediately—a kick like a repulsor field. He pushed back.

A bottle of depil cream abruptly cracked, its viscous contents oozing free.

"Kaj!" Jax said, then more sharply, "Kaj! What's wrong?"

The boy let out a wail that penetrated all the way to Jax's soul. "*Alone . . . alone!*"

Grasping at straws, Jax said, "You're not alone, Kaj. You have me now. You have Dejah and the others. You have the Force."

"The—Force—is doing this—to me!" The words came out in painful bursts, the anguish behind them breaking on Jax's mind like storm-driven wave and wind. "And Dejah—Dejah went away. She doesn't like me!"

Is that what this was about—Dejah? Had she been feeding the boy so much emotional stimulus through her pheromones that her absence brought this on?

"Dejah likes you a lot, Kaj. And she'll be back soon."

There was the tiniest letup in the mounting tension— the screaming of Jax's senses muting to a mere roar. Then the boy shook his head, his fisted hands pulling at his hair.

"Not soon enough. Not—soon—*enough.*" His eyes flew open and he reached up to grasp the collar of Jax's tunic. "Make it stop, please, make it stop! It's *burning* me!"

"What's burning you?"

"The *anger.*"

"Who are you angry with?" Jax asked desperately. "What's made you angry?"

"They sent me away . . . sent me here." He shook his head. "I didn't want to come. If I'd stayed, maybe this wouldn't have happened to me."

"You're angry with your parents for sending you away?"

"No . . . not them. *Him.*"

"Who? Tell me."

"The Emperor. He took everything. The farm, my life, my parents, my world. Everything. *Everything!*"

Jax felt it then—the huge gaping hole of loss and loneliness that lay beneath the anger. He had lost his parents, too, but not like this. Where he had grown up in the embrace of the Jedi, Kajin had simply been thrust out on his own, alone, to be overwhelmed by a power he didn't understand.

The Jedi put his arms around the boy and held him tightly, falling into his rocking rhythm as if they were in a boat on water.

"Not alone," Jax told him. "You're not alone. And if you really want to ruin the Emperor's day, don't let the anger take you. Don't let it win."

"But I can't hold it in."

"Then let it go, Kaj. Don't give in to it. Make *it* give in to *you.*"

The boy gritted his teeth and drummed his heels on the floor. "I don't know *how!*"

"Yes, you do. Yes, you do. Say it, Kaj: There is no emotion; there is peace."

"Peace," Kaj whispered.

"There is no ignorance; there is knowledge." Jax saw the boy's lips move in time to his. "There is no passion . . ."

"There is serenity," Kaj whispered, then repeated, "there is serenity."

"There is no death; there is the Force."

They finished the credo in unison, Kaj's tightly wound body finally relaxing a bit in Jax's arms, the white-hot press of rage cooling. Tears slid from the boy's eyes and dripped to the meditation mat. A moment later he was sobbing, and the threads of anger at last loosened and released him.

Jax felt a trickle of perspiration race down his back beneath his tunic and realized he had broken out in a cold sweat. He heard a muffled noise and looked up to see Rhinann standing in the doorway, a well-pulped domrai fruit in one hand and a sodden spot on the front of his weskit.

"Will he be doing that often?" he asked. "If so, I suggest we store the fruit in an enclosed space."

Jax smiled humorlessly. If Kaj did that often, the fruit would be the least of their worries.

"I thought I'd find you here."

Two steps from the café, Den looked up to find I-Five regarding him placidly.

"And you were looking for me, why?" Den asked.

"I was a bit . . . concerned about your sudden disappearance earlier. It seemed as though you and Rhinann had a disagreement about something," I-Five said.

"Don't tell me you were eavesdropping, too?"

The droid's photoreceptors brightened. "Someone was eavesdropping on your conversation with Rhinann?"

Den shrugged. "I'm not sure, to be honest. But Dejah seemed to know what we'd been talking about, and she would neither confirm nor deny."

"Ah."

The unspoken question, Den figured, was: *What would she neither confirm nor deny?*

I-Five started walking toward the amorphous center of the sprawling marketplace, and Den fell into step. "Where are we going?" he asked.

"To send a message to a friend." In other words, a Whiplash operative.

"Yeah? Which one?"

"Someone who knows a great deal about the UML."

The UML, or Underground Mag-Lev, was a route of egress the Whiplash had used for some time to ferry at-risk individuals to facilities within several of the nearby spaceports where they could be smuggled offworld. Its chief asset, oddly enough, was that it was public enough to be private. You simply melted into the crowds, and if you knew the lay of the tunnels that made up a large part of it, you could disappear and reappear somewhere else in the system in such a way that even surveillance could be defeated.

The secret was a series of secondary tunnels and access tubes that had lain in long disuse and whose very existence had been erased from the engineering records of the world-city. A late high-level Whiplash operative had made certain of that erasure and paid for it with his life. Since the Imperial Security Bureau thought he had been after something else altogether—as had been his intention—they simply assumed they had stopped the assassin and saboteur before he could perform whatever dastardly act he had been contemplating and used his demise as a PR coup: Pity Emperor Palpatine—these black-hearted so-and-sos just kept coming after him like madmen. Would they never learn?

"Travel plans for our Togrutan client?" Den asked.

"Yes. Orto is lovely this time of year."

Den glanced sideways at the droid. "Some part of Orto is lovely at any time of year."

I-Five gave an irritated click. "Don't be dense."

"I'm not. It's just that that sort of inaccuracy sounds really strange coming from you. Why Orto?"

"The music. Our friend feels that the fact of the Ortolans' seemingly universal talent for producing highly affective music would be of great benefit for the young lady in question."

Den thought of Kajin Savaros and felt a little bird of

guilt with tiny, sharp talons roost in his conscience. He said, "Look, there's something I need to ask you about."

"Tuden Sal." The droid looked down at the Sullustan. "I know how you feel about this . . . enterprise. But think about the payoff if I were to succeed."

"Fine, if you'll think about the payoff if you don't. And think about why you want to do it."

"I should think that was perfectly clear."

"It's not. Not considering the risks."

"Why do you think I want to do it?"

"Vengeance?"

That stopped the droid in his tracks, Den was pleased to note. His optics glowed bright with surprise.

"No."

That was it. Just *no*. The droid turned on his heel and continued walking.

Den trotted to catch up. "That sounded an awful lot like denial."

"It was the truth."

"Are you sure?"

I-Five kept walking; Den had to stretch his legs to keep up.

"Whatever else you may think me capable of," the droid said, "I am not given to lying. Who put that idea into your head?"

"What—now I'm not capable of acquiring ideas to put in my own head?"

I-Five mimicked the sound of a supercilious sniff.

"Okay, it was Dejah . . . via Rhinann, or so I gather," Den said.

I-Five slowed his pace. "That's interesting. So they think I'm plotting vengeance on . . . this person . . . because he murdered my partner—my friend?"

"That's the long and short of it, yeah."

"And it hasn't occurred to them that while the work we're engaged in now is annoying and costly to the person in question, this new plan will cut right to the heart of the situation and remove him completely?"

"It's occurred to them. But I guess the question is: why do *you* in particular have to do this?"

"I stand the greatest chance of success simply because of who and what I am."

"Really? I'm thinking they're thinking that maybe Jax has the best chance of success because of who and what *he* is, and because of that extra little something he has. Which has the potential of becoming a much bigger something extra, thanks to you."

The droid stopped to stare—there was no other word for it. "What are you talking about?"

"That vegetable juice cocktail of yours."

"What have they said about it?"

"Not so much said as asked." Den glanced about, then took a step closer to the droid. "They were interested in where it's gone, and seem to have come to the conclusion that you've given it to me."

"Did they say why they were interested in it?"

"I think it basically came down to a fear that when the sky fell, Jax wouldn't have it at his disposal."

"They think I would prevent him from taking it? Why?"

The thought that popped into Den's head unbidden filled him with cold horror. "For the same reason you've taken on the mantle of martyrdom so readily—because *you're* afraid of what Jax might do if he gets the vengeance bug and the bota at the same time. You're afraid he might take it and get sucked into the darkness. This way, he might be thinking about vengeance, but *you'll* be the one acting on it."

There was a long, tense pause during which the sounds, colors, and smells of the bazaar seemed to come to Den through thick wads of padding. In all the universe he could see only this droid—this gleaming metal being—

this *sentient* who was willing to sacrifice himself in a last, lethal act of protection.

I-Five put a hand on Den's shoulder . . . and yanked him out of the main thoroughfare into a dark, grimy corner behind a kiosk that smelled of machine lubricant and dust.

"Kark!" Den squeaked. "What in chaos are you—"

A metal hand clamped over his mouth. "Inquisitors," the droid hissed. He released Den's mouth and allowed him to turn within the confines of their bolt-hole.

The skin at the nape of Den's neck tightened and his dewlaps quivered. There were Inquisitors all right—three of them, moving together in well-rehearsed choreography. Three of them.

"I've never seen them travel together like that," I-Five murmured.

"That makes me feel so much better," Den said.

As they watched, the Inquisitors paused to speak to the weapons dealer across the alley. The booth appeared to be selling domestic water vaporators and distilleries, but everyone who frequented the area knew that that was only a sideline. The Inquisitors were settling in for a thorough interrogation of the visibly terrified Sullustan proprietor, when one of them suddenly lifted his cowled head and turned to peer down the street.

Den felt a wave of chill pass over him. He thanked every Sullustan deity he could think of that he wasn't Force-sensitive.

The itchy Inquisitor then turned and said something to his cohorts, and suddenly all three of them were agitated. They moved off swiftly, almost seeming to float above the pocked duracrete of the bazaar, and disappeared into a lift tube at the nearest corner.

Den shivered. Eerie.

I-Five started in the direction of the Sullustan's kiosk, but Den stopped him. "If they tweaked that guy's warmware, having a droid start asking questions might trip some alarms. I'll go."

I-Five signified his assent and Den dived into the crowd, maneuvered through the stream of taller beings, and approached the weapons booth, shuffling a little and wringing his hands.

"I saw the Inquisitors, *lequana*," he said to the proprietor, using a Sullustan term that roughly translated into Basic as "cave brother." The proprietor still seemed a bit dazed. "Did they tell you who did it?" Den asked. "Did they catch him?"

"Did what? . . . Oh! The murderer, you mean. No, they only asked me if I'd seen someone." His brow furrowed as if he couldn't recall who. Possibly they had wiped that memory.

"Really? They have a description?"

"I . . . I suppose they must have. A human boy, I think they said." He shook his head and shrugged. "Thousands like that in this marketplace."

"Yeah. At least."

Den turned and headed off down the thoroughfare. When he was out of sight of the Sullustan's kiosk, he turned his head slightly and found I-Five pacing him about a meter away.

"Nothing," he told the droid. "If they asked him about anything besides seeing a human boy, he doesn't remember."

"Let's go down a level," I-Five said. He led Den to a lift about two blocks distant—with luck, a safe distance from the Inquisitorial trio.

On the level below they wandered a bit before entering a stygian side alley and making their way into the kitchen of the Emperor's Board, a charity whose impeccable handling of its community service work kept it out of the Imperial eye. The ISB hardly cared who fed the rats as long as they filed the appropriate documentation, which apparently Thi Xon Yimmon did.

I-Five took the lead, presenting himself to the Gungan cook. "I have a price bid for your proprietor on a job he requires performed," he said, his voice free of inflection, like a standard droid.

"From?" the Gungan asked, eyeing Den.

"A certain purveyor of lighting supplies. He tells me your proprietor has a dim corridor he wishes to make passable."

"Oh yes." The Gungan nodded zealously enough to flap his ears and cause his eyestalks to bob up and down. "Yes, me-sa boss is in much need of such. Passage long and very dark. You-sa got the bid?"

I-Five produced a data crystal seemingly from nowhere and handed it to the Gungan.

"When you-sa do the work?"

"Two days at oh seven hundred hours," I-Five said, then uttered three clicks, each one pitched slightly lower than the one before.

The Gungan smiled pleasantly and cocked his head to one side. "You-sa oughta get that looked at, eh? Me-sa take this to the boss."

"One more thing," I-Five said before the cook could pocket the crystal and move away. "Tell the Sakiyan I will see him tomorrow at sunset. He knows the place."

The Gungan nodded his head, causing his long earflaps to dance about his shoulders. "No problem. Me-sa tell him this."

When the Gungan cook had gone to deliver the crystal and the message—which was that the "work" would really be done at 0400 hours, three hours earlier than stated—Den looked up at I-Five with dread tugging at his heart.

"You've decided what you're going to do about the plan?"

"No. But I have given myself a deadline. I will decide by the time I see my contact tomorrow."

"Don't do it, Five. The risk—it's just too big. This whole thing is too big."

I-Five turned to look down at him, optical receptors bright in the dim interior of the charity's back corridors. "With all due respect, Den—and I mean that—I think I'm in a better position to gauge the risks than you are. My processor, in fact, has already calculated all the possible scenarios and variables inherent in my agreeing. I only await the majority opinion of the team before making my decision."

"And?"

"I promise you I will not take on this charge if Jax and the others feel that it's wrong."

Wrong. Not inadvisable. Not illogical. Not stupidly dangerous. Not lethal.

Wrong.

Den shook his head and followed I-Five back out into the street. When droids started philosophizing about morality and ethics, maybe it was time to investigate cyborg implants and a lobotomy.

twelve

It had wafted to him, borne on the winds of the Force, and he had known it immediately for what it was—a release of Force energy that possessed a peculiar edge. Neither of his fellows had noticed it—a fact that gave him a perverse tickle of pride. Not all Inquisitors were created equal, it seemed.

The intriguing sensation grew in strength as they pressed onward, rising several levels to a more affluent sector. As they drew nearer the source, it began to flash across his sight in lambent flurries of sparks. They had just entered a neighborhood in which quartets of resiblocks were built around deeply buried courtyards and plazas when he was brought up short by its intensity.

A shower of sparks all but blinded him, his skin flushed with heat, a strange roaring filled his ears, the tang of ozone was in his nostrils . . . and then it was gone. Completely and utterly gone—as if someone had thrown a thermo-blanket over a fire.

Tesla cast about helplessly and futilely, snarling in the rage of bereavement. "It was him! I know it was him!"

"Pavan?" asked his second, Yral Chael.

"No. Not Pavan. The *other*."

He felt Chael trade glances with the third of their number, a Corellian named Mas Sirrah.

"The prodigy is a secondary target, Probus," Chael

said. "We were specifically ordered to step up our search for Pavan and the droid."

We. The pronoun infuriated him. After his injury at the hands of that rogue—that *boy*—his lord had seen fit to bring more Inquisitors into the game. So Tesla had found himself paired with Chael and Sirrah. He was the nominal leader of the grouping and was, in fact, charged with the prosecution of the search in this sector, but the members of his team each felt they should have been given the lead. After all, hadn't Tesla already proven his weakness by falling victim to an adept who was not even a trained Jedi?

Yes, he'd heard the cascade of innuendo that had torn through the ranks of the Inquisitorius like a flash flood. He'd ignored it. Soon he would silence it.

"What makes you think the two will not be found together?" he asked now. "The boy is a Force prodigy of unbelievable strength. It stands to reason that Pavan would want to recruit him, likely in some vain attempt to resurrect the moldering Jedi corpse."

Again the two other Inquisitors exchanged glances. This time it was Mas Sirrah who spoke. "What makes you suppose that Pavan even knows of his existence?"

"Don't be stupid, Mas. Such a power is like gravity. It will draw Jax Pavan just as it draws me."

During the conversation he had been trying to reacquire the scent of that other Force-sensitive, scouring walls and halls and hidden rooms with his mind and finding only echoes, ghost perfumes. He peered down one long, convoluted alley with the unlikely name of Snowblind Mews . . . but no, the trail was gone—like smoke flayed to transparency by a breeze.

He turned to his peers. "Pavan is somewhere on this level. Maybe he lives here, or maybe he's just hiding here, but he's here now. Stay in the area. I'll report to Lord Vader."

They nodded in unison and glided into the shadows while Tesla pulled out his comlink.

The look on Dejah Duare's expressive face betrayed a jumble of emotions: shock, affront, curiosity, trepidation. She pushed back the cowl of her robe and stared at him. "You want to move to the studio?"

"Not all of us maybe, but at least Kaj and me." Jax hated asking this of her; he could see that it was wreaking havoc on her composure. "I hate hitting you with this, Dejah, and if I felt I had any choice, I wouldn't do it. But Kaj isn't in complete control of his talent, and I need to put him someplace where he stands half a chance of remaining concealed until I can complete his training—or at least teach him how to govern his impulses. Right now the Force is reacting to his every emotion. If he feels anger, the Force amplifies that anger until it's out of his control."

"Are you sure Ves's sculptures will shield him?"

"Not sure, but very hopeful. Especially if I-Five and I can modify them so that the field is widened and stabilized."

Now she was simply stunned. "You want to modify them? You want to *change* them?"

"That is usually what the word *modify* means," Rhinann said from the doorway of the workroom.

Jax lifted a hand to prevent him from saying more— actually putting a bit of the Force into the gesture for emphasis. The Elomin would experience it as the sensation of an invisible hand clamped over his mouth for a moment. His eyes widened and his lips compressed to an even thinner line than usual, but he stayed put. Jax wished he would just go away, but he refused to use the Force for that sort of petty manipulation.

"Surely there are alternatives," Dejah said. "You

could take him to the Whiplash. Don't they have safe houses that—"

"There's no safe house that's proof to a Force prodigy of Kaj's power. They'd have to keep him tranquilized day and night."

"So they keep him tranquilized. You've got him tranquilized now . . ."

"So he can sleep safely. But that's only a stopgap measure. Keeping him that way for any length of time would do him irreparable harm—and only make him more inclined to emotional overload and explosion."

Dejah moved closer to Jax, laying her hands on his arm. He instinctively raised a barrier of tightly woven Force threads against her involuntary assault on his senses.

"Then let's use Whiplash resources to smuggle Kaj offworld. The Togruta is being moved tomorrow morning, right? Can't we move Kaj at the same time?"

Jax shook his head. "Kaj's talent makes him a huge liability, Dejah. We don't have the safeguards in place to move him offworld without tremendous risk to everyone. What I'm asking of you is the only way to minimize the danger. Once Kaj is trained, he'll be able to control his emotions, and then he can learn to control his use of the Force."

She stared up at him for a long moment, her eyes searching his face. Finally she sighed and stepped back, relinquishing her grip on his arm. "Yes. Yes, of course, you're right. I just . . . those sculptures meant so much to me—to Ves. And now they represent irreplaceable financial resources."

"I'll try to use the minimum amount to do what needs doing and try not to modify them irretrievably. It may even be possible for I-Five to memorize Ves's settings and return them to their original configuration."

She nodded. "All right. Yes. Of course you can use the

studio and the sculptures. How soon do you want to move him?" Her gaze flickered toward Jax's quarters where Kaj slept a deep, chemically augmented, and hopefully dreamless sleep.

"As soon as I-Five and Den get back. We'll need to get an airspeeder—" Jax glanced over at Rhinann, who responded with a courtly bow that was somehow laced with irony. It was most often the Elomin's job to arrange for transport and other resources simply because, having been high up within the Imperial apparatus, he knew how to acquire them without drawing undue attention.

"I shall, of course, arrange it," Rhinann said. "Anything else?"

"No . . . and thanks, Rhinann. I don't know what we'd do without you," Jax said.

The Elomin's eyes closed and opened in an almost reptilian blink, his entire body language eloquent of surprise. Then he inclined his head and disappeared into the workroom.

"I won't go with you," Dejah said. "To the studio, I mean. I don't think I could bear to see . . ."

She left Jax to imagine what the end of the sentence might have been. *I couldn't bear to see where Ves Volette died.* Or, *I couldn't bear to see the sculptures that shielded him from me.* Or, *I couldn't bear to see you mangle his work.* In any case, Jax was surprised to realize that he felt a strange mixture of disappointment and relief.

He watched her go into her room, aware of a budding tension that sat between his shoulder blades like an unreachable itch. He hoped Den and I-Five would get back soon. He wanted to go out and look for them, to hasten their return, but knew it would be dangerous to leave Kaj here untended. There was no way to know how long the anti-stim would work on someone with his abilities, or in what state of mind he'd awaken.

*   *   *

Den Dhur was in a black mood. More than any time since he'd signed on with I-Five and company, he felt as if everything was spinning hopelessly out of control. There were too many players, too many half-concealed agendas, and way too many risks.

He glanced up at I-Five, who moved silently beside him as they made their way back to Poloda Place. He had expected that the droid would be more concerned about the sudden interest Rhinann and Dejah had shown in the bota and would confide *something* in him, but even that expectation was doomed to disappointment. After that brief conversation, during which Den felt as if he'd finally gotten I-Five's full attention, it had been business as usual.

They stepped out of the antigrav tube a block from the entrance to the resiblock and made their way west. Den found himself watching passersby. It was an old habit, dating back to his days as a newsbeing—he used to say that he could pick any face at random out of a sea of beings and twirl a story about him, her, or it that, often as not, was remarkably close to the truth. Now, tired of staring at kneecaps, he walked with his head tilted back. It made it difficult at times to keep his footing, but it was also the reason he saw the robed and hooded figure turn from the railing of a balcony two floors above street level in the building they were currently passing. There was no question this time—the iridescent, shifting robes, the cowl, the sense of *presence* . . . this was not mistaken identity.

This was the real thing.

Den stumbled, and I-Five put a hand down to steady him. "Are you all right?"

Den clung to the droid's arm, pretending vertigo, and murmured, "Balcony on the left. Second floor."

I-Five straightened slightly. "Someone just went in-side."

"An Inquisitor. An *Inquisitor* just went inside. He was watching the street. Watching the entrance to the Mews."

I-Five put Den firmly on his feet. "Do tell."

"Don't be so frippin' sanguine about it, Five! Why are they here?"

"I could wager a guess."

Den's heart threatened to shift into reverse. "The kid? You think they're after the kid, or—"

"I think," said I-Five, turning him about and pushing him back the way they'd come, "that we need to find an alternative means of getting into Poloda Place."

The alternative means turned out to be a disguise; not for Den but for I-Five. Back down in Ploughtekal at a shop claiming the finest fabrics in the Zi-Kree Sector, the droid purchased a skinsuit that turned him into a per-fectly credible Koorivar, right up to the multihued spi-raling horn that sat atop his head. It was a large horn, bespeaking great social stature, and the robes that he purchased to go with it expanded on the impression that this was an affluent personage of much wealth and pres-tige.

Half an hour after their initial foray into the Mews, Den and I-Five made their way back again, the Sullustan pretending to be a property agent showing this fine citi-zen available habitations in the area.

They approached the entrance to Snowblind Mews, Den feeling as if eyes were lasering into his back. He saw no Inquisitors this time as they made their way into the alley's mouth, but they kept up their charade anyway. So, despite the fact that he was sweating like a stuck ronto, Den managed to keep his voice energetic and plucky as he loudly described the features of the proper-ties he was proud to represent.

"These conapts are roomy, comfortable, and quite chic when it comes to accoutrements. High ceilings, duracrete floors molded to look like cobbles in the food preparation area—reduces slippage, you know—and sonic or steam showers. Buyer's choice."

"What about natural light?" growled I-Five in a perfect Koorivar accent. "I must have natural light."

"Then you've come to the right agent," Den enthused as they started up the dark winding way to Poloda Place. "I can get you a unit with natural light brought down all the way from the highest levels of the city."

"How is this possible?"

"Oh, the old architects knew what they were doing. The light is channeled by a series of movable mirrors." As Den babbled, having no idea if there was any truth at all in what he was claiming, he peered behind them. No one followed.

"Ah yes, of course. How many rooms?"

"As many as you need. You have a wife? Children?"

At I-Five's nod, Den said, "Well, let me just show you what's up ahead here—a marvelous place for the kiddies to play."

They picked up their pace, Den casting furtive glances over his shoulder. Still no followers.

They emerged into the plaza, and Den trotted to the center to turn in place, arms wide. "You see? Just as I said, room for your children to play—though I wouldn't recommend they be left unmonitored. A number of the units look out on the plaza, of course, and—"

He cut off as his eyes caught on a reflected image in one of the tall, narrow windows. There was an Inquisitor standing in the shadow of an overhanging eave in the building facing their own. He was looking right at them.

Den's stomach abruptly felt like someone had just flicked the ON/OFF switch for Coruscant's gravity.

"Yes, yes, but have you anything on the third level? Something with a window that looks out on this court?"

Den spun to look at the droid, wondering if those omniscient photoreceptors had finally missed something. But then, his hands steepled before him, I-Five made a minute gesture.

"It's your lucky day, friend," said Den. "I have an empty unit on the third floor of this building that just came open. The previous lessees were an odd bunch—secretive, peculiar. One might almost be tempted to suspect criminal behavior." He bustled toward their building as he spoke.

Inside the building it was all Den could do not to race to the lift and throw himself in. Once out of the lift on the third floor, he continued to fight the urge to run, but rather kept prattling about this or that lovely feature of this well-built structure.

At the front door of the conapt, he glanced up at I-Five. If he gave his usual verbal pass code to enter, and an Inquisitor overheard it . . .

The droid pulled aside the sleeve of his robe to display the gleaming tip of one index finger. He would use his laser on lowest power to beam the code into the house computer.

Weak with relief, Den turned to the door and said, "Hatto Rondin," a name he made up on the fly. The door slid open and Den turned to his "client" and bowed. "After you."

Five nodded and entered. Den following. They'd no more cleared the door when Jax appeared, his gaze flicking from Den to the apparent Koorivar.

"Den? Who is . . ." He stared hard at the droid. "I-Five?"

"Gotta love that Force," Den murmured.

"Why are you in dis—" Jax started, then apparently changed his mind. "It doesn't matter. Come on, we need to get Kaj out of here and over to Ves Volette's studio now."

"Yes, it *does* matter," said I-Five, with unbelievably irritating calm. "There is an Inquisitor in the court-yard."

Jax's looked shocked. "I didn't . . . ," he murmured, then clearly did. "The taozin effect. And I wasn't look-ing for it."

"Something happened with Kaj, I take it?" I-Five asked.

Jax nodded. "He had an *episode*. Almost a seizure. He was lonely and angry, and it got to be too much for him. I was wondering if anyone picked it up. I guess I've got my answer."

He turned and moved to the window. Thick and nar-row, the panel of transparisteel ran the entire height of the resiblock, intersecting every floor. Den and I-Five followed to look down into the courtyard. The Inquisi-tor was nowhere in sight.

Which, of course, meant nothing.

"Okay," Jax said. "Rhinann's got an airspeeder wait-ing for us on level seven. We're going to have to make a run for it. Get Kaj into the speeder and—"

"That won't be necessary," said I-Five. "Den and I played the roles of an agent and his client to our unsus-pecting audience. I'm supposedly thinking of leasing this overpriced pile of ferrocrete. If our friend the Inquisitor stays in the courtyard, he will be expecting us to leave at some point. This could work to our advantage."

Den nodded. "I get it. We can provide a distraction while we take Kaj up to the docking station, or—"

"Or," said Jax, "we can take Kaj out right under his nose." He turned to their de facto logistics officer. "Rhi-nann, did the speeder come with a driver?"

"Yes. A protocol droid."

"What model?" asked I-Five.

"It's a threepio."

"That'll do."

"That'll do what?" asked Den. He felt as if bolts of blasterfire were zooming back and forth over his head—a scenario that he had no trouble believing would be reality shortly.

Jax's eyes were alight with something unhealthily close to excitement. He turned to Rhinann. "In about ten minutes, have the driver bring the airspeeder down to the front door."

Rhinann gaped. "Land it in the courtyard? In plain sight?"

"Exactly. Instruct him to come up to this conapt. He'll be taking our property agent and his client off to sign some papers."

Rhinann disappeared back into his lair. Jax was in motion again, this time heading for his quarters. He beckoned I-Five and Den to follow.

"I can explain—" he said to Den, but the Sullustan interrupted.

"I'm sure you can," he said. "What scares me is that the explanations are starting to make sense to me. Even when I'm sober," he added, "which I devoutly wish I wasn't at this point."

"Be as that may," Jax said, "you and I-Five are going to take our Koorivar friend to your office to sign lease papers."

"I may have found a basic flaw in your ingenious scheme—namely, that I-Five *is* our Koorivar friend."

"Not for long."

The scariest thing about the whole maneuver was waking Kaj. Jax did this with his own Force threads tightly held, ready to shield any anomalies. As an added, though possibly useless, precaution, they carried the boy into the living room and placed him on a couch so that the light sculpture lay between him and the forecourt of Poloda Place. *If* the Inquisitor was still there and *if* the cloaking effect worked at that distance and *if* Jax didn't have to resort to extreme measures to calm Kaj, they just might get him out without being detected.

As easy as navigating an asteroid field . . .

thirteen

Den felt as if an army of Inquisitors were stationed in the courtyard, just waiting to pounce on them. He kept his gaze on Kajin as they neared the external door and nearly jumped out of his skin when I-Five poked him in the back of the head.

"Showtime. Start your spiel."

"Uh, yeah." Den wiped his palms on the legs of his pants, cleared his unnaturally dry throat, and launched. "I'm pleased we were able to find a property that fit your exacting needs. My office will have the legal work drawn up by the time we get there."

The faux Koorivar nodded eagerly and patted his hands together. "Excellent!" he said. "And how soon can I move my family in?"

The voice was I-Five's, thrown expertly from the droid's voice generator via tightband hypersonic beam, so that it seemed to be coming from the disguised Kaj, who had awakened by now and been pressed into service as part of their scheme.

"Oh, ah . . . well, pending a check of your funding, we should be able to have you in sometime tomorrow."

"Very good. I'm pleased to do business with you."

They had reached the airspeeder by then, and I-Five opened the doors for his passengers to embark—Kaj first, then Den. He had closed the doors and gotten into the driver's seat when Den saw the Inquisitor. He was standing in the shadows of the building across the way, approximately where they'd seen him before.

Kaj stiffened, and Den knew he'd seen it, too.

"Kick it, Five," he murmured. Then to Kaj, "It's okay, kid. We'll be out of here in a flash. Just sit tight."

But Kaj wasn't sitting tight. He had reached up and was trying to undo the seals on the back of his skinsuit's headpiece. Den put his own hands up to keep him from succeeding.

"Kaj! Just calm down. If you're calm, he won't—"

"I can't fight like this!" Kaj panted. "I have to get—this—*off*!"

The speeder lifted. Simultaneously, the Inquisitor came out of the shadows, his step halting, uncertain. Den suspected he was sensing something but wasn't sure what it was.

The Inquisitor raised his hand, hesitated, reached again toward the rising airspeeder, and froze, his head swiveling away from them.

As the vehicle turned and soared upward toward the skylanes, Den watched the Inquisitor dash across the courtyard in the opposite direction, hurling himself into a Force leap that carried him up toward the resiblock's communal docking stations.

He was in hot pursuit of something, Den realized. Or someone . . .

Jax knew the ruse was in jeopardy when he felt Kaj's psychic gasp of terror. He didn't have to wonder what had caused it, but he knew that he had to act before Kaj did.

He bolted from the conapt, frightening Dejah and sending Rhinann into conniptions of gloom. He went up; the turbolifts were too slow, so he literally flew up the emergency stairs, touching down on the landings only enough to change direction for the next leap.

On the fifth level, he reached out and called to the Inquisitor in the courtyard below, exuding a thin, sharp whiplash of the Force calculated to get the dark adept's attention. He got it all right. Jax felt the other's interest as a sharp tug on his tether.

He cut the thread and leapt away, heading up to the next level . . . in the opposite direction from that which the airspeeder had taken. He let off two more short, sharp bursts of Force energy, then shut down and went literally to ground, taking a lift from the upper levels all the way down to the midlevels of Ploughtekal.

He waited there for some time, listening for other Force-users. When none materialized, he set off for Ves Volette's studio.

Kaj, sans disguise, sat cross-legged in the center of the studio regarding the light sculptures with hopeful eyes. I-Five moved the last of them into place—the last currently functional one at any rate—while Den cataloged how many dormant ones and component parts were left in the sprawling studio.

These were nice digs, no doubt about it. Besides the three-story studio with its overlooking gallery, there were four private bedrooms, a library/workroom, a living room, and a large kitchen. A real kitchen—not just a food prep area with the usual nanowave and conservator. Apparently Ves Volette or Dejah had liked to cook.

Den found himself hoping that Dejah was the cook. If they relocated the entire team here . . . He caught himself. He might not be around that much longer. Depending on the answer he got from Eyar, he might soon be taking off for Sullust and leaving this dangerous, misbegotten, Inquisitor-infested hunk of real estate behind.

"Done with that inventory?" I-Five asked.

Den pulled himself forcibly out of his reverie and

glanced down at the compad he'd been taking inventory on. "Yeah. Think so. We've got three more sculptures in the far corner that seem to lack power modules. A fourth that's down a PM and a crystal, and component parts for maybe two more. I just don't know if the parts list is complete. I found a log record that indicates he kept a small supply of crystals and a few PMs here, but I haven't run across them yet."

I-Five's photoreceptors lit with surprise. "Pilfery?"

Den shrugged. "Or he hid them well. Those particular parts are pretty dear—both rare and expensive."

He threw a glance at the boy within his circle of light sculptures. The rainbow of illumination reared above him into the vault of the ceiling, restless, ever moving, casting light and shadow on everything in the room.

Den shivered, feeling as if he was looking at an analog for their scary guest. Or maybe for the power he invoked. He tried to ignore the crawl of heat across his own face and asked, "Is it working? Can you tell?"

"No. We won't be able to tell until we have a Jedi here to tell us it's working."

"Or an Inquisitor to tell us it's not," muttered Den.

"Will a Gray Paladin do?"

Den spun and stared up at the durasteel gallery that ran the length of the studio. Laranth Tarak stood looking down at them, eddying light from the sculptures playing over her, making her seem to flicker like a candle flame. The radiance shone on the polished railings of the gallery as well, making it look as if she stood on a bridge made of strands of light.

Den was surprised by how glad he was to see her. She represented, he realized, things as they had been, as he had wanted them to be. Sure, she was taciturn and unsmiling and unyielding and uncommunicative. None of that mattered, because she was also unambiguous. Laranth, Jax, and I-Five were the three people Den Dhur felt most at home with. In a bad situation, these were the people he wanted at his side, at his back.

"What are you doing here?" he asked.

"I was in the neighborhood. I sensed an anomaly in the Force."

Laranth left the gallery rail and descended, using the house grav-pad. Stepping off onto the studio floor, she sauntered over to them, her eyes on Kaj. The boy smiled a little nervously and waved at her. To Den's utter surprise, she waved back.

"Interesting," she said, gesturing to the light sculptures. "Wonder why we didn't sense this Force-canceling property in them before now."

"I think they have to be tuned to a specific harmonic," the droid said. "The pertinent question is, are they working?"

She turned her head to look at Kaj, tipping her head to one side. Her right lekku coiled slightly. Then she turned, picked up an electrospanner from a tray of tools, and rolled it between the two light sculpture stands closest to them. "Kaj—lift that."

The boy looked at the spanner. It bobbed up from the floor.

"Hold it there," Laranth told him. She walked the perimeter of the circle. After making a complete circuit, she had Kaj let go of the tool.

"A little gets through," she told I-Five. "But very little. Still, if he were to do something major in there, who knows what might leak out."

"It appears," I-Five said, "that we're going to have to do some adjusting."

Laranth's eyes widened. "Meddle with the art of a deceased master? Dejah's going to allow that? I'm amazed."

"Really, Laranth—sarcasm is so human an attribute."

Laranth ignored him. "Is Jax coming?"

"Jax is here. Good to see you again so soon, Laranth."

Den looked up to the gallery again. Jax was the creature of light and shadow this time as colors danced across his face and set his drab clothing metaphorically aflame. The Sullustan felt a little more secure now that two Jedi were in the immediate vicinity. Not much, but a little.

In the aftermath of Kaj's hasty removal, Haninum Tyk Rhinann sat at his workstation feeling as if someone had immersed him in icy water. They had come that close—*that close*—to being discovered. Oh, he was sure that Pavan would deny this—if he ever returned from wherever he'd gone so precipitously. He would no doubt claim everything had been just fine, under control, and that there had never been any great danger of discovery. But in the proximity of that Inquisitor, Rhinann had felt the cold gaze of his erstwhile master.

He turned back to his workstation, desperately trying to herd his scattered neurons back into some semblance of order. He didn't have the bota. Perhaps he was no closer to knowing who did, though he strongly suspected the little Sullustan. All that foot-dragging and naysaying was most likely just a smoke screen.

But suspicions did him no good at all. The Sullustan was currently out of reach, Inquisitors prowled the streets nearby, and the droid was preparing to put them between a rock and a rancor.

He tried to list his options. Rhinann truly believed that any crisis must be answered with a good list. Creating lists ordered the mind, calmed the blood, lowered the chaos level.

He could run now. That would be safest. But nearness to yet another Force prodigy had reminded him viscerally of what he was missing. That boy—that mere child—

had killed an Inquisitor and had even caused Jax Pavan some concern. If he could experience but a fraction of what it was like to be possessed of such *power* . . .

He could bide his limited time and continue to press Den Dhur about the bota. He had already decided he would ask I-Five. He supposed a direct approach might yield better results.

He turned these ideas in his head for a moment, then blew another high note of exasperation through his tusks. What was he thinking? They had zero chance of remaining hidden from the dark gaze of Darth Vader. Certainly not with that boy radiating the Force every which way, and not with that obnoxious mech evidently determined to make a martyr of himself for Jax Pavan's cause. One way or another, they were going to end up in Vader's parlor, and when they did it would not be pretty. Vader would have Jax Pavan, Kajin Savaros, the sentient droid, the Sith Holocron, the pyronium, and the bota. Rhinann wasn't sure what all that added up to, but he knew it wasn't good. Vader held the winning array, any way he looked at it.

There was only one conclusion that made sense, unpalatable though it was. Rhinann reluctantly realized that he was simply on the wrong side.

fourteen

At 0350 hours, Den and I-Five prepared to retrieve Dejah and tend to the removal of the Togrutan female from Coruscant. In such cases, Dejah's twin talents of telempathy and pheromone production were especially effective. She could not only create an atmosphere of emotional safety that would ease the client's passage off-world, but also knew when that atmosphere needed to be bolstered and when it could be withdrawn.

It was agreed that Jax should stay with Kaj and work on the field generators of Volette's light sculptures. To his surprise, Laranth elected to stay and help him.

Just before he left, I-Five took Jax aside. "I expect my part in this will be completed by roughly twelve hundred hours. I have thus arranged to meet with Tuden Sal late this evening at the Sunset Cantina to give him our answer to his proposal."

The words twisted Jax's gut and made his lungs feel suddenly starved for air. "And what are you going to tell him?"

The droid tilted his head to one side and looked at Jax quizzically. "I said *our* decision and I meant *our* decision. You are a part of this, Jax. Therefore, when I return from this transfer, I think we should talk."

"You realize those words are still scary even coming from a droid," Jax replied. "You'd think a Jedi would be impervious to such things."

"Why so?"

"We're supposed to be centered, brave, in tune with the universe . . ."

"None of which supposes that you're also numb or uncaring. Have you thought about it?"

Jax nodded. He had, mostly while he was supposed to be sleeping. Somehow the thought of I-Five assassinating the Emperor made him think of the bota. And he wasn't comfortable thinking about the bota. It suggested another course to him altogether—one that was fraught with ambiguity and peril.

"I'm torn," was all he said—though he was much more than that, he realized with a jolt. Ambivalence flooded him as if from an unseen cloud. He shook himself. *I must have been too caught up in everything else that was going on to let it get to me.*

That didn't quite ring true. He'd thought about it whenever he'd lain on his bed in an attempt to sleep. It just hadn't penetrated him until now. Not like this.

"I promise I'll give it more concentrated thought. I know I need to. Can I ask what your thoughts are at this point?"

"You can ask," said I-Five, then turned and went to join the others for the Whiplash mission.

Alone with Kaj and Laranth, Jax set his mind to learning the ins and outs of the photonic field generators in Ves Volette's kinetic art. The boy watched, obviously impressed with the ability of the two Jedi to tinker with the devices' mechanics.

"Is that part of your Jedi training?" he asked at one point.

"As a matter of fact, yes." His attention on the guts of the sculpture, Jax moved a fibrous light-emitter array slightly and noted the corresponding movement of a fan of pulsing light in the air above his head.

Laranth said, "It looks as if aiming them is easy

enough, but what about increasing the frequency of the pulses?"

"Why would you need to do that?" Kaj asked.

"The more frequent the pulses, the more solid the wall. It's like weaving a net. The more frequent or closer together the fibers of the net, the less gets through."

Glancing at Kaj, Jax saw the light of comprehension dawn in his eyes. "I understood that," he said. "So you worked on stuff like this in Jedi school?"

Jax and Laranth exchanged glances. "Every Jedi has to build and maintain his or her own lightsaber," Jax told Kaj. "So we learn all the mechanics and physics of it. That's everything from fashioning a hilt to selecting a crystal to putting it together with a field generator not unlike this one." He nodded at the innards of the sculpture's low, bowl-like duraluminum stand.

"But you didn't build *that* lightsaber."

Jax glanced down at the weapon hanging at the belt of his tunic. "No."

"Doesn't it make you feel strange to use that one? I mean, it's *red*."

Jax glanced at Laranth's deadpan expression, then smiled wryly. "You mean because it's what the Inquisitors use?"

"Well . . . yeah."

"It does make me feel strange. I've been meaning to finish the one I started to build myself, but . . ."

But what?

"What's stopped you?" Laranth asked. Her attention was on the selection of tools in Volette's kit.

Good question. What *had* stopped him? "I didn't have a power source that would resonate with the Ilum crystal to generate a coherent field."

Kaj pointed at the open console on the light bowl. "Isn't that one?"

The kid was quick, he had to give him that. Jax

blinked at the core of the light sculpture. The circuit board Kaj indicated was indeed a resonating power source, and he'd known it for some time. He'd also known that these sculptures and their component parts were just sitting here, waiting. Why hadn't he asked Dejah if he could use one of them? She'd offered to sell them for upkeep, let him tinker with them for Kaj's sake, so why not a power source for his lightsaber?

"You're right," he said. "I'll have to ask about that." He sensed Laranth's bemusement and pointedly ignored it.

"What'll you do with the old one?"

Jax could feel the boy's attention on the weapon that hung at his hip.

Kaj continued, "I mean, you'll have to teach me to use one, right? And there's probably not the time or resources to build two . . ."

Jax grinned at the youthful enthusiasm. He wasn't that much older than Kaj, he realized—less than five years—but he felt positively wizened in comparison.

In one corner of the room near Ves Volette's workbench, a ping alerted him to the arrival of a message. With a glance at Laranth, Jax crossed to the workstation to view the source of the message. It was Rhinann.

Jax activated the HoloNet node. "Rhinann, is anything wrong?"

The Elomin's craggy face said that a great deal was wrong. "Pol Haus has contacted us," he said. "He wishes to speak to you."

"Is this about the . . ." Jax glanced at Kaj again. "The matter he brought to us recently?"

"Oh, indeed. He wishes to know if we 'have anything for him on the matter of the rogue Jedi.' Those were his exact words."

Jax felt the "rogue Jedi's" sudden, intense regard. It was not comfortable. "Tell Prefect Haus that we've been tied up with another matter and haven't got anything for him yet. Tell him we still need to research the various connections."

"I already told him that. He wishes to speak to you."

"He's there?"

"Yes."

"I see. Are you . . ." Jax made a gesture with his hand that was Whiplash code for "cloaked" or "cloaking." He hoped Rhinann would take his meaning and make sure his surroundings and location were obscured.

The Elomin inclined his head, then said, "Will you speak to him?"

"Of course." Jax turned his head slightly and signaled Kaj to stay on the other side of the room. Wide-eyed, the youth disappeared behind his wall of woven light.

Haus appeared in the holographic display as a full-sized head and shoulders floating in thin air. "Jax Pavan!" he said in a tone that was almost jovial. "Your associate tells me you've no news for me about the item I'm seeking. Is this in fact the case?"

Jax caught a muffled and miffed *harrumph* from Rhinann. "My associate is apparently insulted that you don't trust him, Prefect."

"It has nothing to do with trust. It has to do with your function in that motley bunch of misfits you call an investigative team. The client has been leaning on me to get results. So far all I've gotten from my informants—and you from yours, I suspect—are looks that say my brain is fried on dreamspice if I think they're going to tell me anything. May I remind you that the closer our client is to me, the closer he is to you?"

Jax took a deep breath. "I understand that part of the equation just fine."

"Good. Remember, this isn't a threat. It's a warning. If the client thinks we're stonewalling him, it will not be good for either of us. Incompetence he will overlook—for a time—but not subterfuge. We need to show him something." Haus tilted his shaggy, horned head and peered at Jax intently. "Do your research, Pavan. But do it soon, or the client is going to force my hand."

"I'm not sure where to start."

"Banthaflop. I know you. That head of yours is as smart as a whip. You'll figure it out."

He was gone then, leaving Jax to stand rooted to the studio floor.

He knows. Somehow he knows we have Kaj.

Jax did need to complete that "research." If he'd read Haus's code right, he knew where he was supposed to do it. He turned to Laranth, who stood by, brow furrowed.

"You heard that?" At her nod, he asked, "Do you know what he's hinting at?"

"Not firsthand. I don't know any more about him than that he's a sector prefect. Obviously we're supposed to construe that the head of the Whiplash knows more."

"Can you set up a meeting with Yimmon? I'd like his opinion . . . about a couple of things, actually."

"Including Tuden Sal's mad plot?"

"Do you think it's mad?"

"Do you care what I think?" There was a challenge in those green eyes.

"Yes, of course I care. How could I not care?"

She shrugged. "When you left me in the medbay, you didn't seem to care. You were suddenly very future-oriented."

"When I left you in the medbay—" Jax began, then remembered that they had an audience: Kaj was watching their interaction with avid interest. Jax nodded at the light sculptures. "We should probably get back to work."

"Yes," said Laranth, deadpan expression back in full force. "We probably should."

fifteen

By the time they had accomplished the task, Jax was so tired he saw floating afterimages of light in reverse colors interacting with the product of their work. But they now had Kaj encircled by a series of half a dozen fans of illumination pulsing so swiftly that they seemed to sparkle.

Pleased with the effect, Jax had Kaj try a series of Force exercises and was rewarded by finding not a single leak. He and Laranth even went up in the gallery and leaned out over the lambent "roof" of the light structure. Nothing of what Kaj did escaped, even when he executed a Force leap that took him up to the level of the gallery rail.

"Am I really safe in here?"

His child-like uncertainty was engaging. Jax grinned. "Yeah. I think you are."

"So what's next?" the boy asked eagerly. "Can you teach me to use a lightsaber?"

Jax's grin grew wider as he glanced at Laranth. He could just imagine what she thought of Kaj's enthusiasm for the Jedi weapon. As usual, her expression revealed nothing.

"You want to talk up the blaster as a weapon of choice?" he asked.

She shook her head. "The philosophy of the Gray Paladins is simply that each Jedi should choose the style of weapon that best suits him or her. From what I've seen of Kajin's 'style' I'd say he may not need any weapon at all."

The boy looked crestfallen. "I like lightsabers."

"Then use a lightsaber, by all means. I'm sure Jax can help you build one."

"Can we use the hilt of that one?" Kaj nodded at the Sith weapon.

"Sure."

"Really? It doesn't have to be—y'know—original?"

"A hilt can be made out of anything the Jedi is comfortable holding," Laranth said.

"Can we start now?" Kaj asked.

"Building a lightsaber? No," Jax said. "I need to—"

"No, I meant me learning to use one."

Jax considered the idea, his eyes roving around the studio for some suitable surrogate for a lightsaber. He found a long piece of duraluminum about two and a half centimeters thick and only a bit shorter than a standard blade. Taking a remote, which he'd packed earlier, from his bag, he entered the cage of light, activated the droid, and tossed it into the air where it hung, humming, awaiting his instructions.

"Is that a toy?" Kaj asked.

"Not exactly. It's a practice droid—a remote. It's what every Padawan starts out with. It shoots EM beams at you, and you try to parry them before they hit you." He gestured Kaj to a place along the sidelines. "Watch," he said.

He closed his eyes, took up the duraluminum rod, and faced the bobbing sphere with it. He gave the activation command, and the little ball shot away from him.

He followed it with the Force, circling, moving as the remote moved. He felt it dart in for an attack, felt the tiny neural net about to trigger a sizzling beam of energy. He moved easily to intercept it with the rod and felt an answering fizz of energy run up the ersatz light-saber to his hands. It tickled, but not unpleasantly; the metal diffused the charge. He continued the exercise, showing Kaj the basic postures and moves of Shii-Cho, not opening his eyes until he had deflected a dozen shots.

Meanwhile, Laranth prowled the perimeter of the light cage, even going up to walk the gallery, scanning for leaks.

"Wow," breathed Kaj when Jax at last deactivated the remote. "That was amazing. You never even *looked* at it."

Jax stared at the boy in disbelief for a moment, then burst out laughing. "After what I saw you do, you're impressed by my fencing with a remote?"

"When I use the Force in defense it's all instinct and desperation," Kaj said earnestly. "I can't control it like that—I just strike out. Even when I use it to do other things like get food or clothes or find a safe haven, I'm never sure of it. I never know quite what it's going to do."

"I understand. Every Padawan goes through that. Every Padawan has to learn his own technique." Jax held the ersatz lightsaber out to the boy. "Try it."

Kaj looked wistfully at the real lightsaber hanging from Jax's belt. "Couldn't I . . ."

"Not yet. As you pointed out, you don't really know your own strength."

"Yeah." Kaj took the rod. "Do I need to close my eyes?"

"Try it with them open for a while. Then maybe we'll try a mask."

Obediently, Kaj mimicked Jax's stance and waited for the remote to engage him. He deflected the thing's salvos well enough from the outset, never letting them touch him. But Jax could see what he meant about the desperation. He wasn't anticipating the remote's attacks using the Force. Rather, he was using the extraordinarily quick reaction times the Force granted him and moving when the blink of the remote's tiny weapons port gave it away. There was a difference, and it could mean life or death in a battle situation.

Jax halted the practice after several minutes and found a sash in Ves Volette's wardrobe that he used to cover Kaj's eyes. Below the makeshift mask, the boy smiled. Jax could feel his eagerness. He wanted a chance to challenge himself, prove himself.

Not waiting for Jax to start the drill, Kaj spoke the activation command.

The remote bobbed into the air and immediately zapped Kaj with a bolt of energy.

"Ow!" the boy yipped and spun around.

"Stand by," Jax instructed the remote, struggling to keep a straight face. "Think of the space around you as a field—a fabric woven by and of the Force. That field joins you to everything else in your environment: Me, the rod, the droid. Let the Force guide you."

"But the remote is a mechanism—it's not alive. How can the Force read the intentions of a mechanism?"

"It's not a matter of intentions, Kaj. Yours or the remote's. The Force exists everywhere—in the present, and also in the past and the future. And the Force can move you in the right direction."

"But the speed—"

"I've been watching you move, Kaj. With the blindfold off, you were reacting to the sight of the beam port opening, and it didn't hit you once. The Force can affect your reflexes so that you can be even faster. Feel the Force, Kaj. Let it guide you . . ."

A slow smile spread across Kajin Savaros's face. He slashed the air with his practice lightsaber. "Let me try again, Master."

Jax felt a warm flush of gratification at the words. Maybe he did have something to teach, after all. He stepped outside the wall of light, called the remote back into action, and watched Kaj dance with it.

It zapped the sleeve of the youth's tunic once, and another time caught his vest. But with a growing smile, the boy parried its bolts, at first hesitantly, than with increasing confidence, dancing this way and that within the circle of kinetic light.

Laranth returned silently to Jax's side. "He's getting cocky," she murmured.

She was right. Jax could tell by the swagger in Kajin's mostly graceful movements. Probably a good time to end the practice, though it might be beneficial for the kid to get zapped once more.

Even as he had the thought, Kaj made a bad parry. A flourish brought his hand too high, and the little floating sphere stung him on the wrist. He cried out and spun after the thing—it dived and got him again on the neck and a third time on the buttocks.

Before Jax could shut the remote down, Kaj roared in incoherent rage and let loose an explosion of Force energy. The hapless remote was blown clear out of the circle of light and the duraluminum rod shot straight at Jax.

If he had not practiced what he'd preached about gauging intention, he would have been skewered. As it was, the rod flew past him, narrowly missing, passing through the exact spot where his heart had been an instant before, and buried itself fifteen centimeters deep in the plasticrete wall of the studio. He turned to see the light bowls supporting Kaj's "safe room" shake violently.

"Kaj!" Jax shouted, reinforcing the verbal command with an application of the Force as he dashed through the veil of light and into the circle. The boy tore the blindfold from his eyes and stood facing Jax, panting and rigid with anger, a hand raised to defend against attack.

Outside the circle, Laranth had her blasters trained on the boy.

"It's just a drill," Jax said. "Just a drill. Calm down."

Slowly the red rage melted from the boy's eyes, to be replaced by miserable fear. "I'm—I'm sorry. I don't know what happened. I just lost it. I'm so sorry."

"That," said Jax, "is what we have to work on, Kaj. You can't use the Force out of anger or hatred. You draw on the dark side when you do that. Remember: There is no passion; there is serenity."

Kaj's shoulders slumped and he nodded. "There is no ignorance; there is knowledge. I need knowledge."

"No kidding," muttered Laranth, holstering her weapons.

Fear flickered again in the boy's eyes. "I don't want to go to the dark side, Jax. I don't want to be like that Inquisitor. I felt him. When he came after me. He was all cold hatred like . . . like a frozen methane lake. He wanted to kill me and he didn't even *know* me. I don't want to be like that. Teach me not to be like that, please." He looked from one Jedi to the other in naked entreaty.

"We'll try," Jax said, looking to Laranth for accord. *If we survive the lessons,* her expression said.

"The good news is that nothing leaked out," Jax continued. "I saw what was happening, but I didn't *sense* it."

"Lucky you," added Laranth drily. "If you'd been blindfolded, you'd be dead now."

And if anyone had told me two days ago that that would be a comforting thought, Jax thought, *I'd've called them crazy.*

*   *   *

They moved to more gentle pursuits after that, the two Jedi putting Kaj through a series of meditative exercises geared to feeling the textures of the world around him, using only the Force. That was far more successful, and Kaj seemed to have left the shadow of his explosive first lightsaber practice behind. They ate and then the boy slept on a couch Jax pulled into the light cage.

"He looks even younger when he's asleep," Jax commented. "Makes me feel ancient."

Laranth said, "You'd never suspect he was capable of blowing this entire building apart, would you?"

Jax chuckled, realizing suddenly how much he'd missed the Gray Paladin. He glanced at her, sprawled with feline grace on a low couch in the upstairs living room, and wondered how he had ever been foolish enough to let her leave. A couple of thoughts collided in his head on their way to his mouth: *Ask her to come back to the team and help train the boy. Ask her what she really thinks of Tuden Sal's plot.*

He opened his mouth to speak—and at that moment, the door in the foyer chimed, then glided open to admit I-Five, Den, and Dejah.

Laranth came to her feet in one whip-like movement. Gone was the relaxed pose; the atmosphere of warm contentment fled with it.

Confused, Jax rose. Clearly, he couldn't ask her anything now. "How did it go?" he asked I-Five.

"It went well. The female is on her way to Orto, where a highly placed family is waiting to embrace her. I note that the building is still standing, so I assume things also went well here?"

Jax glanced at Laranth, but she had retreated from them, her facial expression as impenetrable as a duracrete wall.

"Mixed bag," he admitted. "The bad news is that Kaj had another episode. He got frustrated with the practice droid and destroyed it. The good news is the sculptures didn't let any of that out."

Now Laranth met his eyes, silently noting his obvious omission—how close he'd come to dying.

"You modified them, then?" Dejah asked, sorrow etching her voice.

"If we hadn't," Laranth said coolly, "there wouldn't be a chance that Kaj would ever get trained. Oh, and this place would be crawling with Inquisitors right now." She turned to Jax. "I should go. I'll take Thi Xon Yimmon your message."

"Uh, sure," Jax said. "Let me know when I can see him. It needs to be soon. Today, if possible."

She nodded curtly and left.

"You're meeting with Yimmon?" I-Five asked.

"I need to resolve a couple of things with him." He told them about Pol Haus's message, the unsubtle this-is-not-a-threat speech, the hint that he and Laranth both felt pointed to the Whiplash leader.

The reactions were varied. Dejah seemed eager to get at the truth. Den looked dyspeptic but said nothing. It was I-Five who made a most disturbing observation.

"Has it occurred to you," he asked, "that perhaps this is Pol Haus's way of gaining access to Thi Xon Yimmon? Access he does not already have?"

Jax went cold to the core. "You think it's a setup? That he's hoping to use us to lead him to Yimmon?"

"I don't *think* that, necessarily, but it is a point of consideration."

"Then we have to make sure that when I meet with Yimmon, I'm not followed."

"I believe we can manage that," I-Five said. "I also believe we have an important matter to discuss as a team." He turned to Den, who was hunkered in the chair before the upstairs HoloNet terminal. "If you'd be so kind as to contact Rhinann?"

Den jumped, startled. He'd clearly been lost in his own thoughts. He glanced from Jax to I-Five, then turned to establish the connection. In a moment the Elomin appeared in a life-sized hologram above the holoprojector next to the terminal.

"What's happened?" he asked. "What's wrong?"

"Plenty," mumbled Den.

"Nothing," said I-Five. "We need to consult. I promised to deliver Tuden Sal an answer to his proposition tonight. While that is still hours away, I don't have a firm answer for him. I'd like to know where everyone stands."

"I choose to sit," said Den. He looked up at the droid. "You know my opinion. I haven't changed my mind. This is too dangerous—to you, to us, to Jax, to the Whiplash and everything it represents. I vote no."

"I could not have put it better myself," Rhinann agreed. "I am, for once, in complete agreement with Den. I vote no."

"And I," said Dejah, "vote yes."

Den and Rhinann both reacted to that with stunned disbelief, and Jax had to allow he was equally shocked, though he managed not to show it.

"I realize this is a radical change of mind for me," the Zeltron went on, "but I've thought about this a lot in the last few days and I've come to realize that all we've gone through—the running, the hiding, the concealment of Kaj's talent, now the fear about Pol Haus using us to expose Thi Xon Yimmon and destroy the Whiplash— none of that would have happened if the Emperor was not in power. This Empire is strangling the life out of its people. It must fall, and the sooner, the better."

"Jax?" I-Five was looking at him, expecting an answer.

Jax didn't have one. "That's one of the things I need to talk to Yimmon about, because Dejah's right—what we decide to do will have an impact on the Whiplash and everyone it touches. It will have an impact on everyone *we* touch. After I meet with Yimmon I'll have an answer, I promise."

"Do you really need to do that, Jax?" Dejah asked earnestly. She rose from her chair and came to take his hands in hers, to look up into his eyes. "Don't you know your own heart? Can't you *feel* what's right? Can't you see that the Emperor has to die?"

He did see. He saw it very clearly. Felt it viscerally, but he also knew how seductive the idea of revenge could be. How it could insinuate itself into the heart, and look, sound, and feel like logic, or justice, or righteousness.

He heard Den murmur something acerbic under his breath as he pulled his hands from Dejah's grasp. "I need to talk to Yimmon," he repeated.

Dejah turned and left the room, moving out onto the gallery, where she paused to look down at Kaj through the shimmer of his screening light field. Then, with a glance back at Jax, she went into the kitchen.

Jax pulled his eyes away from her with an effort, returning his attention to I-Five. "Can you wait for me?" he asked simply.

The droid inclined his head. "As you wish."

"Well," said Rhinann gustily, "that's a reprieve, I suppose. Before I go, I have a couple of things to report. One is that there have been Inquisitors in the neighborhood again today. Two or three of them—it's hard to tell. I believe we must abandon this location . . ."

"Yes," said Jax. "I agree. Do you need help?"

"I think I'm capable of managing on my own, thank you. I know how to cover our tracks."

"And the other item?" I-Five prompted.

"A message for Den from an Eyar Marath. Shall I forward it?"

"Don't," said Jax. "It might be traced. Encrypt it, crystallize it, and bring it with you when you come. If that's all right, Den?"

The Sullustan had gone incredibly pale and his dewlaps quivered. He said nothing, merely nodded.

Jax opened his mouth to ask if he was expecting bad news, but before he could say anything, Den slid from his chair and left the room. They heard him take the lift down into the studio.

A moment later, Dejah appeared in the broad entry to the living room. "The kitchen's empty and I feel like cooking something. I'm going down to the market-place," she announced.

Jax was relieved to see her go, hoping that doing something creative might settle her nerves and make her more kindly disposed toward his decision that was not a decision.

sixteen

Jax met Laranth in a corner of the Grotto Room of Sil's Place. Cut out of the ferrocrete substructure of the commercial block above it and fashioned to look like a natural cave, the sub-basement was the only quiet spot the cantina possessed.

Jax got there first, took a corner booth with a table made to look like a squat, flat-topped stalagmite, and ordered a daro root beer. Then he huddled over the pale golden beverage watching the fizz die out of it. It was not alcoholic, but looked as if it could be. He sipped it slowly, savoring the creamy flavor and wondering if Laranth would even show.

He felt oddly hollow inside, as if some part of him were absent—something he was used to having there. And he was uneasy.

Well, there were any number of reasons for unease: Inquisitors prowling Poloda Place, Kaj throwing Force tantrums, Haus leaning on them to expose Kaj, Sal leaning on them to plot murder. And then there was the seemingly trivial friction between Dejah and Laranth . . . and Dejah and Den . . . and Dejah and Rhinann. In fact, the only people who did not seem put off by the Zeltron were I-Five, Kaj, and Jax himself.

He was reminded suddenly of that alien roil of jealousy he'd felt in his gut when Dejah responded to Kaj's neediness. That was just plain weird. Yes, she was attractive, but he had filtered out the chemical portion of that, hadn't he?

He flashed back to the conversation he hadn't quite had with Laranth at the studio—to her comment about their leave-taking in the medbay. There had been a moment in which he had looked into her eyes and known—*known* with the certainty of Force-enhanced intuition—that they were on the same wavelength and that deep beneath the differences in their species, their philosophies, their training, and their personalities, they were . . . what?

He shook his head. It had been such a fleeting sensation. The feeling that he knew her, completely and candidly, and that she knew him with the same stark clarity. That they were, somehow, two parts of a whole that was held together by the Force itself.

Then it had been gone, blotted out by their mutual fear.

And something else.

He recalled it as if it had been yesterday: walking out into the ward beyond the room in which Laranth lay; the filtered sunlight, the others waiting for him, Dejah's sultry laughter, and the feeling that everything would be smoother, easier without the grim Twi'lek . . .

Something cold and insidious crawled up from the pit of Jax's stomach. He took his hands from the chilled mug and sat back in the booth, staring at the play of light through the pale amber liquid. Had he been *manipulated*? Had he *let* himself be manipulated?

"You all right? You look as if your life just passed before your eyes." Laranth, her own large, dark eyes watching his face, slid into the booth next to him.

He tightened his hold on the Force, pulling its fabric around him like a comforting cloak. *Life passing before my eyes? Yeah, something like that.* Something of his life had certainly passed by him so swiftly he had been unable to even so much as touch it before it was gone.

He turned to look at her, caught the honest concern in her eyes. Could he ever get that moment back? "I just had a rather unwelcome realization."

Her eyebrows rose.

He shook his head as if to shake the epiphany away. "This morning you said Kaj was getting cocky. I just realized that I've been cocky, too. And about something a lot more important than a practice droid."

"You're just full of riddles today. You sound like Master Yoda."

He shook his head again, wrapping his hands around the daro root beer. "Master Yoda would never have made this mistake."

She gazed at him, her eyes, he was sure, seeing more than he wanted them to. "I'm sure, if you asked him, that he'd tell you that we all make that kind of mistake once in a while."

He opened his mouth to ask what she meant by *that kind of mistake* when she turned her attention to a couple of Rodians who had just entered the dimly lit grotto, arm in arm. When she turned back to him, he could tell that another of his life's moments had passed. The thought brought with it a tickle of nascent panic.

There is no emotion; there is peace.

"How's your little brother?" Laranth asked, referring to Kaj.

"He's fine. He was playing sabacc with—with the guys."

"He was playing sabacc with the Zeltron."

Had he been that transparent? "Is that a problem?"

"No. In fact, I think it's a good idea. She can keep him calm. She worked wonders with the Togrutan female, by all accounts." She tipped her head toward his drink and raised her voice just a bit. "Why don't you finish that so we can go someplace more private?"

He struggled briefly with cognitive dissonance, confused for half a second by the soft warmth of her voice. The vague static that rose between them when she leaned in close to him.

There is no passion; there is serenity.

He tossed back his drink and grinned at her, falling into his assigned role. "I'll go wherever you want to take me."

She gave him a look that, from across the room, must have looked smoldering. Close up, the effect was somewhat different. More like scalding.

He sobered. "What—too much?" he murmured.

She grasped his hand and hauled him out of the booth. They were making their way out of the cantina when a tall Devish woman passed them in the entry.

"Laranth!" the woman cried with a broad grin. The Twi'lek returned the greeting, if not the smile.

"Who's the new man?" the Devish asked, a suggestive leer on her red, saturnine face.

"Don't know yet," Laranth told her. "But I'm going to find out."

They left the cantina with the Devish's laughter following them down the walk.

"The *new* man?" Jax asked when they'd gone about a block. "Is there an *old* one?"

"I meet a lot of people in that cantina, Jax. Contacts. Friends."

Lovers? he wanted to ask, but didn't.

They went down three levels from the very verges of the spaceport, into a maze of tunnels and alleys so complex that Jax wondered how anyone who was not a Jedi—or at least a Force adept—could find his or her way out again.

When he thought they must be coming to their destination, Laranth stepped into a waiting airspeeder, and they were whisked away to a neighborhood not unlike the one in which Poloda Place was situated. Deep in the crisscross of alleys there was an old theater of the type where live stage plays were mounted to limited audiences. They had been all the rage some four hundred years earlier, but now the old building was long past its heyday and cloaked in grime and faded glory. It had a little art gallery on the first floor where artists unfamiliar to Jax displayed a diverse array of work, including, he noted with interest, some light murals.

Though the medium was the same as that used by the late Ves Volette, the style of display was entirely different. Instead of a bowl from which a fountain of cleverly shaped light sprang, these were affected by having the light leap up the wall from a long, narrow tray or even a bar that housed the emitters and field generators. They were significantly smaller than Volette's work, too, and the generators were miniature.

Still, he caught Laranth's attention and gestured at the works. "Interesting."

"Yeah. I wondered about those myself when you mentioned the plan for the Volettes. They don't have anything like the cohesive power of the fields in his work, though."

"Might do in an emergency."

Laranth shot him a hard glance. "Are you planning on creating an emergency that will test that theory?"

Jax grimaced. "I never plan emergencies. They just seem to happen."

Laranth turned her head away, her right lekku curling and uncurling. She gestured toward what appeared to be a blank wall covered with a spray of light. "Through here."

"Through where?" Jax started to ask, when the Twi'lek stepped through the wall. Correction: hologram of a wall. He followed and found himself in a turbolift tube. He couldn't tell immediately whether they were going up or down. He used a tendril of the Force to find out. It was up, surprisingly.

They stepped out into a hallway that boasted several sets of doors. She led him to the far end of the hall and through a pair of doors that opened with a pop and a sigh.

Den played the holographic message again, heart tripping over itself at the radiance of Eyar's face, the sweetness of her voice. The impact of those things surprised him. He was at least a dozen years older than the Sullustan songstress. Jaded. Tired. Old. But to hear her, see her, made him feel rejuvenated, especially when he considered the gist of her message: "What's keeping you, lover? How soon can you be home?"

Home.

Gods of hearth and hill, but that was a glorious word. Hearing it in his mind, he wondered if he even needed to wait for Jax's decision. Den got up from the workstation and, with a strange, quivering haste, began to pack.

He was just covering all his bases, he told himself. Just preparing for any eventuality. Just packing lightly, the essentials—which were all he ever traveled with, to tell the truth. A career in the news business had taught him to always be prepared to fly out the door on a moment's notice, with never more than a single small valise's worth of stuff.

In ten minutes he was ready. All that was needed was the use of a credit stick to secure a berth on an outgoing starliner. That would take less than five minutes.

He looked about the room and was surprised at how little emotion he felt. He thought of I-Five, his friend. He knew he was being cowardly by leaving without saying good-bye. But he couldn't wait—couldn't take the

chance of losing his resolve. He had to go while he had
the nerve. Because the way things were going, he might
not get another chance.

"Enough adventures," he muttered. "It's time to
rest."

Den walked out the door, which slid shut behind him
with the sound of a forlorn sigh.

The room was comfortable without being opulent,
the colors were rich and warm, the furniture was hand-
crafted. Jax, who had never been here before, was suitably impressed by the room as Laranth led him in—and
even more impressed by its sole occupant.

Seated at the narrow end of a large oval table was the
leader of the Whiplash, Thi Xon Yimmon. A Cerean, he
was an imposing figure, well over two meters tall, his
height accentuated by the tall, tapered cranium common
to his kind, which housed a binary brain. It was this singular feature, along with a preternaturally calm tempera-
ment, that made him the ideal leader for a multifaceted
organization such as the Whiplash. Those twin brains,
able to work semi-independently, effectively allowed
Yimmon to concentrate on multiple subjects simultaneously. Jax had met the man once before and had been
impressed to the point of wondering if Yimmon didn't
have some latent Force abilities. He was known to live
by Jedi principles, at least to some extent. It didn't surprise Jax that Laranth found Yimmon's leadership appealing in the extreme.

The Whiplash leader rose, smiling gently, and held
out a large hand to Jax. The thick fringe of gleaming
blue-black hair that grew from the back and sides of the
Cerean's head was worn long and in ornate braids.

"Sit down," Yimmon said, his voice a deep warm
baritone. "Laranth tells me you have some questions."

"For both of you, actually," Jax said. His glance

caught Laranth just as she turned to leave. She froze, giving him an impenetrable look. At Yimmon's gesture she moved to the table and sat down next to the Jedi.

"Please." Yimmon held out his hands toward Jax, palms-up, as if to receive the questions.

"First," Jax said. "Has Laranth spoken to you about the young adept we've taken in—Kajin Savaros?"

The Cerean nodded. "Yes. An extraordinary young man, by all accounts."

"And a dangerous one," Laranth added.

"And in a dangerous position," said Jax. "The Inquisitors have been rabid to bring him down since he killed one of them. And unfortunately, his Force projections have drawn their notice."

"They've had to relocate," Laranth added. "Vader has ordered the police prefect of the Zi-Kree Sector to investigate the case."

Thi Xon Yimmon nodded. "Pol Haus."

"You know of him?"

"He's served the constabulary well for decades. He's a force to be reckoned with, though I know he doesn't seem it at first blush."

"He's suggested to us that we should find Kaj and turn him in."

"I think you should."

Jax was caught off-balance. "Excuse me?"

Yimmon's eyes glittered with sudden mirth. "Pol asked me if I would be willing to expose our connection. I told him that if he'd be willing, I could do no less. Pol Haus was one of the original Whiplash operatives, Jax. One of the very first. Can you trust him? Yes. You can trust him to do what is best for the Whiplash and the people it serves."

"Then if Kaj's continued existence seemed not to be best for the Whiplash . . ."

Yimmon shook his head. "Perhaps you look for layers

of meaning where there are none. The Whiplash, like the Jedi Order, is built on the conviction that people must be trustworthy in their dealings with one another. He's told me that he means no harm to the adept, and I believe him."

"Why didn't he say as much to us?" Jax asked. "He said nothing about protecting Kaj."

"Not surprising. He's an old hand at giving potential listeners nothing to hear. Meet with him where you can speak freely and plainly and ask your questions there. Even if I'm wrong about him, I think you'd know if he told an outright lie."

If you're wrong? An unsettling thought. "Could you be wrong about him?"

The Cerean shrugged. "Anyone can be wrong about anything. But, while I have known Pol Haus to lie, I have never known him to be dishonest."

Jax blinked at the seeming paradox, but realized he understood what Yimmon was saying. There were lies told with the intent to actively deceive and lies told merely to deflect or protect.

"And that," Jax said, "brings me to my second question—Tuden Sal."

"Also a trusted operative."

"Has he told you about his plan?"

Laranth and Yimmon exchanged glances. Then Yimmon said, "We had spoken of him putting together a special cell that would undertake especially dangerous missions."

Jax knew no other way to say it than straight out. "He wants I-Five to assassinate Emperor Palpatine."

Laranth turned a deeper shade of green, and Yimmon's eyes widened. Neither said anything, but waited for him to continue.

"The rationale is that a droid's thoughts would not be readable by the Force, so his intentions would be

masked and his presence unnoted. He'd be disguised, of
course, to look like a threepio or some other similar protocol droid. And since he has no programming to prevent him from doing an organic harm . . ."

Thi Xon Yimmon was nodding, his eyes veiled. "Yes,
of course. The logic is impeccable."

"But what do you think of the plan?"

"What do *you* think of it?"

"I'm of two minds—almost literally. First, understand
that Sal has been less than trustworthy in . . . well, I
can't talk about my experience, but certainly as regards
my father and I-Five."

Yimmon looked genuinely saddened. "Yes, Tuden Sal
told me quite openly of his betrayal. He feels compelled
to 'set things straight,' as he put it."

"He has very personal reasons for wanting the Emperor dead," Jax said. "His family was torn apart over
it. He had to send his wife and children away to save
their lives—or so he says. And he lost pretty much everything, all in the course of an afternoon—the same afternoon he sold I-Five into service. In the end he didn't
even have the credits from that deal to sustain him. He
blames the Emperor and Black Sun in equal parts, and
since the Empire allows Black Sun to flourish . . ." He
shrugged.

Thi Xon Yimmon nodded. "And to you these don't
seem like good reasons to put your friends in harm's
way?"

"To feed another man's vengeance? No. But he's also
made some points about what the continued existence
of the Emperor means to the Whiplash, to the Jedi, to
the people who live under the Empire's rule. Those are
things I can't ignore."

"And those would be your reasons to allow I-Five to
undertake what would almost certainly be a suicide mission?"

"He's agreed to abide by my decision. I'm just not sure . . ."

"Are those your reasons, Jax?" Laranth asked, suddenly bristling with intensity.

"I . . . I'm not sure I know what you mean."

"You said Tuden Sal was a man bent on vengeance. What about you? Are you bent on vengeance as well?"

He stared at her, feeling as if she'd looked down into his soul and read his deepest fears. He felt Thi Xon Yimmon's gaze on him, too, and resisted the impulse to shield himself from them both. Instead, he gave himself up for their scrutiny. Casting open his mind, holding Laranth's gaze, he said, "You tell me. Please. That's why this decision has been so difficult for me. I'm . . . I'm afraid that my reasons for seeking Palpatine's death might be closer to Sal's real reasons than I know. I've come to understand in recent times that I'm not always honest with myself about things."

He didn't mention that by *recent* he meant less than an hour earlier at Sil's Place.

"I'm a Jedi, Laranth. If I want to stay a Jedi, I *can't* be a man bent on vengeance. I don't think that's what I am, but I can't tell I-Five to do this thing unless I'm sure. Or at least more sure than I am now. He's ready to turn himself into a weapon and put the use of that weapon in my hands."

Laranth held his gaze a moment longer, then lowered her eyes. "There are many reasons why Palpatine should die. He's a blight on the galaxy—he and the Sith. Yes, I know the theories about cosmic balance and the philosophies about the duality of the Force—" She flicked a glance aside at Yimmon as if this was an ongoing discussion. "But I don't believe them. Evil is as evil does."

"Yes," said Yimmon gently. "And if that's so, and if Jax commits himself and his team in an attempt to take

Palpatine's life, then what distinguishes him from those who represent the dark side?"

Laranth's eyes flashed. "Then isn't fighting evil itself evil? When Kaj killed that Inquisitor to save himself, wasn't that act evil?"

"That was an instinctive act of self-defense. Tuden Sal is talking about premeditatedly entering Palpatine's territory and killing him. Hardly an act of self-defense."

"But haven't you always told me that to do battle in defense of others is noble? That even anger can be positive if it is directed at injustice? The Emperor's death would save uncounted billions from injustice, and from the horrors visited on the Jedi, the M'haelians, the Caamasi—and the Force knows how many others."

Her voice was low but impassioned. Seeing again her aura composed of blazing, white-hot strands, Jax felt a resurgence of admiration for the Twi'lek.

Thi Xon Yimmon inclined his head slightly, then turned to Jax. "A quandary. I fear we have given you no solace."

"I didn't come for solace. I came for your thoughtful consideration—for your wisdom. For that, I thank you." Jax stood, bowed respectfully, and left the Whiplash headquarters.

As he went, Thi Xon Yimmon's softly spoken words still rang in his ears: *If Jax commits himself and his team to Palpatine's assassination, then what distinguishes him from those who represent the dark side?*

He had no answer to that.

seventeen

"Do you think the Sullustan has it?" Rhinann pitched his voice low so that only Dejah, alone in the kitchen with him, would hear.

She glanced at him from the corner of her eye as she continued to chop silverleaf into a salad bowl. "If he does, he's taken it offworld with him," she said. "And no, it's not among his personal effects—I checked. If he has it, it's on his person." She looked at the wall chrono. "And along about now, I'm guessing that his person is on board a starliner headed back to Sullust."

Rhinann felt a shot of cold run from his horned head to the soles of his feet. "Are you sure?"

"That he's gone or that he's gone with the bota?"

"Both."

"I'm sure, on both counts. It took him quite some time to screw up his courage to leave, judging from the trace smells he left behind."

Rhinann snorted an involuntary arpeggio. "Why would he have to screw up his courage to *leave*? It's staying here that's dangerous."

"Yes, but that's the problem inherent in attachment. He's in love with the Sullustan woman he just heard from—or at least he thinks he is—but he's also loyal to I-Five . . . and Jax, too, when it comes to it. He loves them. He's attached. He was at home with them—at least he was before I came along." She smiled and shook her head. "That's the problem with these so-serious species. They become attached to the things they love and never understand that if you lose one love object, you must simply find another."

Rhinann tilted his head to one side. "Odd. I'd always thought of Zeltrons as beings of immense passion. Yet at the core, you're quite bloodless, aren't you?"

She didn't seem insulted. "Not at all. But our passions are usually very immediate, and—" She sliced the last of the vegetation into the bowl and set down the knife, brushing her palms together to dust them free of residue. "—they are many."

"Yet you seemed quite attached to your deceased partner. Or at least Jax imagines you were."

The red eyes went out of focus for a moment and seemed to be staring at some point in space or time that Rhinann couldn't see. "I was. Ves was a creator. He breathed out great pieces of art the way other beings breathe out carbon dioxide. It was exhilarating to be around him, to watch him work, play, whatever you want to call it. It's also exhilarating to be around these Force slingers . . . when they're not hiding out. I wish I could have been here while Jax was working with Kaj early this morning." She shrugged. "But the Whiplash mission was pretty exciting, too . . ."

"You're a thrill addict. Is that why you changed your mind about the Emperor's assassination? Hungry to be in on a harrowing plot?"

"Now, that was insensitive." Tuden Sal entered the room before Dejah could fire off a response that matched the look of annoyance on her lovely face. *A pity,* the Elomin thought. He enjoyed nettling her.

"I am simply grateful," Sal continued, "that Dejah Duare has agreed to support my proposal."

"Much good it will do you," Rhinann said. "I suspect

that, when Jax Pavan returns and finds you here, he will feel ambushed."

Before he could continue, Dejah's chin tilted up and a smile curved her lips. "He's here," she said and hurried to the living room.

Tuden Sal and Rhinann followed. "This should be interesting," the Elomin said casually, but the emotions roiling in his breast were far from casual.

You can get out, he reminded himself before he started to hyperventilate. *You can get out anytime you want.*

As he entered the room, he saw to his surprise that Den was there as well.

Jax was both surprised and puzzled to find Tuden Sal and the others waiting for him when he walked in the door of the studio. He read the room quickly, noting that Rhinann and Den were arrayed at the rear of the group—separate from it in a way that it did not require a Jedi to interpret. The group had bisected along lines of conviction: I-Five's point of view he knew, and Sal's. Dejah . . .

He read her most carefully—the bright inquisitive eyes, the shimmer of agitation, the way her gaze darted from him to Sal. He saw the subtle threads now, too, as they reached out toward him. She was not simply exuding pheromones, she was *willing* them to affect him. How had he been so blind to them before?

"Where's Kaj?" he asked I-Five.

"Dejah cooked him a meal. I expect that will occupy him for a while."

There was no sense in prolonging this. Jax turned his attention to Tuden Sal. "A wise man asked me a question not long ago. He asked me if I countenanced the same sort of tactics that Palpatine and Vader would use, how I would distinguish myself from them. I didn't have an answer to that question. And, in the absence of that answer, I can't give my active approval of this . . . mission."

There was a flurry of startled words, and Jax found himself assailed anew by the strength of their emotional reactions. Rhinann and Den were literally gaping at him, while Dejah took a step backward, visibly stunned and bewildered.

Jax started for the entry to the gallery. "If you'll excuse me, I have to call Pol Haus."

On his way to his room, he glanced down to the studio floor where Kaj was in the midst of what seemed a very fine meal, indeed. The aroma alone made Jax's stomach growl, reminding him how long it had been since he'd eaten. The boy paused long enough to smile up at him, a look of contentment on his face.

I'm glad someone's happy, Jax thought.

He went into his bedchamber, intending to close the door behind him, but Dejah took up a spot in the doorway before he could.

"You're making a mistake," she told him. "This plot of Sal's is the best way of restoring the Republic and putting an end to Palpatine's cruelty."

"I-Five is an independent being, Dejah. He can make this decision on his own."

"He refuses to. For all that he swears he's owned by no man, he certainly seems to be owned by you."

"That's not fair to either me or I-Five."

"So you're just going to go along, like always, solving cases for Pol Haus and pecking at the Empire's armored flank until you exhaust yourself?"

He met her gaze, feeling a warm rush of heat as he did. She was fully armed, he realized, and probably always had been where he was concerned. Why? Was it so important to her that she have a fleeting physical relationship with a Jedi that she'd intentionally numb him to what was going on around him?

"Is that what I'm doing, Dejah?" he asked. "Is that what we are—me, Laranth, Thi Xon Yimmon, the entire Whiplash? Just annoying little gnats buzzing around a juggernaut we can never hope to bring down?"

She advanced into the room, fists clenched, fire sparking in her eyes. "I'm no military strategist, Jax, but even I know that if you want to take down a superior force—be it a beast or an army—you take off its head. No other strategy makes the least bit of sense when you have such meager resources."

He smiled wryly. "You've been talking to Sal."

"Yes. And I think what he says makes a lot of sense."

Jax nodded. It did make a lot of sense. In fact, Sal was right. That was the textbook strategy under the circumstances. "Did you bring him here?" he asked mildly.

"He brought himself here. I simply let him in."

He gestured at the HoloNet node in the corner of his room. "I need to talk—"

"To Pol Haus? So you said. What are you going to do, give Kaj up to him?"

"No. Thi Xon Yimmon believes Haus is trustworthy. I want to give him a chance to lay out his ideas."

"You're going to betray that boy."

Jax felt a stab of unease. "I would never do that. I hope you won't suggest to him that I would."

She seemed crestfallen and contrite. "I'm sorry. That was a stupid, indefensible thing for me to say. I'm . . . I'm just not used to feeling like this."

She might have said more, but I-Five announced his presence with that peculiar throat-clearing sound he'd cultivated. With a last glance at Jax, Dejah excused herself and slipped out of the room past the droid, who watched her leave with an expression that somehow managed to be speculative.

I'm not used to feeling like this. Jax suspected that meant the Zeltron was simply not used to being told no. She was used to getting her own way. He realized he was disappointed on two counts—disappointed in Dejah for directing her wiles at him and at himself for not realizing it.

Jax stowed his thoughts and looked at I-Five. He took a deep breath. "I'm sorry, I-Five. I just can't—"

"You don't need to apologize to me, Jax. You don't owe me—"

"I owe you my life several times over."

"But you *don't* owe me the sacrifice of your principles. You are a Jedi Knight. If you feel giving your approval of Sal's plan is too close a brush with the dark side, then I would never ask you to make yourself part of it. I was merely going to observe that, whatever stand you take, I believe your father would be proud of you."

Jax sat down heavily on the bed, suddenly feeling physically weary. And no wonder—he'd slept little in the last several days, barely remembered to eat, had played hide-and-seek with Inquisitors, done training sessions with Kaj, and gone for a walkabout with Laranth. Add to that all the emotional turmoil . . .

He sighed. "My father. Just once, I-Five, I wish I could ask my father for advice."

I-Five's reaction to the words was sudden and unexpected. He jerked upright, his optics going intensely bright, and said in a mechanical monotone, "Message Mode Ninety-nine. Recipient: Jax Pavan. Sender: Lorn Pavan."

A tiny projection port on his chest plate activated, shooting out a beam of multicolored light that resolved into a full-sized hologram.

Jax found himself looking into his father's face.

It was a face he knew and yet didn't. He saw something of it when he looked at his own reflection, but the cheekbones were a little broader, the chin maybe a bit stronger. Lorn Pavan's hair was thick and dark, like his son's—or rather, Jax's was like his father's. His eyes were a clear, dark brown.

"Jax," said this ghost from the past. A pause, then, "Son." The dark eyes sparkled with incipient tears. "Wow. I'm going to hope that you and I are sitting and watching this message together and having a good laugh, but I'm going to bet that we're not. For whatever reason."

He hesitated, rubbed the palms of his hands on his pants, glanced up. "Blast it, I-Five. This is harder than I thought."

There was a momentary pause as Lorn gathered his thoughts before he looked up again. He was gazing into I-Five's photoreceptors—Jax knew that intellectually, of course—but it seemed as if he were looking right at Jax.

"Okay, look. The thing is, I'm about to go after this guy—this Sith—and I wanted to—to leave you a message. Just in case . . . By the time you get this I'll probably be up to my armpits in trouble—so what else is new?—and I don't know if I'll be able to make it to the Temple to see you."

His gaze became suddenly imploring, almost desperate. "Look, Jax, I wish I could reassure you that I'll come out of this alive. The truth is I'll be lucky to come out of it in one piece, given this Sith's predilection for taking heads."

He took a deep breath, fidgeted, and wiped his palms again. "So you're wondering why your old man has to go off and play hero. Why he has to try to take out an enemy that's been pretty close to unkillable up till now. Well, it's like this. I don't want to be a hero. In fact, I don't think there's any way I could qualify as one no matter what I did. But someone I knew was the real article, and I kinda feel obligated to carry on where she left off. Her name was Darsha Assant, and she was a Jedi. She was also the bravest soul I've ever known."

Amazed, awed, Jax slid forward on the bed until he was on his knees before the hologram, seeing his father from the perspective of the small child Lorn Pavan believed he was talking to.

The hologram licked his lips, the tears in his eyes close to falling. When he spoke again his voice was rough with emotion. "I know that, given what you've probably heard about me, it's hard to believe I could feel that way about a Jedi. Well, the Jedi be damned—I'm doing this for a friend, for Darsha. And because I want you to be proud of me."

The message ended, the hologram seemingly sucked back up into I-Five's holo-emitter, and Jax still knelt on the floor feeling . . . bereft.

His father had gone after a Sith. Had fought him and died. He had done it for love. For the friend he had just lost; for the son he had lost years earlier. He had done it because there was no one else who could or would.

"Jax?"

He felt the touch on his shoulder and marveled anew at how gentle his metal companion—his metal *friend*— could be. He looked up into the droid's face and said, "My father was a hero."

"Yes. He was."

Jax rose, realizing his face was wet. He wiped it on the sleeve of his tunic. "We're going after the Emperor, I-Five."

The droid's display of surprise seemed to involve his entire body. "Why?"

"Because no one else can."

—[**PART II**]—

THE TIES THAT BIND

eighteen

Jax's sudden reversal was inexplicable and devastating to Rhinann's fragile peace of mind. He vaguely heard the whys and wherefores—something about a message from Jax's father, a message that was no doubt a trick played by that wretched, conniving droid—but he tuned them out and went to his own quarters where he did the only thing he could think of that would both calm him and allow him some clarity of thought.

He made a list.

He itemized the reasons for and against I-Five having either hidden the bota or given it to various members of the team. Roughly half an hour of this pursuit left him with several strong possibilities. Too many, in fact.

First, hiding the bota made no sense at all. The recent forced move from the apartments on Poloda Place revealed the bankruptcy of that stratagem.

Second, it made no sense for the droid to keep the bota himself. He'd be a fool to carry it into enemy territory where it could be lost to the last person on the planet he wanted to have it.

Dejah's reaction to his revelation about the bota rang true. He was positive that she'd known nothing of it before.

That left Jax and Den.

Den's protests to the contrary, Jax could hardly be expected to resist the temptation of taking the bota, but

Rhinann suspected that I-Five—who was loyal to a fault—no doubt trusted the Jedi's professions of self-control. In fact, I-Five likely believed that if his assassination attempt failed, Jax having the bota would be the only way to salvage the operation.

Den was leaving. Dejah had been sure he'd already left, but the Sullistan had made it clear that his mind was made up. Perhaps it was I-Five's plan to have him take the bota with him wherever he was going. Certainly Rhinann could see a certain advantage to getting the substance away from people who were likely to come into close contact with Inquisitors, Darth Vader, or the Emperor. If the assassination plan went horribly awry, Den Dhur could pop out of hiding and get the bota to one of the Jedi or, failing that, use it as leverage to secure their release.

So which was it? The Jedi or the Sullustan?

He suspected the Jedi and hoped for the Sullustan, for surely it would be easier to get the substance away from the latter.

Rhinann considered his options. They were two: leave and forever give up the possibility of experiencing the Force, or stay and await an opportunity to remove the bota from whoever had it.

He had waited so long, borne so patiently with danger, served the "cause" so selflessly, that leaving now seemed a waste. Besides, escape was but an airspeeder ride away, thanks to a grateful soul within Black Sun whom he'd had occasion to befriend. The service came at a price, but it would be worth it. The airspeeder, which would bear him to the spaceport in less than an hour, was available at a moment's notice, day or night.

Stay, then. He might even be able to persuade the carrier of the bota that giving him the stuff in a dire situation would be the best way to preserve it. Now, if only a dire situation would present itself.

* * *

"You shouldn't be involved, Jax."

Jax kept his eyes and mind focused on the little field generator he was in the process of prying from the light sculpture on the living room of their abandoned conapt.

"I'm surprised at you, I-Five. You saw that hologram my father left—"

"Actually, I didn't. Lorn had put me in autonomic mode for its delivery. It was set to play when triggered by a certain phrase. One of the few ways I can still be manipulated like an ordinary droid."

"Whatever—you heard me describe it. How can you listen to that and expect me not to be *involved*? My father wasn't even a Jedi, and he went after a Sith warrior."

"And died." I-Five bit the words off as if saying them was painful. "I lost your father because of his foolish human heroics. I will not—"

"Five," Jax cut in. "If my father hadn't indulged in his foolish human heroics, if he'd let you go with him, you wouldn't have been on Drongar to get the bota . . . and you wouldn't have been around to introduce me to him. Now let me finish this or we may find ourselves making small talk with the Inquisitors."

The droid subsided with a series of grumbles worthy of Rhinann. For some reason, it made Jax want to laugh. For all the danger they faced—which he had insisted on being an active participant in—for all the complications they'd embroiled themselves in, he felt an absurd lightness of spirit.

It was due in part, of course, to Lorn Pavan's ghost-image in I-Five's holographic data files. He felt connected to that long-dead man. He was a member of a family. He had seen his father's face, heard his voice, and what had always been an abstraction to him had become real.

It raised questions in his mind, to be sure. Questions about the real necessity of removing Padawans from their families and creating a completely new context for them. Why couldn't the Jedi have family *and* Force? If they were successful in removing Palpatine—in *killing* Palpatine, he corrected, unwilling to indulge in euphemisms—might there be a future Jedi Order in which Padawans were allowed both? A future in which there was enough allowance for diversity that even Gray Paladins might be willing to proudly call themselves Jedi Knights?

I-Five said, "Are you finished with that? You've been staring at that generator for exactly seventeen-point-oh-two seconds. May I remind you that we were to meet Pol Haus at oh eight hundred hours?"

Jax looked down at the gleaming object in his palm. He hadn't even noticed he'd removed it from the emitter array. He laughed.

"Yeah. Sorry. Lost in thought. I imagine Haus will wait for us if we're a little late. After all, he's kept us waiting on occasion." Jax pocketed the generator and followed I-Five to the rear exit of the conapt—an antigrav lift that went straight up to the docking stations.

I-Five shot a look back over one shoulder, a maneuver that required him to pivot his head almost entirely to the rear. "I wouldn't remind him of that if I were you."

Kaj was happy just to be in motion again—to be able to use his arms and legs for more than fencing with the stinger droid. He had felt a little naked at first, strolling along between Rhinann and Dejah with not a single light sculpture in sight. In fact he had been certain they must have misunderstood Jax when he said he thought Kaj didn't have to spend all his time in the light cage. But even the tired little Sullustan had been of the opinion that it was okay for him to poke his nose out and explore "the digs," as he called them.

"But to go outside," Kaj protested. "That's not quite the same as just hanging out in here. I mean, in here I'm close enough to the shield to dive back inside."

"Have you felt the need to dive back inside?" Dejah had asked him. "You've been working with the Force, using it, exercising it. My senses tell me you don't feel the pressure you did to hold it in; that you aren't so afraid of an explosion." She'd smiled at him engagingly, and he had admitted that what she said was true.

And so Kaj let himself be talked into a sojourn to a small local bazaar where Dejah bought him roasted takhal nuts and some sweet ice to wash it down with. Rhinann, he understood, was using the opportunity to touch base with several of the team's street contacts to gather intel about what had been going on in the Zi-Kree Sector where the Inquisitors still prowled.

Kaj found this all very exciting, and by the time they were making their way back up from the local marketplace, he had become quite comfortable.

Working with Jax was good for him, he realized; he was gaining not merely knowledge but a sense of *belonging,* a sense of purpose, even. He was on his way to becoming a Jedi. With the exception of that little explosion the day before, he'd been in complete control of his talent. Even Jax had said he was learning quickly.

He was having daydreams of battling at Jax's side, wielding a lightsaber the color of a twilight sky, of flying in controlled leaps from cloudcutter to cloudcutter, when Dejah, walking placidly beside him, went suddenly stiff.

He stopped and looked up. "What?" he asked, looking at her face. She had paled and was staring into the oddly canted window of a storefront to their left.

She turned back to peer up the street behind them. "I thought . . . I thought I saw something."

"Could you be a little more unenlightening?" Rhinann asked.

She shot him an uneasy glance. "I thought I saw an Inquisitor—reflected in the window there." She nodded at the storefront.

Rhinann jerked his head around and followed her gaze back up the street. Kaj looked, too, feeling a horrid, cold tingle gliding up his spine. He saw several hovertrucks, some rickshaw speeders, and weavers, and a good many people of all species. He saw no Inquisitors.

He reached out tentatively with the Force—just a trickle—and probed their back trail. He was about to announce that Dejah had been mistaken when he felt it—the questing sense of another Force adept, seeking. Seeking *him*.

He withdrew his touch as if scalded. "She's right. There's at least one there. I felt him."

Dejah stared at him, horrified. "Did he feel *you*?"

"I don't know."

She grasped his arm and wheeled him about. With Rhinann panting and worrying behind them, they quickened their pace. But it was no good. Kaj knew as they rounded the corner onto the block that housed the studio that that questing intelligence had felt his minute touch.

The Inquisitors were coming.

The studio was empty, right down to Kaj's little sanctum. And if that were not unsettling enough, the living quarters were vacant as well. They were also neat and tidy, something that did not tally with the idea of an Imperial home invasion. The doors were unbreached, the locks locked, and everything in its place.

"One message on the HoloNet," I-Five said, turning from the terminal in the studio. "Pol Haus, verifying that he'd be here, though possibly a bit late. Of course,

I'd have to check the nodes in the individual rooms to be sure."

Jax gazed down at the droid from the gallery, feeling the beginnings of relief. "That's probably what spooked them—the thought of a visit from Pol Haus with Kaj here. They must have figured they should remove him until we're sure of Haus. I should have thought of it myself."

"Whistling in the dark, are we?"

"Doesn't that make sense to you?"

"Just because it makes sense doesn't mean that's the way it happened."

Jax closed his eyes and felt the room. No, there was nothing here. No fear. No residual ghost of the Force having been used . . . He opened his eyes and looked at I-Five.

"If they'd been taken forcibly, Kaj would've shattered the place and sent out a blast of Force energy that I would have felt all the way from Poloda Place. They've taken him out to keep Haus from seeing him, that's all."

I-Five made a percussive sound not unlike an exasperated sigh. "As you said, it makes sense."

"Look, can we not indulge in this nonsensical behavior? I can hear you rolling your photoreceptors all the way up here."

"What nonsensical behavior?" the droid asked. "*I'm* not the Force-sensitive who's insisting on playing an active role in a plot in which having a Force-sensitive present is suicidal."

Jax only heard half of what I-Five said. The other half was drowned out by a silent scream that sent the Jedi reeling against the gallery rail.

Kaj!

Jax pulled himself upright and bolted for the studio door, vaguely aware of I-Five calling his name. He approached the corner toward the antigrav lift in the outer corridor and felt the presence of another, advancing on the corner from the other side. Taking no chances, he drew and ignited the Sith blade, and cleared the corner wielding it in a two-handed grasp.

Pol Haus stared at him from the middle of the corridor, his hand hovering above his blaster. His eyes widened at the sight of the lightsaber in Jax's hands.

"Have I come at a bad time?"

Kaj stood frozen on the worn duracrete of the walkway, knowing there was no escape. For him, perhaps, but for the two people with him, who had no Force abilities, there could be only one outcome.

He remembered the night his parents had decided to send him away. Stormtroopers had come to the village of Imrai, and with them a single Inquisitor. He recalled his parents' fear that his tiny, nascent display of Force sensitivity—a sensitivity that had first shown itself as an instinct for what was wrong or right with a food crop and an uncanny ability to empathize with and heal sick animals—would be noticed.

As clear as the scene on this dirty street was his memory of the moment he had seen his first Inquisitor. He and his mother and father had just exited the trading post in the village center, having bartered a portion of their fruit crop for machinery. His mother had looked up, seen the disturbance at the fringes of the village, and clutched his arm.

"Bey," she'd said—his father's name. Just that, no more, but the quiet terror in her voice had chilled Kaj's insides to absolute zero.

He had looked up just in time to catch the glance they exchanged over his head, had seen the naked fear in his mother's eyes, and the blaze of rage in his father's that quickly dimmed to despair.

Now he looked at Rhinann and Dejah and saw that

same exchange of glances flash between them as he felt
their fear.

No. They would not suffer because of him. He simply
would not allow it to happen.

He turned to Dejah. "They're coming from two directions. There are two behind us, one straight ahead."

"Oh, demons of chaos!" moaned the Elomin. "We're
cut off. We can't get back to the—"

"We can't go back to the studio anyway," Dejah told
him tersely. "They'd follow us."

"You can," Kaj said. "I can't. It's me they want."

He glanced down the street, taking in the people, ve-
hicles, storefronts, cross-alleys—the entire scene. He
could see them all with incredible clarity, as if he had a
hundred eyes and the multitasking brains of a Cerean.
The Inquisitor ahead of them was high up and half a
block away, but moving ever closer. The two behind
were at street level and would come around the corner
any moment.

"See that café three doors up across the street?" he
asked.

Rhinann and Dejah nodded, following his gaze.

"It's really crowded. Go in there and mix. Between all
the confusion and me, they won't notice you."

Rhinann was in motion before he'd finished speaking,
but Dejah hung back, dread straining her crimson features. She put a hand on Kaj's arm. "Let me stay with
you, Kaj," she begged. "I can use my abilities—"

He grinned fiercely. "I'm not gonna let them get that
close. Now go! Please," he added.

She went.

Kaj flitted into the street, blocking himself from the
eyes of the two Inquisitors behind by the simple expedient of falling into pace with a slow-moving hovertruck.
If he was lucky, he could remain hidden in its lee until he
bypassed the third Inquisitor's lofty position. He clamped

down hard on his thoughts, his emotions, his impulse to use the Force. The words of the Jedi mantra cycled in his head:

There is no emotion; there is peace.

He checked his passive awareness of the third Inquisitor. Like a rock in a stream, the Inquisitor's taozin amulet parted the water of Kaj's regard, leaving a strange, warped shimmer in the world. He was almost past it, walking calmly in the shadow of the hovertruck and feeling a quivering elation, when someone stepped out of the doorway of the café.

It was the Twi'lek, Laranth Tarak. Surprised, Kaj stopped walking.

Laranth saw him, recognized him, and stepped out into the street, her brow furrowed with concern.

"Kajin, what are you doing out here alone? Where's Jax?"

"I'm not alone. Dejah and Rhinann were with me, but there are—"

She cut him off. "I can feel them." She glanced up and down the street. He saw her expression change as she glanced down the street behind him, and knew she was seeing them. He could almost see them himself, reflected in her eyes.

She grasped his arm and spun him around, aiming him at the apothecary. "Walk," she murmured, then slipped her arm around his shoulders.

"There's one right above us," Kaj told her.

They were passing the apothecary, still shielded from the two Inquisitors behind them by the lorry, when a figure in a shimmering, scarlet robe dropped out of thin air to block their path.

Kaj looked up into the face and felt as if a shaft of ice had been driven through his heart. The pale, burning eyes that stared back at him, triumph in their chill depths, belonged to a man he thought he had killed.

His reaction was swift and involuntary. Even as Laranth fired her blaster, Kaj flooded the street with a dam-burst of Force energy, throwing the Inquisitor a dozen meters. The blast from Laranth's weapon sizzled past the spot where he'd been standing and burned through the cargo compartment of the hovertruck. The lorry burst into flames.

Someone screamed, and the street scene dissolved into chaos.

nineteen

Jax's first view of the scene on Gallery Row was from inside the first-level entrance of their building. What he saw—and felt—made his blood run cold. People fled something that was going on farther up the block near the corner with a main cross-street—Rainbow Parkway it was called, though it had no park, and no rainbow had been seen by the citizens of this level of Coruscant for uncounted centuries.

Until now.

Now they saw a display of the Force that shot brilliant ribbons and pinwheels of power in every direction—an explosion of variegated energy near the corner of Rainbow Parkway and Gallery Row—an explosion being generated by more than one Force adept.

He hesitated, checking the street for angles of egress. He did not want to be seen coming out of this building or sensed coming from this direction. Pol Haus and I-Five caught up with him as he was considering his options.

"I take it we have a situation," Haus said.

"There's a Force battle going on down there," Jax said.

"Our rogue adept?"

"Yeah. And at least three others, maybe four. Hard to tell when some of them are wearing taozin."

"And you need to get there without being noticed."

The eaves and buttresses of the buildings were his best chance of that. Maybe if he worked his way down a back alley toward the corner . . .

"We'll take my speeder." Haus was already on his way toward the rear of the building, along a corridor that housed a warren of small studios and conapts.

Jax turned and sprinted after him, leaving I-Five to bring up the rear. "You can't be seen with me."

Haus let out a dry laugh. "No kidding. I've no intention of it. But I can lend a hand . . . or an airspeeder."

With the three of them squeezed into a speeder built for two, Haus darkened the windows and darted the vehicle down a long, dank alley that roiled with greasy fog. He came out on Rainbow Parkway and turned a sharp right, then stopped his speeder at the corner, tucking it skillfully beneath the buttressing of a tower that housed three restaurants and a purveyor of artist's supplies.

"This is as close as I dare get," he told Jax. "But if you like I can at least keep the Imperial goons out of it. Tell them the Inquisitors are on it and don't need their interference." He grinned, showing sharp white teeth. "I try to run interference between the Inquisitorius and the Imperial regulars whenever I can. It's good for department morale."

Jax popped the canopy and leapt out of the speeder. "Thanks. I-Five, why don't you stay—?"

"As if that would *ever* happen," the droid retorted, extricating himself from the small cargo area behind the passenger seat.

Jax threw him a grim smile and darted to the corner, drawing his lightsaber as he ran. The street was emptying quickly of its last few inhabitants, leaving as audience only the people trapped within the businesses on either side. He took in the scene at a glance: Kaj was about twenty-five meters distant on the right side of the street. Jax realized with a jolt that Laranth was with him. The two stood in a strangely distorted bubble of air—a Force shield that Kaj was using to hold off the two Inquisitors prowling just beyond its perimeter while he stared up into the smudgy air, looking for something.

Jax's hesitation was minuscule—only long enough for him to assess the situation—then he ignited his lightsaber and hurled himself at the Inquisitors, hoping that with their attention on Kaj, they'd never see him coming.

In the same instant that he saw Jax's crimson lightsaber out of the corner of his eye, Kaj beheld the resurrected Inquisitor above him on a high, narrow ledge high up across the street. That he'd wounded him horribly in their previous meeting was obvious from the scars on the man's face and the unadulterated hatred in his eyes.

He glanced at Laranth, then flicked his eyes upward to telegraph his intentions. She, too, had seen Jax round the corner, and stepped lightly toward the Inquisitor to her right, leveling her blasters at him.

Kaj shut down his Force shield and leapt straight up into the twilight.

From where Rhinann cowered in the apothecary, peering out through the thick transparisteel, it looked as if the boy had taken flight or simply teleported. One second he was there, staring upward, the next he had rocketed out of sight, leaving Laranth at the mercy of the two Inquisitors.

Even as Rhinann was reacting to that, Jax's lean form soared into the picture from the left, his blade a slash of gleaming red against the window. One of the Inquisitors spun to engage him, while the second was forced to somersault backward to flee a blast from Laranth Tarak's weapons. She charged after him, disappearing from view.

Rhinann twisted around to look at Dejah. "We've got to get out of here. Surely, there must be some way we can slip out—"

"Are you mad?" she asked. "That street is a war zone. The most intelligent thing we can do is stay here and hope that Jax wins."

Rhinann snorted his disagreement and, seeing that Jax was battling his adversary into the middle of the street, started toward the door. As it slid open before him, the façade of the building began to crumble.

Rhinann quickly changed his mind and dived for cover.

Jax didn't have time to think about where Kaj had gone. He met the Inquisitor blade-to-blade in a sizzle of brilliant energy. Within the obscuring cowl of his robe, the Inquisitor's face showed momentary astonishment that the lightsaber locked with his was the same shade of gleaming crimson. His astonishment lasted but an instant. Then he was all business.

He parried Jax's first stroke, but he had leaned away from the attack and put himself at a disadvantage. Jax pushed him back toward the middle of the street in the direction Laranth had dashed after the second Inquisitor.

This would be a test, he knew, of his raw talent and his training. The Inquisitors were said to have received advanced instruction from Darth Vader himself, and were rumored to be far more powerful than the Jedi by virtue of their not being limited by what they thought of as a pacifist philosophy.

Jax suspected this was little more than propaganda aimed at inspiring fear—the Emperor would hardly care about truth in advertising—but even so, he could feel the tentativeness of his own strokes, as if he were fighting a complete unknown.

He rejected his own trepidation. He'd fought Aurra Sing and Prince Xizor—he doubted this one could do anything more unexpected or accomplished than those two.

He feinted, his blade meeting the Inquisitor's blade at the hilt. Continuing the movement, he swept it down and around, catching the adept's robes and charring them. Simultaneously, he leapt, using the point where the two lightsabers crossed as a fulcrum. He somersaulted through the air, landing lightly on the far curb. The moment's respite gave him a chance to look for Kaj. He glanced upward just in time to see the façade of the building housing the apothecary ripple like the surface of a stormy lake. Masonry began to rain down from above, narrowly missing the charging Inquisitor.

Still there was no sign of his boy.

Kaj came to rest in the high support scaffolding of the apothecary building. He barely noted that he'd leapt many times higher than he'd ever managed before, but was pleased with the vantage point. He'd seen Scarface just *there*—across the street on that ledge, several stories down.

He was gone now, but to Kaj's eyes, he left an oily smudge in passing, not unlike the phosphor-trailing spotted slugs back on his parents' farm. Mind going back to that day—the day the Inquisitor assigned to his village had taken their farm—Kaj aimed his stored outrage at this Inquisitor.

His eyes followed the slug trail along the ledge. It stopped abruptly. So he'd leapt from there to . . . Kaj swept the front of the building, seeing no movement, catching no recommencement of the trail.

Where had he—?

The realization struck Kaj as suddenly as if someone had flung open a window in his mind. He leapt again, arcing across the street to a higher ledge even as a bolt of Force-lightning struck the spot where he'd stood, dancing across the durasteel frame of the scaffolding.

Kaj's heart hammered in his breast. *Frip,* but that had been close. He'd forgotten the taozin's deadening effect. He leapt a third time, straight up, and lost himself in the shadows beneath a docking station. He did not lose track of the Inquisitor, though. Nor had the Inquisitor lost track of him. Scarface had dropped to the buttress he'd just fried with his Force-lightning and was taking aim at the docking station.

Kaj shielded with one hand and held the other out, cupped to collect whatever there was that could be collected. He needed ammunition—the energy and matter in the air would provide it.

The salvo of Force-lightning from the Inquisitor enveloped the docking station and sundered it, exploiting every crack and crevice in its aging fabric. It blew apart dramatically, chunks of duracrete flying in all directions. Beneath it, in his Force cocoon, Kaj waited until he was sure the docking station had shed its last loose piece. Then he dropped his shield and thrust energy and matter away from him in a huge wave, sweeping everything in its path directly at the Inquisitor.

Masonry bombarded the scaffold, carried on a tide of Force energy. The solid surface beneath it heaved, then rippled like a banner in the wind. Bits of the façade broke loose and fell away, crumbling beneath the metal buttressing until the huge bolts lost their grip on the masonry. With a groan of surrender, the scaffolding toppled toward the street, carrying a trail of debris with it.

At first Jax wasn't sure who had fired the volley; then he saw the flutter of scarlet robes among the falling debris. The Inquisitor who only seconds ago had been charging him had vanished. Taken out by the debris? Unlikely. He was too resourceful for that.

Jax dodged back under the overhanging eaves of the building behind him, scanning the sidewalk for Laranth. He saw her just up the street to his left, craning her own neck to see where her opponent had gone. She didn't see him leap from the concealing debris, because she was spinning toward Jax, leaving her own flank exposed.

In an instant too brief to measure, he saw what Laranth saw—the cloaked figure atop the overhang, lightsaber drawn, preparing to plunge it downward through the duracrete into the top of his head. His reaction was instantaneous: he dodged sideways, shoving his own weapon up through the ledge and raking it sideways with a strength borne of desperation. It parted the duracrete as if it were a dense, heavy liquid. There was an answering shriek of agony from above him.

A split second later he heard Laranth's blasters fire. He turned and saw her adversary evade the shot, catching one bolt with the blade of his lightsaber and vaulting backward into the street. A large chunk of masonry rolled from atop a heap of rubble to obscure him from view.

Jax somersaulted out from beneath his protective overhang, angling toward Laranth, but ready to defend against attack from above as well. He rolled to his feet just as the wounded Inquisitor reared up for another attack. His left leg was gone from the knee down, leaving a charred stump, but he was not about to surrender. He loosed a charge of Force-lightning from his free hand and dived at Jax like a stooping raptor.

It was a shrewd move. Jax was forced to parry the lightning with his lightsaber and was out of position to defend against his enemy's blade. Time slowed to glacial speed. Jax knew that if he leapt out of the way, the second Inquisitor, hidden in the rubble on the street, stood a very good chance of striking him down.

He'd have to take his chances with the lightning.

He dropped to his knees, hoping the Inquisitor wouldn't be able to adjust his flight. There was a strange, sharp tingle in his Force sense and a split second later a thin line of blue-white energy cut through the thick air and made the wisdom of his maneuver academic. The beam severed the Inquisitor's sword arm at the shoulder. The Inquisitor was carried to the ground several feet past Jax on his own momentum. His arm and weapon took their own trajectory.

A second laser beam sliced through the Inquisitor's throat, stopping his howl of pain.

Jax looked to the source of the blasterfire. I-Five stood, gleaming, in the dust and debris, the index finger of his right hand still aimed at the crumpled enemy.

"Thanks," Jax murmured, then realized that his awareness of Laranth through the Force was gone. He pivoted, lightsaber still armed, and was flooded with relief to see her racing toward him.

The relief was short-lived. The second Inquisitor had moved since he'd gone to ground, covered by the fury at his cohort's death. He fell on Laranth from a ledge above the sidewalk, aiming one bolt of Force-lightning at her unprotected back and a second at Jax and I-Five.

Jax leapt, trying desperately to angle himself above the flow of searing energy. But he knew even as his feet left the ground that he would be too late to save Laranth.

Kaj had touched down gently amid the debris, senses thrumming, waves of Force issuing from him like ripples from a pebble in a still pool.

Oh yes, his enemy was still here somewhere, still *present*. And if his sense was true—and he knew it was—the taozin ward had been destroyed or stripped away.

He heard and felt the battle going on down the street as he searched the rubble, seeking the Enemy. All of the anger he'd felt over his parents' dispossession, all the loss of being sent away from them to Coruscant, all his hatred of the Imperial Order roiled beneath his breastbone and he invested it in this quest. If there was any life left in the scar-faced Inquisitor, Kajin Savaros would extinguish it.

He followed the dark ripples in the Force to a twisted mound of wreckage where the bulk of the scaffolding had fallen, letting the pure flow of energy seep in among the randomly toppled blocks and struts. He felt frustrated. The trail told him the Inquisitor was nearby, and the inconstant Force energies told him the man still lived, but something was obscuring his ability to sense it clearly and find it.

But wait—there was movement in that wreckage, a flutter of power like a flame fighting to take hold. Kaj moved closer, his eyes on the spot where the Force emanations were strongest, where Scarface struggled to rise.

A tug at his senses caused him to pause and glance across the street. Laranth Tarak had turned to run toward where Jax and I-Five stood near the body of another Inquisitor. Kaj allowed himself a moment of fierce celebration, then saw the danger Laranth was in.

In the duracrete barrow, not two meters away, the third Inquisitor used the Force to thrust rubble away from him.

Torn, Kaj swung back toward where his enemy rose, again, from what should have been his grave. He knew he had the means to send him back again—once and for all this time.

But the Inquisitor high above Laranth's head had leapt, Force-lightning sparking from his hands in two deadly, dancing streams.

Kaj turned and raised his hands, delivering a massive

Force-push from every angle against the Inquisitor. One moment the Inquisitor was falling toward Laranth, power streaming from his hands—the next he was simply gone. Where he had been there was only a fine swirl of ash. In seconds it, too, was gone, tugged apart by the air currents above the street.

Laranth had half fallen against a slab of tilted masonry and was staring up into the empty air; Jax and I-Five raced to her side, hurling aside obstacles as they ran—Jax using the Force, I-Five using his innate strength.

Kaj breathed out a sigh of relief; the Twi'lek would be fine.

He swung back to his own target now . . . and found it gone. He swept the area with the Force, uncaring at that moment if every Inquisitor in the sector felt him.

It did no good. The Inquisitor was gone.

He let out a roar of rage that embedded a meter-long twist of durasteel in the nearby building.

Far up the street, Probus Tesla, propped painfully in a deep window embrasure, watched as the Jedi and the droid he had sought gathered their companions and disappeared from sight.

His first impulse when he had emerged from the rubble—where he had lain twisted painfully despite his effort to cocoon himself—was to continue the fight, to let his sheer rage empower him. But then he had seen that boy—that untrained adept—use the Force to . . . atomize Mas Sirrah. Destroy him so thoroughly that not even an echo of his Force signature remained. It was as if he had never existed.

In his entire tenure as an Inquisitor, Tesla had never seen the Force used in such a way.

And there was something else he did not understand. For a moment, as he struggled to free himself from the rubble, he had felt an odd new presence in the Force, like an echo or a mirror image in an imperfect surface. When he had at last pulled free of the debris, he had seen only Jax Pavan, the droid, the Twi'lek, and the boy, all of whose signatures he had sensed before.

At first he'd taken it as Mas Sirrah's death echo, then realized he had felt that, too—*after* this odd phenomenon. There was but one conclusion he could come to: the strange Force echo was from the droid, I-5YQ.

So Tesla had taken the moment of distraction caused by Sirrah's suicidal ploy not to attack, but to flee.

It was galling, and he thought of following the outlaw Jedi and the peculiar droid, but that would only delay a complete report to Lord Vader. That was his duty, he told himself. As much as he thirsted for revenge, he understood that revenge must wait. He needed to report to his master. There was too much here he didn't understand. He trusted Lord Vader would.

He shifted slightly on the ledge and a searing pain ripped down his side from ribs to hip. He realized only then that a piece of durasteel had pierced his side, and he was bleeding badly. Once again, he would need to be dragged to a healer.

He swallowed his shame at this second defeat, used the Force to slow the flow of blood, and sent out a call for help.

twenty

Jax decided they should make their way back to the studio through the rear of the apothecary, picking up Dejah and Rhinann on the way. The human proprietor of the business—large, impressive, and incensed by the damage to the front of her building—posed a minor problem, however.

"Are you one of them frippin' ghosts?" She placed herself firmly in Jax's path, hands on ample hips, and glared at him.

Jax frowned. "One of . . ."

"I believe she means the Inquisitors," said I-Five placidly.

"No. No, I'm not. You can see—no robes." He held his arms out from his body, emphasizing the ordinariness of his well-worn tunic, pants, and scuffed boots. What Inquisitor would be caught dead in such a mundane outfit?

"Well, they were sure fighting somebody," the apothecary said dubiously. "Are you sure it wasn't you?"

"We didn't see who they were fighting," Jax said, then added with a subtle change of tone, "and you didn't, either."

"*I* didn't see who they were fighting," the woman said.

Jax shrugged and smiled. He and his company hurriedly left out the rear of her shop and thence home by a winding route. They could hear PCBU sirens blaring down the block as they stepped through the rear doors. The doors slid shut, cutting the sound off.

Pol Haus stood waiting for them.

"I thought you were going to keep the sector police out of it," Jax said as they headed for the lift.

The Zabrak prefect raised his eyebrows. "I did. But when I intercepted a call from one Probus Tesla, an Inquisitor by trade, calling for assistance, I had to take a chance it was over and call my forces in. It'd be pretty suspicious if I hadn't, wouldn't it?"

Jax had to admit that it would.

Safely in the studio, there was only one question on Jax's mind—one he was sure everyone else shared. He turned to Kaj, who sat in the sanctuary, and asked, "What did you do to that Inquisitor—and how?"

The boy shrugged, smiling wanly. "I used to have to bag swamp rats at home. Keep them out of the granary. You pop the alpha female in a sack and take her out in the swamp somewhere and her whole warren will follow. So I popped him in a sack. A very tiny sack."

Dejah stared at the boy. "But how?"

Kaj's smile wavered. "I . . . I don't know. I've never done that before. I just—" He swallowed convulsively. "I just imagined catching the swamp rat and . . . look, it was an Inquisitor. What does it matter what happened to it?"

Jax drew in a breath. "*He,* Kaj. Not *it.* Inquisitors are people, just like us."

The boy reddened and shook his head. "No. Not just like us. They're evil. *He* was evil." He went to his couch then and lay down on it, turning his back on the others.

Jax gestured for the rest of them to take their discussion upstairs and out of Kaj's sight and hearing.

"What now?" Laranth asked when they'd reached the living room above the studio.

"Yes," Rhinann echoed, "what now? Despite your Jedi manipulation of that storekeeper, you may well have blown our cover with your pyrotechnics—"

Jax wheeled on him. "*My* pyrotechnics? I wasn't the one who took Kaj out of the gallery for walkies. Couldn't you have just hidden him in the studio or one of the bedrooms?"

The Elomin's face went blank. "Hidden him? Why—?"

"That was my fault," Dejah said quickly, her crimson gaze flickering to Pol Haus. "I was afraid maybe the prefect would come with force. Or that if you told him about Kaj, he'd want to take him in." She looked up at Jax earnestly. "I didn't want that to happen to him, Jax. I suppose it was silly of me . . ." She trailed off, lowering her eyes.

"It happened. We'll deal with it," Jax said. "But Rhinann is right about one thing. At the very least we will have called their attention to this area and invited closer inspection. We need to move Kaj again."

"You could let me take him," Pol Haus suggested.

Everyone turned to look at him.

He held up both hands as if to deflect their gazes. "I have no intention of turning him over to Vader. I realize," he added, his eyes on Jax, "that I haven't had sufficient time to prove my good intentions. Though I did help you today at some risk to myself."

"Pardon me for saying this," said I-Five, "but you might also have done that purely for the expedient of gaining our trust. When you called in the sector police to the scene of the 'disturbance' just now, you may also have given them this location."

"I might have," said Haus imperturbably, "but I didn't. Forget I made the offer. But I'm here now. If I can help out with this . . ."

"Wherever we move Kaj," said Laranth, "we'll need to move at least some of those sculptures with him.

Which could look suspicious if they went to the wrong place. As it happens, I know of an art gallery that would make a perfectly fitting home."

She was perched on the ledge of a wall niche in which one of Ves Volette's colleagues had painted a mural in morphing pigments that framed her in a kaleidoscopic display of dancing color. Something about her being there bothered Jax, but he couldn't put his finger on what it was.

"You want to send him to Yimmon?" This from Pol Haus.

Jax glanced at him. "You . . . you know where—"

"Where the Whiplash is centered? Yes. And Thi Xon knows I do. Does that help set your mind at ease, young Jedi?"

Jax ignored the question, because he'd just realized what was wrong with the grouping in the room. "Where's Den?"

The Sullustan always favored the highest seat in the room, which in their new environs put him where Laranth was perched. Jax recalled, suddenly, the too-neat room down the hall. The room with not a personal artifact in sight.

I-Five moved before Jax could, and was in the journalist's quarters several seconds ahead of him. When Jax got there the droid was just standing in the center of the room, staring at its pristine neatness. It looked as if no one had ever slept in it.

"He's gone," said I-Five. "He's really gone this time." The droid seemed, for once, at a complete loss.

"I'm sorry, I-Five. I guess this is my fault. The vote . . ."

"No, it's mine. He's been considering leaving—going home to Sullust to marry Eyar Marath—for some time now." I-Five set his shoulders in a very human gesture. "I should have anticipated it. I should have . . ."

"Talked him out of it?"

The droid emitted a tiny metallic sigh. "Not if it was what he really wanted. A home. A family. I suppose he'd fooled himself long enough that he had that here."

Jax grimaced. "We've been a pretty dysfunctional family of late."

"Yes. We have been." I-Five turned his head to look at Jax. "But a family, nonetheless."

Jax held his breath. There it was again—that odd Force echo. Just as he'd felt . . .

He put his hand on the droid's gleaming shoulder. "Five, I can *sense* you. Right now. And before—in the street—just before you killed that Inquisitor. You felt . . . fear then. Fear for me." As he said the words, as his memory played back the images and sensations, he knew it for truth. "Now you're feeling pain. Loss."

The droid's head tilted slightly to one side. "Yes. I am."

"Don't you see what that means? You can't just walk into Imperial headquarters unnoticed. You can be sensed through the Force, I-Five. You'd never get near the Emperor."

"But you said it yourself: I was—*am*—feeling strong emotions. In Imperial headquarters I won't be. I'll be a good little protocol droid, going about my business—"

Jax put both hands on I-Five's shoulders and met him eye-to-optics. "Until you get into the same room with the Emperor. Then what? Then can you promise me that you won't feel anger? Loss? Pain? That the thought at the forefront of your mind won't be to avenge my father's death?"

"I can—"

"*Promise me?* Because if you can't promise me that in all honesty, I can't let you do this thing."

The droid literally shivered. "You can't *stop* me."

Jax shook him hard enough to rattle his frame. "This isn't about independence and free will and the prerogatives of a sentient. It's about . . . it's about *family*. It's about me needing you because you're all the family I have left. And inside that metal heart you hold the only image I have of my father. If you die—"

"I can put the hologram on a crystal—"

"But you can't put *you* on a crystal! Look, you told me that I had to stay alive because I was needed. Needed to train a new generation of Jedi. Well, you're needed, too. To help keep me alive."

I-Five blinked, his photoreceptors going off and on quickly. Jax felt a pulse of emotion from the droid once again—stronger now than before. But it wasn't fear or loss this time.

It was anger.

"If you go into Imperial headquarters leaking like that," Jax said, "they'll be on you in a Coruscant minute. It's suicide."

"Then I suppose we must come up with a different plan."

"Maybe. But first, we have to move Kaj."

twenty-one

"Then Jax Pavan still lives." Darth Vader stood with his back to Tesla. His posture, like his voice, gave no indication of stress or inner turmoil. Only his gloved right fist, held at his side, worked rhythmically. The Inquisitor, fresh from the healer, was certain he could hear the tiny servo-mechanisms in the bionic digits click and hum with the motion. Was Vader intending to wrap those cybernetic fingers around his neck? Would the statement *Jax Pavan still lives* be Probus Tesla's epitaph?

"Yes, my lord," Tesla said. He made his voice as colorless as possible. "I felt it was best to bring report of these startling developments to you without delay. If it had been only Pavan I had to face—"

"You should be thankful, Tesla, that neither you nor your cohorts killed him. I would have been most displeased. And you were correct in assuming that this information is invaluable to me."

Vader turned and regarded the Inquisitor with gleaming, featureless eyes. "You have done well."

Tesla dropped to one knee, relief flooding him. "Thank you, Lord Vader. I am gratified."

Vader made a dismissive gesture. "Clearly their combined forces are considerable—and unexpected. The depths of this young adept's powers are unknown, which is to say they are incalculable." The helmeted head tilted slightly to one side. "You felt nothing when Mas Sirrah was taken?"

Tesla had never known his master to show any uncertainty. The thought that this adept's abilities baffled his lord both intrigued and excited him.

"Nothing. It was as if he had been . . . erased."

Vader nodded. "And you are certain this other phenomenon—this Force echo or reflection you spoke of—was the droid?" There was, to Tesla's further surprise, a note of puzzlement in the deep, well-modulated voice.

"As certain as I can be."

Darth Vader moved to stand directly before Tesla in a whisper of dark robes, looking down at him. Tesla saw his now-bald pate and scarred face reflected in the surface of his master's lenses.

Vader extended a hand over the Inquisitor's head. "Give me your thoughts, Tesla. Let me see what you saw, hear what you heard, feel what you sensed."

In Tesla's mind the rhythm of the words was a chant, an incantation. His lord meant to read him, to touch his mind directly. The very thought was intoxicating. He felt the touch within his mind and quivered with a strange elation.

He recalled the street, viewed from his perch in the buttress far above. The barrage of matter and energy that hit it. His fall into the wreckage. That strange tingle of his Force sense just before Mas Sirrah died. And then, what he beheld when at last he rose from the rubble— where he expected to see another Jedi, he saw instead the protocol droid.

Tesla knew a moment of doubt. Perhaps Pavan had created the echo?

"Don't." Vader's voice was in his head now, reprimanding him. "Don't edit what your senses told you.

Don't qualify it. Jax Pavan is a Jedi—a Force adept. Was this the signature of a Force adept?"

It wasn't, and Tesla knew it. He remembered the rest of it then, up to the point when he escaped the blasted street. When Darth Vader withdrew his touch, Tesla nearly wept with bereavement.

Vader was silent for a long while. Silent and unmoving. Then he turned and strode back to his cloaked window. The sun was setting, turning the tops of the cloudscraping buildings copper, their windows glittering like gems atop the scepters of giants.

"What have we found here, Tesla? A Jedi who eludes every attempt at capture—no, two—there is also the Twi'lek woman. Add to them a rogue adept with unheard-of abilities and a droid that possesses a Force signature . . ." He swung back to look at the Inquisitor. "I am more determined than ever to capture them. All of them. Other intelligence I have received leads me to believe that the boy is the key. If we have him, we will have them all."

Tesla, still kneeling, looked up at his master. "What would you have me do, my lord?"

Vader beckoned his acolyte to rise. "I would have you arrange for the boy's capture."

"But . . . Lord Vader, his abilities—"

"Must be circumvented. There are ways we can do that—with an ally in the right place."

"Have we such an ally, my lord?"

"It seems we do."

twenty-two

Laranth volunteered to remove Kaj to the Whiplash headquarters. Jax at first insisted on going with them, but Laranth argued that his discovery of I-Five's presence in the Force made consulting with Tuden Sal of greater importance.

"Don't you trust me to get Kaj to Yimmon safely?" Laranth had asked him, her face an emotionless mask.

"Trust isn't the issue. You have to know that. I trust you with my life. *Have* trusted you with it," he added, meeting her gaze. "I wouldn't be standing here talking to you if I hadn't."

"Then what is the issue?"

What *was* the issue? He wasn't afraid for Kaj, really; the boy's gut instincts had so far proven themselves effective at self-preservation. The issue was Laranth. It was for her safety that he feared.

He responded, somewhat lamely, "I just think two heads are better than one."

Laranth opened her mouth to say something, then shook her head. "We'll be fine, thank you."

And so he'd sent them off to Thi Xon Yimmon while Dejah arranged for the removal of the light sculptures to the gallery in the Port Sector—with an escort of hand-picked police droids from among the Zi-Kree Sector security contingent, led by Pol Haus himself. The sculptures would take some time to arrive and to set up; until then

Kaj would be warded by more low-tech means. Based on the boy's certainty that the Inquisitor pursuing him had lost his taozin artifact in the fall of debris on Gallery Row, Laranth had dispatched a swarm of the youngest Whiplash mudlarps—waifs who lived by pilfering and whose presence poking among the rubble would thus not be remarked upon—to find it. The dried and powdered taozin skin nodule wasn't sufficient to cloak a power like Kajin's from Vader if the former should have a major tantrum, so to speak, but Laranth was satisfied that it would do until she could remount the light sculptures.

Jax saw her and Kaj off with a sense of foreboding, and told himself it was merely because he and Laranth had something unfinished between them. He was experiencing the irrational human fear that he'd never get the opportunity to finish it.

He glanced at I-Five as the two walked side by side through Ploughtekal Market's lowest level on their way to a meeting with Tuden Sal. A continuously shifting rainbow of neon splashed over the droid's metal sheathing as they walked. *A being of many colors,* Jax thought philosophically. A being who was at the moment, he knew, also suffering from unfinished business. Den Dhur had left behind no message, no explanation, no indication of what he'd been feeling in the days before his departure. Even Laranth had said farewell from her medcenter bed before she'd left.

No, he told himself, *you're wrong on both counts.* Neither Den nor Laranth had been reticent about expressing their feelings about the course things were taking. He and I-Five had simply been too busy, too focused . . .

Who was he kidding? He'd been too *blind* to notice. And too muddled by Dejah's veil of pheromones. That knowledge ate at him now, seeping into his soul. What must Laranth have thought—for him to go in moments from that intimate touch they'd shared in the medcenter, to practically forgetting she existed.

He recalled the moment now and suspected he knew what had happened. Dejah had entered the waiting area outside Laranth's room. With her telempathic abilities she would have felt that strong flare of sudden awareness, of emotion, when he'd entered the room, moments later . . .

He'd seen the look on the Zeltron's face when he and I-Five had left for their assignation just now. She had been hurt and puzzled because she could feel him blocking her aggressively, allowing her to get no sense of his emotions. He'd felt some remorse for that back at the studio. Now, twenty minutes and several kilometers away, he no longer did.

That bothered him. It hinted that, though he blocked her with a strong and trained will, she was still able to affect him. He felt a tickle of anger, as much at himself as at Dejah's meddling, and turned it aside.

There is no passion; there is serenity.

Right.

They reached their destination—a seedy dive that billed itself as an "inn." Jax followed I-Five to the end of the main corridor where it took a left turn and opened onto a broader hallway flanked by what the proprietor termed "conference rooms." The one in which they found Tuden Sal had just enough room in it for a low table and four hassocks. The table was arrayed with a selection of food that looked not at all appetizing to Jax, who was glad he'd remembered to eat something on their way through Ploughtekal. Even the provender offered by such dubious establishments as Max Shrekk's "Mystery Meat" Pies Emporium looked better than the glop Sal was noshing enthusiastically on. Hard to believe that this same man had been the owner of a popular upscale restaurant some two decades ago.

Jax sat, while I-Five remained standing. The Jedi accepted a cup of steaming red leaf tea and sipped it, then set the cup down and said, "We have a problem."

Sal's eyes narrowed. "I heard about the ruckus down on Gallery Row. That was you, then?"

"During the *ruckus,* as you so quaintly put it," I-Five told Sal, "Jax discovered that I generate a sporadic Force signature."

Tuden Sal's face was a stupefied blank. The first emotion to display there was disbelief. He looked at Jax. "You what?"

"I was under attack—" Jax began.

"An Inquisitor was half a second away from running Jax through. I prevented him. I was in the grip of rather strong emotions at the time."

"Which I felt," Jax added.

Sal gaped. "Strong emotions?"

"I was terrified of losing him, if you must know."

"The long and short of it," Jax said, "is that I-Five can't guarantee he'd be able to keep his emotions in check if he got close to the Emperor. He's not the ideal assassin you thought he was."

Sal's face flushed a darker shade of bronze. "You're sure of this?"

Jax shook his head. "How can one be sure? But the fact that there's a reasonable doubt of jeopardy is enough to call it off."

The Sakiyan's eyes narrowed again. "Are you the only one who felt it? Did Laranth sense it as well?"

"She was having her own difficulties at the time," I-Five noted drily. "We were under attack by several Inquisitors."

"I heard the rumor, but I didn't believe it. You fought the Inquisitors—in the *open*?" Sal shook his head. "That's another strike against our plan. But perhaps that's what you intended."

Now it was Jax's turn to stare in surprise. "Excuse me?"

"You've really been against this mission from the beginning, haven't you? Why? Is it because of your father?"

Jax leaned forward. "What are you accusing me of, exactly?"

"It isn't difficult to parse. You engage in a public battle with Inquisitors, thereby drawing attention to yourself *and* I-Five, then claim that, as a result, you can sense him through the Force." He spread his hands. "No one else has claimed they can sense him."

"That's a ridiculous accusation," said I-Five. "If anyone was going to bear you ill will over Lorn Pavan's death, it would be me. And ultimately it was Senator Palpatine who had him killed, through the Sith assassin. Research tells me that the assassin, or at least a Zabrak with similar ritual tattooing, was later killed during a fight at a power station on Naboo, so there goes any chance for revenge against him. That leaves Palpatine.

"Jax didn't engineer yesterday's incident. We were drawn into a fight with the Inquisitors to prevent the capture of a friend."

"Another Jedi, no doubt."

"A potential Jedi," said I-Five.

"Ah . . . or a potential Sith, then."

Jax shifted uneasily, remembering the ease with which Kaj had sent the Inquisitor into oblivion. He'd felt the hot wash of hatred that preceded the act. "Not if we can help it," he said. "But that's neither here nor there. I did not blow our cover yesterday, nor am I making up what I felt. I-Five can be sensed through the Force. How, I don't know . . ."

"He's a *droid*," Sal said. "He can act like a droid and—"

"*Act* is the operative term," I-Five interrupted. "The only way for my intentions to be clear of falsehood would be if someone were to strip my cognitive module down to my basic programming kernel—"

"Ah! Of course!" cried Sal. "That's what we'll do."

"In which case, I would no longer be able to carry out the directive," I-Five finished. "My BPK does not permit me to injure a sentient being."

Sal looked glum, then brightened as he snapped his fingers. "What if you had a handler? Someone who went with you and remote-switched off the BPK when you were close enough to the Emperor to complete the mission."

Jax shook his head. "Too risky. At that last moment, when his sentient overlay was reinstated, it's likely his module would overload and flare out."

Sal shrugged. "But then it would be too late—for the Emperor, at least."

"Yeah. And maybe too late for I-Five as well."

Sal shrugged. "So what? The handler simply reinstates the program. A clean-slate override."

"Not simply," objected Jax. "You have no idea what you're dealing with here. If ever a droid was more than the sum of his parts, it's I-Five. I don't want to take the chance of a reboot causing him to lose whatever part of him might go beyond code."

Sal stared at Jax. "You're not seriously suggesting that I-Five has a *soul*?"

"I'm suggesting that he might not be the same droid we powered down. And that's not all. Emperor Palpatine is the head of the Sith Order. If you think the Inquisitors are deadly, the Emperor is exponentially more deadly. Quicker, more focused, more powerful. In that split second that I-Five's BPK goes offline, the Emperor could very well sense it and retaliate before I-Five has a chance to do anything."

"You don't know that. Palpatine won't be expecting anything. And the droid doesn't need to be that close to him—a laser shot from the gallery when the Emperor is on the floor of the Senate, for example . . ."

"Such a scenario might possibly work, but there's always Darth Vader to worry about."

"But the droid could—"

"The droid could fall apart from metal fatigue waiting for you two," I-Five cut in. "Let's assume for a moment that we can get me past surveillance." He looked at Sal. "What were you thinking?"

Tuden Sal was suddenly animated. "It's a simple plan. And because it's simple, I think it stands a high chance of success. Palpatine attends the Senate 'debates'— bootlicking fests is more like it—on the last day of each week. The number of protocol droids in the Senate Hall at those times is mind-boggling. They're everywhere— interpreting, carrying messages, serving tea—we should have no difficulty getting in as attachés of whatever delegation I-Five tells the security system we're with."

"And as the handler, where would I be?" Jax asked.

I-Five reacted strongly to that. "Jax, you can't. You're a Jedi. A wanted Jedi. Even if you wore a skinsuit, you'd be in danger of being read. You'd jeopardize the mission."

Jax thought about it. "I could be one of The Silent, perhaps. They travel heavily enrobed and no one notices." Then an epiphany struck him. "Got it. I'll go in as an Inquisitor. Totally appropriate as a Force-sensitive."

"And where would you get an Inquisitor's robe?" the Sakiyan asked.

"I don't know, but I'm sure Rhinann does. And I think I may even know where I can get some taozin. I already have a Sith blade."

Tuden Sal nodded. "Yes. It could work. The citizens' galleries have an unobstructed view of the Emperor's Senate platform."

"Which is protected by a repulsor shield *and* an EM shield," I-Five objected, staring at Jax as if he'd gone completely mad.

"I'm a Jedi. I can defeat both."

"Perhaps. But doing so will cause you to light up like a supernova to the other Inquisitors."

Jax shrugged. "There'll be too much pandemonium because the Emperor will be dead."

I-Five's photoreceptors met Jax's eyes straight-on. "I," said I-Five, "am supposed to be keeping you alive. Remember?"

"Then you'd better make it your best shot." Jax turned to Tuden Sal. "Are you convinced yet that I haven't been trying to sabotage your mission?"

The Sakiyan didn't answer that; instead he said, "Palpatine's next appearance in the Senate is in two days. Will that give Rhinann enough time to get an Inquisitor's robe?"

Jax stood up. "Let's find out."

"You want me to get *what*?" Rhinann was aghast. As he had long suspected, the Jedi had completely lost his senses.

"An Inquisitor's robe. Can you?"

"Preferably without alerting the entire Inquisitorius as to its destination," I-Five added.

Rhinann fixed the droid with a baleful glare. "They won't even know it's missing. When do you need it?"

"Within the next two days."

Rhinann felt the building sway around him. "That soon?"

"If you can't do it," Pavan said, "perhaps I'd better seek another source."

Rhinann stiffened. No Elomin could stand to have his professional integrity thus impugned. He knew that Pavan knew this, and was using it to manipulate him, but knowing that didn't help. "I can do it. It's just . . . so soon." The Elomin moved to the HoloNet station in the living room and jacked in. "By the way," he said as he began his egress into the Inquisitorius node, "I was monitoring the ISB traffic this morning. The droid has been made. The surviving Inquisitor sensed him during the incident yesterday."

He saw Pavan and I-5YQ exchange glances, and felt a glow of satisfaction. "Hmm. Yes. A bit more alarming a prospect now, isn't it?"

To Rhinann's surprise, the Jedi merely shrugged. "I'm not surprised, but Tuden Sal might be. Let him know."

Rhinann swung around to stare at the daft human. "So you're still going through with it? What can you be thinking?"

"That the ISB will be looking for a Jedi with a sentient droid and what they'll get is an Inquisitor with a garden-variety threepio."

They left him to his ministrations then, descending into the empty art gallery—most likely, the Elomin thought, to continue the process of planning their own funerals.

Still, Rhinann reflected, it might not be an unmitigated disaster. I-Five would surely make certain that, under these conditions, Jax was the one carrying the bota. The more Rhinann thought about it, the more sense it made as a contingency plan. The bota would provide backup. If I-Five were discovered or the plan went awry in some other way, Jax would take the bota and complete the mission.

Elegant. It also clarified what Rhinann had to do. He must grease the gears for the assassins' entry into the Imperial headquarters.

And he must make sure that he was one of the assassins.

twenty-three

Kaj liked being with the greenskined Twi'lek. She was his idea of a Jedi—stealthy as the wind, lithe, smart, brave, mysterious.

"You're different," he told her as they made their way together from the safe house he'd spent the night in through the maze of alleys that led, eventually, to the gallery/theater above which Thi Xon Yimmon's sanctum was located.

"From what?"

"From Jax."

"Jax is human. I'm Twi'lek."

"That's not what I meant."

"Jax is male. I'm female."

"Well, yeah. I kinda noticed that."

"I'm green. Jax is a sickly shade of beige."

"Now you're teasing me."

"I never tease."

"You keep saying that, but you tease me. And sometimes you tease Jax."

Laranth turned her head to look at him. "Don't tell him that."

Her eyes were a stellar shade of green—like the twin stars that rose in the winter evenings just after midnight in the southwestern sky over his parents' farm.

He grinned at her. "I won't. What I meant was you're

not what I expected a Jedi to be. Well, neither is Jax, really."

"I'm not a Jedi. I'm a Gray Paladin." The green eyes darkened. "So what did you expect Jedi to be like?"

"All serious. Well, you're serious, but I mean like . . . like the monks in the healing orders."

"The Silent?"

"Yeah. I mean, Jax is all into teaching me how to be still and calm and all, but he's . . . *Jax*." He paused a moment then asked, "How do *you* do it? How do you keep from letting the anger get you?"

"You're feeling angry right now?" She swept him with her emerald gaze, and he knew she was reading him—as much as she could, considering the fact that he was wearing the Inquisitor's taozin necklace. Rhinann had told him the Inquisitor's name: Tesla. He'd remember that.

"No, I'm not angry now. It's . . . it's partly what they did to my parents."

"The farm?"

He'd told her about that. Now he just nodded. "And partly it's just . . ."

"Maybe it would be better if you didn't think about it."

"Is that how you deal with it? By not thinking about it?"

She gave him a long, disconcerting look. "I seem angry to you, do I?"

"Yeah. Especially when—"

He didn't finish the sentence. Stepping out into the intersection of four narrow corridors, he found himself knee-deep in some sort of weird fog. It lapped languorously around his legs like subliming CO_2.

"Hey, what is this stuff?"

Laranth stared down at the rising mist, then swore.

Spinning back the way they'd come, she drew her blasters and took one step, then stopped.

"Inquisitors," she snarled and turned again.

Kaj's blood pumped harder. "It's okay. I can take care of them."

"No, you can't." She took the right branch of the intersection. It was blocked not a meter and a half from the junction by what looked like a block of solid ferrocrete.

Kaj stood in the center of the intersection watching the fog rise, catching the scent of it. He knew it was a drug even as the first wave of vertigo hit him. He saw Laranth tear by him in a curling wake of the stuff, futilely checking the center and left-hand corridors.

She staggered as she came back into the junction, swore again, and bolted back the way they'd come. The logic of that hit Kaj as his knees buckled. Their captors had all the time in the world to completely plug the corridors ahead of them with objects they'd be unable to manipulate, but their back trail would have to be guarded. His first impulse had been right, he thought as the fog seeped into his mind. He should've turned around and blasted them.

He tried to summon the will and focus to do that now, but his mind would not cooperate. He felt as if his body had been disconnected from his brain and the different parts of his brain blocked from communicating with one another.

He fell into the swirl of mist, watching Laranth's silhouette move away from him through it. He heard the hum of lightsabers and saw red flashes.

How would Jax find them? How would he even know what had happened to them?

Pebbles.

The answer came from a simple childhood tale about a young sister and brother whose evil father took them out into the fens to lose them, lest they grow to adult-hood and fulfill a prophecy that foresaw his demise. They had dropped pebbles along their trail to find their way back.

Kaj had no pebbles, but he did have a taozin chain. With his last shred of focused thought he wrenched the thing from his neck and tossed it behind him.

Jax couldn't have said where the dream twisted and became a nightmare. It wasn't a Force dream, just a reel-ing off of recent events seen in strobe-like splashes of color and movement. Then, with a suddenness that thrust him into a half-waking state, the entire atmo-sphere of the dream altered, becoming viscous, fluid, and terrifying.

He plunged through layers of oily cloud in a cold, narrow place that was as dark as an Inquisitor's heart. He was dropped into a maze to run blindly here and there, seeking escape. But escape was barred at every turn and someone or something was seeking him, draw-ing ever nearer in the dark.

He dragged himself to wakefulness, a chemical taste in his mouth. After a moment, he recognized it.

Spice gas.

He sat up, the oppressive foreboding he'd felt since yesterday now a crushing weight that sat in the middle of his chest. He rose and pulled on his tunic. Any more sleep was out of the question. He'd go see Thi Xon Yim-mon. He checked the wall chrono. If he went now, he could help Laranth align the light sculptures.

He hung his lightsaber at his belt, arranged his vest over it, and went out onto the upstairs gallery. I-Five looked up from his inspection of the cloth Rhinann was holding out for him. The Inquisitor's cloak, Jax realized.

"Where are you off to?" I-Five asked.

"I'm going to check on Kaj."

"We are scheduled to meet with Sal again shortly to fi-nalize—"

"I know. I'll be late for that, I guess."

The droid blinked. "Jax, may I remind you that we're plotting to assassinate the Emperor, not planning a fam-ily picnic."

Jax hesitated. I-Five was right, but the nightmare still sat on him—*in* him—making his thoughts slow and dis-jointed. He took a deep breath. "I think I felt a distur-bance in the Force. I was asleep, so it's all muddled up with a dream I was having."

Rhinann turned to I-Five. "Can you translate that into Basic for me, please?"

I-Five sounded annoyed. "It's Jedi for something bad has happened." He thrust the cloak back into Rhinann's arms and came to stand below the balcony, looking up at Jax. "Kaj?"

"I'm not sure. I want to go check."

"We have a HoloNet node," said Rhinann, gesturing at it.

As if on cue, the HoloNet pinged to signal an incom-ing message. Rhinann moved to the floating station in the corner of the gallery and checked the source.

"It's Thi Xon Yimmon." He looked up at Jax.

"Open the link."

By the time Thi Xon Yimmon appeared, Jax was standing on the projection pad, facing him. One glance at the Whiplash leader's gaunt face made every atom of his body chill.

"What's happened?"

"The worst, I'm afraid. Kaj and Laranth have been captured."

Jax realized he was using the Force to hold himself upright, his legs suddenly feeling unequal to the task of bearing his body's weight.

"How?"

Yimmon glanced to one side. "As near as we can tell an ambush was set up along one of our approach corridors beneath the spaceport. A little-used one we selected especially for the purpose of moving Kaj. I can't tell you how it was done. Somehow they must have incapacitated Laranth and the boy or . . . or worse."

Jax closed his eyes and reached out, uncaring just now if some nearby Inquisitor should feel the brush of his mind as it touched the fabric of the Force.

"No," he murmured. "No, they're alive. I would have known it if she . . . if they were killed. There would be an echo of their life forces. I felt *something,* but didn't know what it was. I think they were drugged. Spice gas. I woke up just now tasting it."

"That, at least, is good news. They were late getting here so we sent out search teams. We'd never have even realized what had happened to them or where if one of our teams hadn't found this." He reached to one side, and a hand laid something in his. It was the taozin ward Kaj had been wearing. The woven chain was broken.

Jax felt as if a metal band were being ratcheted tightly around his chest. He forced his mind to prioritize its thoughts, not according to his personal dictates, but according to the greater good. "Do you think you're in danger of being discovered?"

"The ambush point was some distance from here—in fact, Laranth and Kaj had barely entered the tunnels and might have taken any number of different routes once they got past this particular juncture. I think the ambush was set up by someone with only a cursory knowledge of our routes of access."

I-Five made a strange sound. "Set up by whom? Only a handful of people knew who Kaj was and that he was being moved today. Only Whiplash operatives, as you point out, know your routes."

"Yes. Which leads to the unhappy conclusion that the

person or persons who arranged this are in Whiplash confidence, but only up to a point."

The thought sent Jax's mind reeling. "Someone like Pol Haus?"

"I would not believe it of him," Yimmon said. "Or perhaps I would merely not want to believe it of him. He is an old and trusted friend."

"May I remind you," I-Five said, "that Pol Haus knows about the art gallery. If he had wanted, he could have given up the entire organization."

Another possibility occurred to Jax that was chillingly reasonable. "Unless all he wanted or needed to do was pacify Vader, which was pretty high on his priority list if you'll recall. He may not be allied with the Empire, but just trying to keep the peace. In fact, he might have reasoned that giving up the 'rogue adept' was the best way to protect the Whiplash from discovery. He may very well have seen Kaj's presence there as a threat to *his* old and trusted friend."

As Yimmon digested that, Dejah stepped onto the holoprojector pad at his end of the transmission. "Jax, Yimmon has told me that some Jedi possess the power of psychometry. Do you?"

"I have some ability. I've rarely used it."

The Zeltron lifted the taozin ward from Yimmon's hands and held it out. "Would you be willing to try? Even I can sense *something* about this necklace. Some . . . emotional resonance from it. Maybe you could divine more."

Jax nodded. "We'll come at once."

Yimmon agreed immediately. "We'll send runners to all the access points on the outer perimeter. You choose which one you use. Right now that's the only way to make sure there won't be another ambush."

With those chilling words, Thi Xon Yimmon ended his transmission.

Rhinann lifted his arms in a gesture of dismay. "We'll come at once? May I remind you—"

Jax was already on his way to the lift. "I-Five and I will go. You contact Sal. Let him know what's happened. Tell him . . . tell him things have changed. Our assassination plot just became a rescue operation."

twenty-four

Kaj woke from a nightmare to find himself lying in an elegant yet spartan room. His head hurt, his vision was blurred, and he had no memory of coming here.

Cold panic shot through him then, from top to bottom. He had no memory of *anything*, beyond his name. He was Kajin Savaros. Beyond that, his past was a void.

He looked around the room. The walls were soft, deep blue-gray, the sparse furniture black.

He listened to the room. It was not completely silent, but breathed gently with the slow, regular influx and outflow of filtered air. There was a pleasant scent in it that reminded him of . . .

He racked his brain. Water. It reminded him of water, flowers, and the green scent of home. But where was home?

Was *this* home?

He sat up, his head throbbing, and swung his legs off the couch. The fabric of it was soft beneath his fingers. He dug his fingertips into it, trying to concentrate.

Nothing came.

Maybe that was the wrong thing to do. Someone had told him once that when you wanted to remember something, you should take your mind off remembering.

He couldn't even remember who'd told him that.

Panic clotted in his throat, making it hurt, making his eyes sting with tears.

Stop it, he told himself. *This is silly. You're in this nice place. Someone put you here. You're not hungry, so you've been well fed. Someone is taking care of you. You're okay.*

He had a sudden, blinding recollection of cadging food from kiosks in a dingy marketplace. It was gone as swiftly as it had come.

He got to his feet with care, wobbling a little as he moved toward the door. It did not open at his approach. Was he a prisoner?

He glanced to either side, looking for a control plate. It was on the right: a gleaming octagon of metal set flush with the wall. He waved his hand over it, and the door slid back with a sigh.

He gasped aloud at the beauty of the room beyond the door. It was large, elegant, and decorated in the same shade of blue-gray as the bedchamber. Paintings and sculptures decorated it. The wall he faced was a curving panel of transparisteel that looked out on all the splendor of the city.

The City.

He searched for a name. Imperial Center. He was in Imperial Center. He still had no idea of who he was, beyond his name, but being this high up, in a building whose windows looked out upon gleaming spires, soft white clouds, and golden sky, he must be someone of importance.

There was a soft rush of air and a door opened to his right. A man stepped through it; a tall, thin human, with a bald head and a face covered with pale scar tissue. Kajin held his breath on a stab of recognition. He knew this man, but could not remember how he knew him.

The man hesitated in the doorway a moment, as if taken aback by the sight of Kaj, then smiled. "You're awake. I'm pleased."

"Was I . . . was I asleep long?"

"I'm afraid so. Over a day. We were worried about you."

"Why? What happened to me? I don't remember."

The man's eyes were sad. "That's probably for the best. You've had quite an ordeal."

Kajin swallowed. "What ordeal? What happened to me?"

"The Jedi tried to capture you. They nearly succeeded, too. They had spirited you away underground when we caught up with them."

Darkness. Running back and forth in darkness with the walls closing in. A woman. A greenskinned Twi'lek. "No, you can't," she'd said. She'd stopped him from doing . . . something.

He rubbed at his temples. "There was a woman. A Twi'lek."

The man's eyes were chill. "Yes. She was one of them. A Jedi. Don't you remember?"

"I-I told you—I don't remember anything."

Running. Fear. Wanting to do something—what was it?

"I seem angry to you, do I?" She'd asked him that. Why would she ask him that?

He was angry now. Frustrated.

The man in the doorway held his hands out in a placating gesture. "Please, Kajin. Don't upset yourself. The Jedi drugged you. It may take some time for your memory to return."

"Who are you?"

The pale gaze flickered as if in disappointment. "I'm Probus Tesla. Your teacher."

"My teacher." He had had a teacher. He remembered vaguely. A gentle voice prompting him, encouraging him. The soft touch of another mind . . .

There is no emotion; there is peace.

No face came with the memory. He gazed at the bald man. "Then who am I?"

The smile was back, warm and comforting. "You, Kajin, are one of the most promising initiates of the Inquisitorius. Which is why the Jedi sought to capture you."

The Inquisitorius.

The ripple of iridescent robes. The flash of a crimson lightsaber.

"Sith," the boy said. "I'm a Sith."

His teacher's smile broadened. "Good. You do remember."

twenty-five

The Inquisitor stepped out into the skyway that terminated in the plaza in front of the Imperial Security Bureau and strode with studied confidence along its length. The personnel who passed him tilted their heads in deference to his apparent station and moved on. Not one of them raised their eyes to try to see his face within the obscuring cowl. Apparently even Imperial operatives were so awed by the Inquisitors that they averted their gaze.

This was a plus.

Jax's goal was twofold—to see how well his disguise worked with no one else's life on the line, and to see if proximity allowed him to sense Kaj.

Laranth he'd had no trouble sensing, though the nature of her contact had been disturbing in the extreme. It had come in a burst of mingled defiance and pain and had left him shaken to the core. He suspected she had been provoked into the brief contact; her captor wanted him to know where she was.

She was there. In that obsidian monolith across the golden surface of the plaza. Jax could see his own reflection in the front of the building as he crossed the plaza— or rather he could see the reflection of a tall, slender Inquisitor moving with cloud-like grace; one among several passing to and fro.

He watched as a pair of them, their robes coiling like sanguinary smoke about them, giving them the appearance of crimson ghosts, entered the broad doorway of the ISB. The bureau had become a home away from home for their order—the offices of the Inquisitorius were here, but the order itself was centered in a temple several kilometers away.

The two Inquisitors he watched entered the building without any sort of security check. Jax slowed his pace. Could it be that easy? He thought of Laranth—of that frantic burst of pain and desperation he had felt through the Force—and experienced the urgent desire to walk straight through those doors, find her, and take her out—*now.* The knowledge that she was in there and had been tortured with enough force to break that iron will, even for a moment, was agonizing.

He swept the place with tendrils of Force. He found Laranth amid the weird, dead echoes from the taozin wards worn by roughly a dozen Inquisitors. It was a tangled presence, its threads looped and knotted, but it was there. *She* was there.

Of Kaj Savaros, however, there was no sign.

Jax moved slowly along the front of the building to a lift on the far corner, scanning as he went. Nothing, nothing, and more nothing. Then, abruptly, his regard slipped past another signature of coiled strength. Dark strength—as black and hard and gleaming as this edifice.

Vader.

He withdrew his touch gently and took the lift down several levels before making his circuitous way back to the Whiplash.

"What does it mean?" Tuden Sal glanced at the others in the room—Jax, I-Five, Rhinann, Dejah, and Thi Xon Yimmon. His gaze lingered on Jax.

"It means we can't go through with the assassination attempt," Jax said. "If we assassinate the Emperor, we would lose any chance of ever getting Laranth and Kaj back alive."

"You're sure they're alive now?"

Jax fingered the hilt of his lightsaber and found it comforting. What would Laranth say about that? He hoped he'd get to find out. "I can sense Laranth, but not Kaj. Which means one of three things: Kaj is drugged, he's dead, or he's not in the ISB detention center."

Dejah put her hands to her mouth. "You don't think he's dead?"

Jax shook his head. "As I said before, I would have felt that. And it makes no sense for Vader to take him just to kill him. He's too much of an anomaly for that— too potentially useful to him. They'd want to turn him to the dark side. I also don't think he's still drugged. Vader's no fool; he knows that long-term deep sedation can wreak havoc with the Force in an adept."

"Then what are the alternatives?" asked Thi Xon Yimmon.

"I think they're keeping him somewhere else and that they've found some way to damp down his powers."

"Correct me if I'm wrong," said I-Five, "but this would seem to put paid to our idea of a rescue mission."

"Pretty much."

"I don't understand," said Dejah, frowning. "Why would that be?"

"They aren't together," Jax explained. "We could go in to get Laranth, but I'm pretty sure we won't find Kaj in the same place."

Dejah made a frustrated gesture. "But surely, even if we can only rescue Laranth, it's worth the risk?"

Jax threw the Zeltron a sideways glance. "I hadn't thought you cared all that much for Laranth."

"You've got it backward—*she* doesn't care much for *me*. I'm fine with her, although I find her a bit grim. But you . . . you care for her. That's enough reason for me to want to get her back."

Jax shook his head, partly in negation of the words, partly in negation of the manipulative wash of pheromones that came with them. "We can't just barge in after her. She . . ." He pressed his lips together, shoving the agony of her last touch away. "I think they're using her as a beacon. Trying to get us to go in after her. I can get into the building as an Inquisitor, but I'd never convince anyone I had the authority to remove the prisoner. If they were just stormtroopers guarding her, that'd be different. But they're Inquisitors."

I-Five said, "You're saying they're using her as bait. Not Kaj. Interesting."

"Bait," repeated Rhinann. "For the rest of us."

"Well, more specifically, for Jax and me." I-Five looked at the Jedi. "And perhaps of the two of us, Darth Vader would be most interested in me—if not for what I am, then most certainly for what he thinks I have. I think we should suggest a trade: me for Laranth and the boy."

There was dead silence in the room. Jax finally found his voice. "That's insane."

"I think not. Nor am I suggesting that we actually give me over to Vader. My thought is that with your disguise—which apparently works admirably—we might enter under false pretenses."

"Enter where?" asked Yimmon. "You can't be proposing to go into the ISB."

"If Vader wants me—and the bota, of course—we may have some control over the exchange point."

"Even so," Yimmon argued, "Vader can't be trusted to keep to a bargain. It would be a trap."

"Of course," I-Five acknowledged. "That's to be expected. We'd consider that in our plans."

Tuden Sal looked as if he had swallowed something

particularly sour. "And may we include in those plans some way of getting the Emperor to the exchange point?"

Jax opened his mouth to say something terse about the new goal of their mission, but I-Five spoke first, his gaze on the Sakiyan.

"I fully expect that the lure of the bota will do that. Consider that, when it comes to that rare and mysterious substance, Palpatine and Vader may find themselves in competition. I would think the Emperor would be adamant about being in on the exchange to be certain the bota falls into his hands, not his lieutenant's."

The Sakiyan snorted. "If, indeed, he even knows about it."

"I can make certain that he does," said Rhinann quietly.

"And can you get through to Vader and make our proposal?" Jax asked him.

The Elomin nodded. "Yes. It may be my complete undoing, but I'll manage it."

"Use the HoloNet system back at the studio. That way, if they trace you . . ."

"I had that in mind."

Jax found himself wondering what else the Elomin might have in mind. He was, after all, a former associate of Darth Vader's—his amanuensis and adjutant. Jax was not completely on board with the idea that their mole was Pol Haus. Haninum Tyk Rhinann was also a possible candidate.

It was with that unsettling possibility in mind that, once the group drew up the exchange proposal for Darth Vader and sent Rhinann off to deliver it, Jax took I-Five aside for a private strategy session.

In the end, the idea of the exchange was accepted and the conditions discussed. The very first condition was that the arrangements be finalized by Jax himself, via the HoloNet. Rhinann, saying he feared some sort of trickery on Vader's part, removed Ves Volette's floating HoloNet station from the gallery to an abandoned conapt in a neighboring sector. It was from that anonymous location that Jax now stood, face-to-holographic-mask, with the Dark Lord.

Even as a hologram Darth Vader managed to project an aura—a presence—of towering darkness. The effect was even more pronounced when he spoke.

His words were brief and to the point. "Jax Pavan. You have what I want."

"The feeling—and the situation—is mutual," Jax replied. "Laranth Tarak . . ."

"Is here." Vader stepped to one side with a sweep of his robed arm. A light went on behind him, and the holoprojection expanded to show the Twi'lek huddled in a small, doorless holding cell, her hands bound in electromagnetic force shackles. Her lekku, Jax saw, were encircled with some sort of flexible metal bands along which tiny ribbons of light raced. He'd never seen anything like them before, but he could guess their purpose. He fought a tide of nausea and schooled his face and his racing heart to calm.

There is no emotion . . .

Laranth almost undid him when she looked up at his holographic image, her eyes dull and unfocused. He clenched his fists, fingernails biting into his palms. The pain was good. Centering.

There is no emotion . . .

"If you've harmed her . . ."

"Spare me your empty threats, Pavan. She is merely restrained by the fruits of the Imperial research program. Twi'leks, it seems, make use of their lekku for a number of Force-related activities. When the bands come off she will be as she was."

Jax tore his gaze from Laranth and straightened his shoulders. "Your conditions?"

Vader didn't waste time. "The droid will wear a restraining bolt."

Jax feigned reluctance. "Why? What can you possibly fear from—?"

"I *fear* nothing. The droid will wear a restraining bolt. He, like your young adept—or should I say your Padawan?—is both unknown and unexpected."

Jax projected barely restrained anger and bowed his head. "Agreed." There wasn't a restraining bolt made that could control I-Five, but Vader couldn't know that. "Where is Kaj?"

"I'm sure you understand that we had to handle him differently. He is safe and well cared for. I am somewhat reluctant to give him up."

Jax said nothing. He folded his arms and waited.

"This will be only a temporary truce, Pavan. Once I have what I want from the droid, our game will recommence. You'd do well to simply surrender to me now."

"Sorry, Vader. I'm not part of the deal. I'm willing to sacrifice the droid, not myself."

Vader cocked his helmet slightly, the movement conveying a sense of amusement. "An odd attitude for a Jedi."

"Ultimately, he's just a mechanical device."

Vader's laughter seemed to roll directly from his chest plate. "You believe that no more than I do." He made a broad gesture of dismissal. "Enough of this. Let us conclude our arrangements."

Jax barely heard him; his gaze had been drawn again to Laranth. She had squeezed herself into a corner and turned her head away from him, pressing her face into the wall of her cell.

Vader noticed his concern. "Such devotion. Does she distract you? That is easily remedied." He made a subtle gesture with his hand, and the cell and its pathetic inmate dissolved into darkness.

"Is that better?" Vader asked, his voice mockingly sympathetic.

It wasn't better. Seeing her like that was horrific, but not seeing her was far worse. With an effort—

There is no emotion . . .

He drew a cloak of detachment around himself and went on with the negotiations.

"You surely don't mean to return the boy to them," Tesla said as soon as the holoprojection of Jax Pavan had disappeared.

Darth Vader turned his helmeted head to look at his acolyte. "Is he here, as I requested?"

"Yes, my lord."

"Bring him."

Tesla did as required, going to where he had left the young adept studying a holocron of the early Sith Masters, and escorting him into the Dark Lord's presence. Tesla had explained to the boy who Darth Vader was, of course, and as he expected, the youth was suitably awed in his master's presence.

Even awed, he dared to speak first. "You're . . . you're the one who rescued me from the Jedi, aren't you?" he asked.

Vader inclined his head in agreement. "I could not allow such a thing to happen to you, Kajin. We were greatly disturbed by your kidnapping. I have brought you here so that you can see one of the rebels who tried to take you from us." He turned and, with a wave of his hand, lit the alcove where Laranth Tarak lay in her fetal curl.

The boy glanced from Tesla to Darth Vader—then, with surprising boldness, approached the cell. "This is one of the Jedi?" Then, "Yes . . . yes, I remember her now. In that tunnel. She was . . ."

The Twi'lek, hearing the boy's voice, turned her head to look at him. Her eyes cleared slightly, and her lips formed his name. Kaj stiffened, his back going ramrod-straight. He held his ground, though, Tesla noted, and the woman's gaze as well. His face screwed into a mask of fury as the boy spit out a single word:

"*Jedi.*"

Tesla met his lord's veiled gaze and smiled.

twenty-six

I-Five would be escorted by Dejah Duare, who stood the best chance of keeping Kaj calm, and Rhinann, whose reasons for volunteering were vague at best. He had gone to such great lengths to hide out from the Dark Lord that it was hard to explain to his cohorts why he suddenly was willing to march into harm's way.

He tried out a number of explanations in his own mind that sounded disingenuous even to him: loyalty to Jax, a secret fondness for I-Five, a desire to flaunt his alliance with a Jedi to a master who had abused his sensibilities tremendously. None sounded believable, and so he'd come up with something a bit closer to the truth.

"Frankly," he'd told the gathered plotters, "I am hoping to turn this into a strategic ploy. Vader will recognize me, of course, and might be persuaded to think that I am a mole of sorts and thus might be useful to him in finally capturing Jax and shutting down the Whiplash. Besides," he'd added, wrinkling his nose in disgust, "I wish to acquit myself better than that cowardly Sullustan has done. I refuse to be so spineless as to abandon my companions."

The little speech seemed to go over well enough with the group, and Rhinann threw himself into the final arrangements for the exchange. He believed that now, finally, the bota *must* surface, and he would be the last person anyone would expect to snatch it *and* use it.

The exchange point was to be the control tower of a spacecraft hangar in an abandoned military complex. Tuden Sal had selected the place, which had to have caused Pavan some unease. Sal was yet a newcomer to the Whiplash and, though Yimmon and even Laranth trusted him, the fact of his previous betrayal of Jax's father must make it hard for the young Jedi to have the same amount of faith in him.

Rhinann thought it ironic that Tuden Sal had not volunteered to be part of the mission, though I-Five still intended to assassinate the Emperor if the opportunity presented itself.

The Elomin was not sanguine about their prospects, but he had made copious mental lists of all the things that could go wrong, and so felt himself well prepared for whatever they might encounter. Nevertheless he was surprised almost immediately upon their arrival at the tower. As he and Dejah led the droid from their airspeeder, they found themselves in the company of a trio of Inquisitors. The adepts flanked them as they approached the lift that rose to the control room.

Rhinann reacted in a most undignified manner, all but hiding behind the droid. Dejah took their appearance somewhat more calmly, expressing only mild annoyance that she and Rhinann hadn't been warned of the extra precaution on Vader's part. I-5YQ, disguised as a protocol unit of the 3PO line, said nothing, as befitted a droid wearing a restraining bolt. It had agreed to have its cognitive module wiped down to its basic programming kernel and the data stored within the bogus restraining bolt. At the proper moment, someone—Rhinann didn't know who, in order to keep Vader from plucking the knowledge from his mind, if it was to be Dejah, or Jax, monitoring from a distance—would reactivate the droid's higher brain functions so it could complete its mission.

"You will accompany us," one of the faceless beings said simply, then swung away to lead them into the lift.

"You could have warned me they were there," Rhinann told Dejah between clenched teeth.

"What makes you think I knew they were there?"

"I seem to recall you commenting that taozin doesn't impede telepathy. I assume these fellows are emitting some sort of brainwaves. Possibly they even have emotions."

The Zeltron glanced at him out of the corner of her eye. "Indeed they have."

"Cease talking," said one of the Inquisitors. Rhinann felt their eyes on him as they stepped from the lift and crossed the empty chamber that had once directed Republican spacecraft, and which was now home to dust, grime, and insects.

Rhinann saw Laranth standing within some sort of force field spun between a series of portable emitters. Her wrists were shackled, and there was some sort of winking device attached to her left lekku—an electromagnetic pulse emitter, he guessed, intended to disrupt her brain's interaction with the mysterious fleshy tendril. She looked angry, he thought. But then, when had she not?

There were three figures standing just beyond her at the window that overlooked the distant hangar floor: the boy Kaj, Darth Vader—and Emperor Palpatine. The Emperor was seated in a hoverchair at the center of the little group, looking arch and cold. Vader was . . . well, Vader. He had not changed one bit since the last time Rhinann had seen him. The boy, meanwhile, was dressed in a uniform of Imperial black against which his pale skin and hair were shockingly bright. Oddly, he did not look happy to see them.

It took an enormous effort for Rhinann to stay on his feet—at the sight of Vader all of his old panic had settled on him, to such an extent that the chamber literally grayed out for a few moments. He felt himself swaying, and commanded himself fiercely to get a grip.

He glanced at Dejah. The Zeltron stood on the opposite side of I-Five, her eyes wide with terror, her gaze fixed on Vader and the Emperor, her breathing quick and shallow. He looked at the droid next. What was it waiting for? Why didn't it fire at Palpatine? Hadn't the upload been accomplished?

The answer came in a most unexpected way. The Emperor smiled and steepled his fingers, then winked out like a dying star—chair and all. He had been no more than a holographic image.

Rhinann had the absurd desire to laugh.

Darth Vader, a hand on Kaj's shoulder, surveyed them through his insectoid lenses. Then he moved toward them with languid, menacing grace, his robes whispering softly. "Haninum Tyk Rhinann. I am surprised to see you here. I would not have taken you for either a hero or a fool."

Rhinann had no reply to that, being too terrified to speak—nor, he knew, would Lord Vader have expected one.

Vader approached them, stopped and surveyed them all for a moment. Kaj stood a few steps behind, his expression neutral. Rhinann wondered at that, but only vaguely—there wasn't much room in his head for anything except terror at being so close to Vader again.

After an endless moment of silence, Vader addressed himself, not to Rhinann, or to I-Five, but to Dejah. "Which of them has the bota?" he asked.

"I don't know," she said calmly. She turned to look at I-Five. "I tried to discover that, but I-Five is terribly clever about such things. I can't really rule out the possibility that he still has it."

Rhinann was surprised at how little surprise he felt at this evidence of Dejah's betrayal.

"On the other hand," she said, turning away from the droid and looking at one of the Inquisitors, "he might have given it to the Jedi."

Rhinann caught a hiss of breath from the Inquisitor.

Dejah approached the scarlet figure, her expression sweetly melancholy. "I'm sorry, Jax," she said gently. "I really am."

twenty-seven

Blood thundered in Jax Pavan's ears—so loudly he barely heard what the Zeltron woman was saying to him.

"Please understand that this isn't personal, Jax. Or political, for that matter. In fact I'm grateful to you for introducing me to the Force. I've never been so near a Force adept before. I had no idea of the sheer sensual power of it. It's the most intoxicating thing I have ever encountered. I had thought Ves's creativity was heady, but this—" She drew in a long breath. "—this power you and Kaj and the other Jedi wield . . . it's beyond my experience." She looked demurely through her lashes at him. "Like I said—I'm sorry."

Jax pulled back the cowl of the Inquisitor's robe. From the corner of his eye, he caught the echo of the motion from one of two real Inquisitors in the room— Probus Tesla, if the scarring on his head and face were any indication. He stared into Dejah's eyes.

"No, you're not," he said.

She shook her head sadly. "If you'd been willing to meet me halfway, this wouldn't have been necessary. But you kept withdrawing from me, holding me at bay. You wouldn't let me in. You wouldn't let me taste the Force in you." Her lovely mouth twisted. "All that Jedi circumspection, that moral code, kept you from letting me touch you—kept you from touching me. But—"

"But Probus Tesla, unlike me, is not bridled by moral limitations."

She smiled, her gaze caressing the keloid ridges on the Inquisitor's face. "Yes. How did you know?"

"I suspected something was amiss when you stopped importuning me with your pheromones. At first you shifted your desire to Kaj, but when he disappeared, you needed another source. Who better to make an alliance with than the Inquisitor who was hunting me?

"But you had to prove your sincerity. So you gave them Laranth and Kaj. You told them where to find the boy and the Paladin."

She looked puzzled. "But—I was so careful—"

"I told you about the Force dream I had, in which I smelled spice gas. The scent of your pheromones was there as well."

She appeared about to reply, when Vader interrupted. "This is all vaguely interesting and amusing, Pavan," he said. "But it has gone on long enough." He extended a black-gloved hand. "Give me the bota—now."

Jax laughed without mirth. "Why? You're not going to let us go no matter what I do."

"I will not let *you* go, but I will let *her* go." Vader dipped his head toward Laranth.

"Why would you do that?"

"Because it is easier than the alternative—dissecting you all, piece by piece until I find what I'm looking for. Something you know I'm capable of doing." He made a careless gesture with one hand and Laranth stiffened, her head thrown back, her eyes wide with sudden pain.

Beneath his robes, Jax triggered the remote that would, in theory, restore I-Five's higher cognitive functions. The droid, however, gave no indication of any change. Jax felt fear stab his heart. Had he been right? Had I-Five lost some ephemeral part of himself that he could never regain?

"Tell the droid to give me the bota, Pavan."

"The droid doesn't have it," said I-Five suddenly. Both hands came up in a lethal gesture, lasers firing. The beams sliced toward Vader . . . and stopped mere centimeters from his outstretched hand.

"Interesting," he said. "I read your intention even as you were forming it. Not as a current in your positronic matrix, but as an *emotion*. You were protecting what you hold dear. You truly are a remarkable machine."

"Forgive me for not being gracious enough to thank you for the compliment," said I-Five.

"Understand me, tin man. If you do not release the bota to me, I will force you to watch as I destroy Jax Pavan and Laranth Tarak. There will be nothing left for you to protect."

There was a strange psychic reverberation that seemed to come from everywhere at once. In the wake of it, Jax felt Laranth's mental touch and glanced at her. Vader had released her from the grip in which he'd held her and she was staring at Jax fixedly. When his gaze met hers she made a subtle gesture, her eyes dipping toward the tip of her right lekku, which, lying over her shoulder, nudged the belt at the waist of her tunic.

He understood the message immediately—*she* had the bota. Laranth was I-Five's secret accomplice. Which made perfect sense. She was accessible to the team but no longer part of it, and she was, of all Jax's associates, the most completely trustworthy.

Jax's mind scrambled for an epiphany. Holding Laranth's gaze, he gave her the tiniest nod and a little nudge with the Force.

Her eyes widened in disbelief.

Jax opened his mouth to speak when a force like a giant invisible fist struck him and hurled him back against the wall. He was pinned there, spitted, while every nerve ending in his body exploded and burst into flame. A scream was wrenched from his throat before he could stop it.

"Stop it!" Laranth snarled at Vader. "I have the bota!"

Vader let Jax go, and he collapsed to the floor in a heap. He lay against the wall, watching as Vader relieved Laranth of her shackles and dropped the shield. The Twi'lek reached down to a pocket on her belt and removed the skinpopper containing the single dose of bota extract. She held it out to Vader.

He took it and reactivated her cell in one fluid movement. Caught once more in the field, Laranth was slammed to the floor.

Again, Jax felt that peculiar quiver of dread in the Force, but had no time to question it. Vader had moved to stand over him.

"And now, if you would return the pyronium . . ."

There was no sense in prevaricating. If he pretended not to have it, Vader would simply turn him inside out and take it. He reached into the Inquisitor's cloak, fielded it from the inner pocket of his vest, and handed it over.

"And lastly, the Sith Holocron." Again, Vader held out a gloved hand.

Jax shook his head. "I don't have it."

"He's telling the truth," I-Five interjected quickly. "Jax gave that to another member of our team who is . . . no longer with us."

"Oh yes, the Sullustan muckraker. Where is he?"

"On his way to his homeworld by now, I should think."

The gloved hand clenched into a fist, making Jax steel himself for the continued flaying of his nerves. He was surprised when Vader simply shrugged off the inconvenience, as if the Sith Holocron were of little importance.

Of course, Jax's epiphany could be pure wishful

thinking. His assumption that Vader would need the holocron to tell him how to use the power of the pyronium might be a false one. He thought Vader a man of supreme hubris, but who knew—maybe he was merely confident and would simply know how to use the pyronium once he had an unfettered connection to the Force.

Jax glanced at Dejah. Her face was that of a zealot in the throes of meditative rapture. Rhinann, too, seemed utterly focused on Darth Vader as the Dark Lord looked down at the two items in his hands.

"You can have no conception of what you have given me," he told Jax. His tone was exultant. "The bota will purify and exponentially increase my connection to the Force, a transformation that will be maintained and strengthened by the energy latent in the pyronium. The Sith Holocron contained instructions written long ago by Darth Ramage, a Sith scientist, which would have been a useful addition to the combination, but not essential. I will simply have to divine what the connection is between these two forces."

"How did you find out I had them?" Jax asked. He picked himself up off the floor with some care, his nerve endings still feeling the sting of remembered agony.

"I knew you had come into possession of one of the items—and when I traced the tangled history of Lorn Pavan's droid, I knew there was a good chance you had the bota as well. As for the other, it was mere suspicion on my part. Thank you for confirming it."

He swung back to circle around I-Five next, the skin-popper of bota in one hand, the pyronium in the other. "And this creature; a sentient droid? I am curious to know how such a feat was accomplished."

"That knowledge," said I-Five, "is lost even to me. I doubt you'd figure it out."

Vader shrugged off the droid's scorn. "No matter.

When I have made use of this, I suspect I will possess even that knowledge."

He stepped carelessly back to the center of the room as if to pose before the great transparent expanse of the window, still considering the objects in his hands. He looked at his Inquisitor and said, "You are blessed, Probus Tesla. Today you will witness my utter triumph."

Before Jax could guess what he meant to do, Vader had emptied the contents of the skinpopper into a receptacle on his chest plate.

"Master!" cried Tesla, starting forward.

The Dark Lord held out a hand to stay him. "Merely an analysis, Tesla. I would not be so foolish as to—"

Vader stopped abruptly. His helmeted head tilted back in surprise. "What—?"

He was quiet, almost contemplative. "Interesting . . . ," he said softly. "I seem to have somehow—"

Then he stiffened, as in sudden pain. Of a moment, his armored form was covered with crackling blue energy. The Dark Lord began to jerk spasmodically as the energy intensified.

Jax quickly sloughed the Inquisitor's robe and ignited his Sith blade. Neither Vader nor anyone else in the room seemed to notice.

The Dark Lord continued to stand, rooted to the spot, staring at the frenetic patterns of light that chased over and around him. A shock wave of Force hit Jax then, a sense of *intensity* beyond anything he'd ever experienced. For a fleeting moment he understood what was happening, realized he was experiencing the faintest echo of the unimaginable connection that Vader was feeling—the connection with the Cosmic Force.

Jax raised his lightsaber. This was the time to act.

He had no chance. Locked in some sort of dark fugue, Darth Vader began hurling Force energy in every direction at once, as if he fought an army of swarming enemies. But the blows were random, spasmodic, striking the walls, the ceiling, the floors. It was as if the Force struck through him, using the Dark Lord as a puppet—or, more appropriately, as a weapon.

One of the first volleys struck the control room window, shattering its vast expanse into myriad tiny shards. They ballooned outward and fell like a rain of deadly stars to the ground. A tattered console chair tore from the floor and went flying at I-Five. It caught him on the right shoulder and flung him backward, pinning him against the rear wall of the room and crushing his chassis. The durasteel frame of the chair embedded itself in the ferrocrete, effectively pinning I-Five there.

The EM field around Laranth fell and the pulse emitter that had been scrambling her Force sense dropped from her lekku to the floor. Freed, she dived for Kaj, who huddled in a corner by the window, quaking, pale, and seemingly helpless.

Rhinann scurried for cover behind a ruined control console. Dejah still stood in the center of the room, a mere meter and a half from the heart of the storm. Her face was rapt, smiling, her large eyes bright with pleasure.

"Dejah!" Jax shouted at her. "Dejah, get out of the way!"

She turned back to give him a coy glance over one shoulder, then advanced even closer to the embattled Sith, lifting her arms as if to embrace him. She was embraced by the Force instead—a burst of Vader's unstable power hurled her across the chamber, to impact with bone-breaking force against the wall. Jax didn't need the Force to tell him she was was dead.

He had no time to be stunned. He struggled to parry the random blasts, but Vader's instability was roiling the Force so badly, a few blasts got through. One was enough to crush the third inquisitor.

Jax finally resorted to shouting, "Laranth! Cloak him!"

She tried. She attempted to envelop Vader in a bubble of seamless Force energy, but she, too, found handling the Force as difficult as Jax had. He felt her frustration as broken threads of quivering energy.

No matter. Lightsaber flashing, Jax began to inch toward the Dark Lord.

The Inquisitor, Tesla, immobilized by shock, seemed to come to himself suddenly. He ignited his own weapon and met Jax blade for blade, intent on keeping the Jedi from his obvious purpose. With the place coming down around them, and with no way of reaching Vader, Jax found himself in a standoff with the Inquisitor.

He glanced at Kaj, huddled with Laranth in their corner, face white and terror-filled. What had Vader done to him, to keep him from even attempting to use the Force? How had the Dark Lord turned him from an unpredictable and implacable enemy into a pet he dared let out of its cage? Jax knew he'd never get any answers to those questions if he couldn't end the stalemate.

Above the sizzle and clash of the two crimson blades, Jax heard a blessed sound behind him: the whine of I-Five's laser. The droid had freed himself and was working on the doors. Jax caught his breath when he saw the condition his friend was in—one arm all but severed, dangling by a few wires, and most of his upper torso crushed. He'd had to drag himself to the doors, and his single functioning laser was sputtering badly. Nevertheless, he persevered.

Marshaling all his energies, Jax bore down on the Inquisitor, pushing him back toward his dark master. He handled the Sith blade as if it were an extension of his body, as if his mind wielded it without the intermediary of his arms and hands. Thrust, parry, thrust; high to low, then high again.

Tesla, his face shiny with sweat and twisted into a rictus of pure rage, tried to hold, but was forced to give ground. His gaze bored into Jax's as if he might do him physical damage with that as well. Jax knew he wanted to.

Back and back, closer and closer to Vader the two fought, until a clever feint by Tesla pulled Jax slightly off-balance. The Inquisitor's grimace became a death's-head grin of elation. He shifted his blade to one hand and whirled it in an arc toward Jax's side.

A glancing blow of Vader's erratic power struck the Inquisitor and tumbled him, head over heels, into a tangle of wrecked machinery and optical fibers. His lightsaber extinguished and spun away, clattering to the floor.

Jax abruptly found himself facing Darth Vader with nothing but his lightsaber. Opportunity or disaster? he asked himself.

Vader's helmeted head turned toward him, half obscured by the frantic flow of Force static. Every nerve ending in Jax's body tingled with the regard. He raised the blade and saw the mirrored movement of Vader's hand.

Vader issued two words; Jax couldn't tell if he heard them with his ears or through the Force: *You cannot.*

A warning? A hope? A lie? Before Jax could answer with word or lightsaber, the doors behind him slid open.

Jax saw Vader's head tilt toward the doors, and swung his blade in an overhand arc. It struck the envelope of Force cocooning Vader and ricocheted as if it were made of mere metal. The shock of the contact numbed Jax's arm and hurled him to the floor.

"Jax!" The voice was Laranth's, calling from behind him; he turned and scrambled to his feet. Through the open control room doorway he saw Thi Xon Yimmon, Tuden Sal, and a team of Whiplash operatives that included, incredibly, Den Dhur. They were armed to the teeth, fangs, and mandibles.

Laranth stood just inside the door, one hand extended toward him. Next to her Tuden Sal struggled to remove Kaj without hurting him; the boy seemed intent on getting to Vader. He was screaming inarticulately; what it was Jax couldn't make out above the booming sounds of Vader's Force blasts. As Jax stumbled toward them, reaching for Laranth's outstretched hand, Kaj broke free of Sal and darted past him. Before Jax could react, the boy was slammed by Force energy and wrenched off his feet. Vader had effectively roped him with a lash of pure energy and was dragging him inexorably toward the blasted-out window.

Jax leapt after the boy, blade upraised—only to be lassoed by another energy lash from Vader.

twenty-eight

No.

It could not end like this. His chance—his *one chance* of experiencing the Force, wasted.

Wasted.

Rhinann didn't understand what had happened or why the bota hadn't affected Vader the way the Dark Lord had obviously expected it to—the way any of them had expected it to. The Sith Lord had not become the exponentially augmented, god-like being of supreme control that the rumors of the bota's properties had suggested. He had become instead an unstable locus of power, spitting out death and destruction.

And now, with Jax Pavan and Kaj Savaros tethered to him with chains of unbreakable energy, Vader backed toward the shattered control room window, showing every intention of destroying the Jedi and the boy.

Such a paltry use of that stupendous gift.

Rhinann could no longer bear it. "It should have been *mine*!" he shrieked, and hurled himself from his hiding place directly at the Dark Lord.

He had nothing but brute strength on his side, but he knew the weaknesses of his ex-master's person. Vader's energy was now totally focused on Jax and the boy. Rhinann shot toward him and battered at Vader's breathing apparatus with clenched fists, trying desperately to damage it.

The move, unanticipated and unexpected as it was, distracted Vader. He lost his Force grip on both Jax and Kaj and took several steps away from the Elomin, teetering on the brink of the broken window.

It was a long fall, and Rhinann suspected that was where his life would end, but he no longer cared. He ripped at the chest plate with clawed hands, shrieking his anguish again and again. "It was *mine*! *It was mine*!"

He felt Vader's hands close around his neck and looked up to see his own ravaged face reflected in the obsidian mask. "You stole my life," Rhinann gasped as the fingers tightened. "I shall have yours in payment."

He lunged; they toppled over the broken sill together, tumbling into the cavernous space beyond. Rhinann never felt the impact. He attained his experience with the Force for one brief, shining moment, feeling an echo of it gust through him as it reduced him to dust.

The control room was silent but for the sound of labored breathing and Kaj's whimpers. There was movement behind him; Jax felt hands touching him, lifting him up. Laranth's hands and I-Five's good one. He clung to them and let them right him, then nodded at Kaj, who lay huddled on the floor nearby.

There was a babble of sound then as the rescuers flooded the room with bustling intent. I-Five turned to face Den, who was hovering behind him holding a blaster rifle that was almost as big as he was.

"Do you even know how to use that thing?" the droid asked.

Den looked down at it. "Well, I'm not sure. Shall I point it at your thick metal skull and find out?"

"It's good to see you, too," I-Five said softly.

"Likewise." The Sullustan peered closely at the damaged droid. "Isn't that the same arm that Wookiee pulled off when you were drunk on Drongar?"

"Hold on," said Jax, feeling a sudden tension in the atmosphere of the place. He glanced about, seeking the fallen Inquisitor, Tesla. He had vanished.

Not good.

A cataclysmic burst of Force energy from the hangar floor threw the dimmest recesses of the control room into blinding brilliance. The entire building rocked.

"Out! Get out!" Jax dodged a piece of falling ceiling plate and glanced around for his lightsaber. It might be a Sith blade, but it was all he had right now. He saw it lying on the blasted floor. Next to it lay the pyronium crystal Vader had taken. Jax whipped out taut threads of Force energy and called both objects to his hands. Then he sprinted for the open doors as the chamber disintegrated about him.

twenty-nine

Den and I-Five, in the manner of old and comfortable friends, easily fell back into their accustomed, seemingly dysfunctional relationship. I-Five teased Den about returning. Den accused the droid of being feckless and inept without him to offer wise counsel and practical advice.

The droid had availed himself of the talents of a number of mechanics and designers in the Whiplash during the course of his repair, and as a result was as good as new—better, in some ways. In addition to the twin lasers and the interfacing spike, he now possessed a veritable transforming arsenal in his hands, including a monofilament line capable of supporting over a metric ton, a small but efficient automatic slugthrower, and the ability to shoot streams of various nonlethal soporific gases.

Jax knew something of apology and confession had passed between I-Five and Den, but he refused to pry. Den did admit to all that he'd been sitting in the spaceport fuming and vacillating when he realized that, as fond as he was of Eyar Marath, and as cozy as was the thought of a comfy cave on Sullust, this wretched planet with its artificial tunnels and its dangerous inhabitants was where his heart was.

"While I was with you guys—arguing, frustrated, ready to strangle the droid *and* the Zeltron—I thought about Eyar in moments of angst. While I was on my way to her, I thought about you guys nonstop. I finally realized that meant something. It meant *this* was home, because this was where I was the most alive. The most *me*. I don't know who that old codger is that wants to do nothing but lie around Eyar's family cave being sage, but he's not Den Dhur."

Jax and Laranth spent over a week working with Kaj, trying to restore his memory and banish the falsehoods Vader and Tesla had implanted in his mind. He was torn, one moment hovering on the verge of knowing Jax and Laranth as friends, the next cowering from them in abject fear and begging for Tesla.

It was Thi Xon Yimmon who suggested that they send the boy to the Togrutan healers and The Silents on Shili, adding that between the planet-grounded Force adepts and the strange, unspeaking monks with their soothing, therapeutic presence, he might more readily heal, as well as regain conscious control of the Force. In destroying the boy's memory, Vader seemed to have wiped from Kaj's mind the very meaning of what it was to be a Force-sensitive. The Force in him was like a skein of tangled threads, knotted, frayed, their connections obscured. As much as Jax hated to admit it, he knew Yimmon was right—there was nothing he could do for Kaj here. Here, Jedi were still marked for death. Here, they would still have to hide. That was no environment for the boy.

Jax had given momentary thought to leaving Coruscant and traveling to Shili with Kaj, but he knew he could not. He was committed now—he and his companions— to doing what he'd come to realize was his life's calling: helping the downtrodden and the helpless, and helping to build a larger and more far-reaching rebellion against the Emperor.

So it was that, with some sense of having failed, Jax sent Kajin Savaros through the UML to a waiting tramp freighter in the company of one of The Silent. Then he returned with Laranth to their new environs in a Whiplash safe house.

"You didn't fail, you know," Laranth told him as they walked the alleys on their way to their new home. "You weren't at fault. Dejah just wasn't capable of putting anything as abstract as loyalty ahead of her own gratification. You couldn't have anticipated that."

"Yes, I could. I *should* have. But I was so sure of myself. So sure of my grasp of the Force, that I didn't realize what she was doing to me—to us. I was completely taken in by her, Laranth, to the point that I . . ." He let his voice trail off.

"You gonna finish that thought?"

He glanced aside at her. "I let her wrap me in a veil. Pheromones and pride. Bad combination. I got so caught up in the cosmic idea of being someone's Jedi Master that I forgot what it meant to be a Jedi Knight. I forgot *you*. I don't ever want that to happen again." He hesitated. "When you were in the medcenter . . ."

"That was then. This is now."

He stopped walking and turned her to face him. "No. I'm not going to accept that. That was then *and* now." He struggled for words. "We . . . I . . ."

"Eloquent, aren't we?"

"Laranth, stop it. Don't make this so hard. You know what I'm trying to say. You can *sense* what I'm trying to say."

And suddenly he knew she could because, in the space of a breath, she had let him in. He was swept up in a strange, heady recursive emotional loop. A Force-enhanced empathy.

He looked at Laranth and saw himself as she saw him and was awed by the emotions that he evoked in her. He experienced the echoed revelation of that in her as she caught the tenor of his feelings and explored the texture of his innermost being.

He moved past the reserve and the hurt and the careful defenses she had erected and felt her breaching his barriers in return.

When they came fully back to themselves they were standing in a stygian alley, foreheads touching, fingers entwined, quivering.

"What was that?" Laranth murmured. "What did we just do?"

"I was about to ask you the same question."

"I know. I don't know what to call it."

Jax exhaled. "Let's not call it anything for now. Okay?"

"Okay."

They separated, physically at any rate, and began walking again by mutual agreement.

"While we're on the subject of mysteries," said Laranth, and Jax smiled. "What made you take a chance that the bota would push Vader over the edge—literally as well as figuratively?"

Jax was quiet for a few strides, then he said, "It's a debate as old as the Force itself: Is it generated by and for living beings, and so subject to their desires and their demons, or is it transcendent—something ineffable that we can only hope to glimpse occasionally in its entirety? Something that's not meant to be experienced in its entirety. As long as there are living beings to wonder about it, the question will exist."

"Be careful what you ask for, you might get it? That's not an answer. It's just another question."

"There's also another factor—the fact that I-Five had been carrying the bota around for two decades. True, it had been processed, and was much more stable than in its raw state, but still—I was betting that such a complex molecule was starting to fray a bit around the edges." He shrugged. "Whether you opt for the mystical explanation or the practical one, Vader wasn't expecting a bad trip."

"You were betting our lives," Laranth said. She didn't smile, but there was amusement in her thoughts.

Jax marveled at their texture and nuance. "What choice did I have?" he asked. "He could have killed us all in a breath, using just the Force he has access to every day. I had to gamble that, at the very least, the bota would make him lose track of the ephemeral world and give us half a chance to escape."

He didn't mention the third factor: this was the first time he'd been this close to Vader, close enough to touch him. And though he hadn't dared to try to probe the man, he'd noticed something about the patterns of Force that had swirled around the Dark Lord. Patterns that seemed strangely, unbelievably, familiar.

Master Piell had told him once that the moiré swirlings of the Force were as individual as a person's DNA. He could not be sure—and likely he'd never know the truth—but, if Master Piell was right and those patterns were not to be duplicated . . . well, it had been enough to gamble on.

He had evidence through the Force that Anakin Skywalker was still alive. And the Anakin he knew, steeped though he had been in the Force, would not have had the self-knowledge to realize what the bota might mean for someone with his particular set of character flaws.

Yes, it was a mad thought, but it was a thought Jax dared to have because of something Darth Vader had said: *And now, if you would* return *the pyronium . . .*

"Do you think he's finally dead?" Laranth asked, breaking into his thoughts.

Jax shook his head. "He's harder to kill than that. But I think maybe the game has changed. And that could be good news . . . or bad."

"But you'll still stay." It wasn't a question.

He didn't reply. What was there to say? Inquisitors or no, Vader or no, the Emperor or no, Jax couldn't conceive of anyplace he'd rather be, any job he'd rather be doing. For better or worse, this was home.

They'd reached their new domicile while he'd been thinking, and when they entered, they found someone waiting in the front room, talking to Den and I-Five.

Den introduced the newcomer, who seemed to be a Mirialan, judging by his facial markings. "This is Chan Dash. He's got a problem that we might be able to help with."

Jax nodded. But as he was about to speak, he suddenly felt the Force surge within him, higher and stronger than he had ever felt it before. It was as if those threads which some believed vibrated throughout all of time and space, forming the fabric of reality itself, had suddenly seized him and lifted him, almost instantaneously, above—no, *outside* the world that he knew, and carried him to some metaphysical vantage point. For one timeless moment, Jax beheld the spectacular galactic whirlpool itself, which simultaneously being *connected*, somehow, to each and every being within it.

It lasted a millisecond; it lasted an eternity. Then, just as abruptly, he was back.

Was this what Barriss Offee had experienced when she had taken the bota? Had he been, for the length of a heartbeat, connected to the greater, unifying gestalt that the wisest of the Masters called the Cosmic Force? If so, how? Vader had used the last of the bota; there was nothing he could think of that could possibly have triggered this, except—

Except the Force itself.

Jax felt a sense of great contentment, of purpose. He didn't know why the Force had elected to grant him that vision, but he suspected a reason. He suspected that it had been to show him without a doubt where, in the immensity of the galaxy, that Jax Pavan belonged.

Tell me something I don't know, he thought.

He realized that Chan Dash, as well as his team, were beginning to regard him strangely. The silence was beginning to stretch.

Jax shook the Mirelian's hand and gestured to a chair. "Sit down, please," he said. "Tell me how I can help you."